THE POWER GAME

THE POWER GAME

A WASHINGTON NOVEL

Joseph S. Nye, Jr.

PublicAffairs
New York

Book design by Jane Raese
Text set in Janson

Library of Congress Cataloging-in-Publication Data
Nye, Joseph S.
The power game : a Washington novel / Joseph S. Nye Jr.—1st ed.
p. cm.
ISBN-10 1-58648-226-2 (HC.)
ISBN-13 978-1-58648-226-8 (HC.)
ISBN-10 1-58648-420-6 (PBK.)
ISBN-13 978-1-58648-420-8 (PBK.)
1. Politicians—Fiction. 2. Foreign relations—Fiction. 3. Washington (D.C.)—
Fiction. 4. Power (Social sciences)—Fiction. I. Title.
PS3614.Y4P68   2004
813'.6—dc22
2004053163

FIRST EDITION

FOR MOLLY

PREFACE

I HEARD IT ON THE CAR RADIO, the president's decision to fire me. I was driving along the George Washington Parkway half listening to the 7:00 A.M. news, trying to concentrate on the traffic and wondering if I should cut across to a side street to beat the lights in downtown Alexandria. At first I was only vaguely aware of the usual phrases: "informed sources," "White House will announce," "removal of the State Department official responsible . . ." But I snapped to attention when I heard the words "nuclear weapons," "terrorists," "Iran," and "Pakistan." Then finally my name, Peter Cutler, and then "uncertain about whether the Justice Department will be asked to investigate . . ." My face grew hot. Could this be true? There must be some mistake. They would have told me first.

I slammed on the brakes, barely avoiding a car that had stopped for a red light. Leaning forward, I rested my head against the wheel. Damn. So they decided to blame it on me.

The car behind me blasted its horn, announcing that the light had turned green. I let out the clutch too quickly and my car jerked forward.

Traffic crept along Washington Street. The sun glared off the row house windows, and I pictured people listening to the radio behind each pane. Soon everyone would know.

I thought back to the day a year earlier when the president had appointed me. My picture had appeared in the *New York Times* and the *Washington Post*. Some of my colleagues at the university had feigned disdain while others were openly envious. Now they would smirk.

A line of red taillights lengthened in front of me. I was hitting all the lights wrong. Should I even continue to the office or just turn around and go home? But why return? With Kate gone, I hardly spent any time there. Half the furniture was missing, along with her paintings. The refrigerator stood empty most of the time.

When I reached the State Department, the guard waved hello, scanned my pass, and lowered the metal barrier to allow me into the basement parking. Did he know? As I exited the elevator and walked down the paneled hallway, former secretaries of state stared down at me, fixed in pigment within gilded frames. William Jennings Bryan. He broke with Woodrow Wilson in 1915. What did he feel at that moment? Cyrus Vance. What must he have felt in 1979 when he resigned over Iran? I stopped outside my door and glanced at my name above it. The sign had a momentarily reassuring effect. It had appeared soon after the Senate confirmed me as undersecretary. How long would it take the system to remove it?

My special assistant looked up as I entered the outer office. He often sat at my secretary's desk until she arrived at 8:00, handling the phones and underlining the overnight intelligence reports and press clippings so that I could absorb the main points before the morning staff meeting with the secretary of state.

"Morning, Tony. Any calls?" I tried to make my voice sound normal but looked at him closely to see what he knew.

"Hi Peter," he replied in his casual way. "I just got in. I'll have this for you in a few minutes. I was out late last night and slept through my alarm this morning. Sorry."

"No hurry. I may skip the secretary's meeting."

I entered the inner office before he could reply and shut the door after me. The sense of panic rose again. It crept up my gorge, pulling my guts into my throat, choking me. The pulse in my forehead throbbed. I looked for a moment at the deep leather couch and thought of lying down. Of course not. Instead, I forced the lump in my chest back down toward my stomach and sat at my big mahogany desk. Unlike career bureaucrats, I had arranged the desk to face the view, leaving my back to the door. This eccentricity had been the occasion of many little jokes by visitors who warned about "never turning your back in this town." I had laughed politely.

I stared out the window. The sun's red stain was beginning to burn through the haze, casting a pink glow on the marble columns of the Lincoln Memorial. In the park between the department and the memorial, a few joggers were making the rounds. Would I be here in the afternoon to watch the softball lots fill up?

Swiveling away from the view, my eyes rested on the only painting in the room, a copy of Winslow Homer's *Casting to a Rise*. A solitary figure sits in a small boat on a still lake, the long loop of his fly line arcing toward the faint circle made by a rising trout. The lake is shrouded in mist, and the blurring of greens and grays suggests perfect calm. On the most trying days, a glance at this scene centered me. It was everything Washington was not. But this morning it didn't work.

I turned on the television in the corner of the office. A newscast was starting on CNN. I sat very still. Tornado in Texas. Six deaths. Suddenly my face dominated the screen. A large red map of Iran, Pakistan, and Afghanistan was behind me. It was footage from a press conference I had given earlier that year. I was talking but I was voiced-over. An announcement was expected from the White House later in the day. I closed my eyes and exhaled sharply, clicking the machine into silence. I turned back toward the window and lay my head on the desk.

I thought of the stories about the suicide of a White House aide back in the Clinton administration. His body was found near the Potomac. "I was not made for life in a city where ruining people is considered sport," his note had said. Jim had told me about learning the news at a Georgetown dinner party. One of the White House people had received a call. Teasing erupted as he left the table with a slightly self-important swagger. The other guests speculated. A foreign crisis? A congressional vote? A breaking scandal? The longer he was away, the wittier the remarks became. But the jokes stopped short when he returned to excuse himself. Jim said he looked defeated and pained, like a child who had been struck in the face without knowing why. The party broke up quickly.

A light knock on the door. I quickly picked up some unclassified papers from the inbox, then turned slightly to face Tony, who held a handful of intelligence reports in black covers labeled with code words.

"Here's the overnight take," he said. "Are you all right?"

"I'm fine. Why do you ask?"

"Oh, nothing." He hesitated. "Some of that stuff is a little nasty." He gestured toward the pile he had just delivered.

I nodded, not knowing what to say.

"You're definitely not going to the morning meeting?"

"Don't know yet. Let me read this stuff first."

After he shut the door, I opened the cover of the first report, a long cable from Islamabad. I stared distractedly at the blurred lines of capital letters. I couldn't concentrate. The secretary's conference room was just down the hall. The other undersecretaries were bound to know, but no one would say anything. I could not bear the idea of sitting at that big table. I would try to see the secretary privately.

A light buzz and a bright red dot blinked on my phone. I hesitated before picking up the receiver. It was Julie, my secretary.

"The White House. Mr. Reese."

I pushed the blinking button and heard an operator ask, "Mr. Cutler? One minute for Mr. Reese." Then the raspy voice of the White House chief of staff came through the line. "Cutler, the president wants your letter of resignation on his desk by noon today. Is that clear?"

"Can I see him first?"

"You've done enough damage already," Reese replied. "The decision is final."

"You can't single me out," I almost shouted into the phone. "I'll call a lawyer."

"Listen to me, Cutler," he broke in. "If you go quietly, we won't turn this over to Justice. Otherwise. . . ." He let the sentence hang.

"There's no case."

"Don't be so sure." Reese sounded angry. "Your files are being sealed. Fax the letter to me in the next hour."

"This is no way to treat. . . ." But he had hung up.

I buzzed Julie and told her to get me an urgent appointment with the secretary. A few minutes later, she relayed the news that his schedule was too full to fit me in.

How typical. It's not as though we were close; I was a White House political appointment. But we had worked together for over a year and a half. Now he was acting like a coward. He knew I had a good case, and that was why he didn't want to hear it. He didn't want to spend his precious political capital on a lost cause. He would let me hang out to dry on the White House line. I had no choice. I had to call Jim.

I started to buzz for Julie but changed my mind. I dialed the number myself.

When we entered government together, Jimbo and I made a pact to answer each other's phone calls first. Some days I would return to the office from a trip or testimony on the Hill and find a list of thirty or forty e-mails and dozens of calls to be returned in the half hour of free time before some interagency meeting or a visit by an important ambassador. I knew Jim's desk was just as bad. At such times, our little pact was crucial. I waited while the number rang.

"Betty, it's Peter Cutler. Is he there?"

"Just a minute, Mr. Cutler, while I see if Mr. Childress is available." The phone was silent for a long time.

"I'm sorry, Mr. Cutler." Her voice had that treacly official singsong. "Mr. Childress will be tied up in meetings all day."

I slowly lowered the receiver onto its cradle.

Grabbing a pad of lined yellow paper from the top drawer of my office desk, I dated it August 31 and scribbled a few lines.

"Dear Mr. President. I hereby tender my resignation at your request. It has been a privilege to serve in your administration. I have always done my best to serve you well. My intentions were good. I thought at the time that my actions were justified. I deeply share your concern about terrorists and the spread of nuclear weapons. If we part with differences, please know that it is only because I tried to do what I thought was right. Sincerely, Peter B. Cutler."

I stared at the dark pencil lines on the yellow paper. So much more I could say. Who would have thought it would end this way? Or so quickly. Less than a month earlier, I was riding high, a major player in the Washington power game. Now I was out. Fired.

Exhaustion swept over me. The tensions of the last month had sapped my last drops of energy, and I was still suffering from the bug I had picked up on my recent trip to India and Pakistan. I felt light-headed. I pulled out a handkerchief and blew my nose. A sharp pain shot through my ears.

Before the ringing sound inside my head could subside, the phone buzzed, and Julie announced that John Marcus was calling from the *Post*. I told her that I was not taking any more calls and asked her to send in Tony. Without looking up, I handed him the yellow piece of paper.

"Have Julie type this and fax it to Reese," I said. "Then get me some boxes. I want to be out of here in an hour."

Tony glanced at the few lines and looked up, puzzled.

"This is totally unfair," he sputtered. "They can't blame this on you. You're the most decent guy in this damn government. We can prove you weren't even involved at the end."

He looked at me expectantly, but I had nothing to say. I thought of a comment Jim once made. "Nearly everyone in Washington will betray you given the right circumstances."

"No, we can't," I replied to Tony. "Please hurry."

I stared out at the monuments. The rosy glow had faded to stark white as the sun began its daily bake of the city. I needed to escape Washington before the swarm of news locusts descended in full force.

Tony reappeared with some cartons.

"Thought you might use these for the stuff in your desk."

I thanked him and he left quietly.

Julie came in with the letter and put it on the desk for my signature.

"I'm so sorry, Peter," she said over my shoulder as I fumbled for my pen. "You've been a wonderful boss. Nicest I've ever had."

"Thanks," I said in a choked voice. I turned only halfway as I handed back the letter.

She hesitated and then added, "The people from security have come to seal our classified files."

I nodded and turned back to the window. "I'm going home. Please tell people you don't know where I am."

The door clicked behind me. I threw some books into the boxes and scooped out the contents of desk drawers. Tony could send them later. I jammed a few personal papers in my briefcase, closed it, and moved to the door.

I turned for one last look and noticed the Winslow Homer print on the paneled wall. I had almost forgotten it. The fisherman leaned forward in his boat, frozen in optimism, casting into the blue-gray mist. I walked over to the wall, lifted it gently from the hook, and placed it upside down under my arm.

The roads were nearly empty as I drove home. I was no longer in a hurry. The sun had turned the parkway into a shimmering black strip. I fumbled in the glove compartment but could not find my sunglasses. The glare hurt my eyes, and my headache throbbed. I pulled into my driveway, turned off the engine, and rested my head on the steering wheel. Finally I forced myself to get out of the car.

The phone was ringing. I dropped my briefcase and the Homer print, fumbling anxiously for the key. A spark of hope ignited. Jim. He had changed his mind. I finally got the door open and rushed to the phone. I picked it up and heard a dial tone. I slumped into a kitchen chair.

The phone rang again. I jumped to pick it up before the second ring, but it was a reporter asking for a reaction to my dismissal. "No comment." I slammed down the receiver. Another call. Channel 4 wanted to send a crew to tape an interview. "No." After the fourth call, I took the phone off the hook and piled old newspapers over the receiver to deaden its buzz.

As I went out to retrieve my briefcase, I noticed a van with the letters WRC-TV turning the corner onto my block. I hurried back into the house, went to the living room, and closed the venetian blinds. I drew the curtains in the bedroom. The doorbell rang. I stood frozen, heart pounding, wondering if they had seen me. The bell rang again, and then a knock. I waited until I finally heard steps going back down the walk before gently lifting one blind and peeking through the slats. Damn. The van was still parked in front of the house.

I went back to the kitchen and looked in the refrigerator. It was nearly empty. An open pack of hot dogs, some stale bread, a six-pack of

Diet Coke. Now I lived mainly on Diet Coke—or any other source of caffeine. A box of crackers sat on the counter. It didn't matter. I had no appetite.

I sat on a kitchen chair and rested my head on the table. The Formica was cool against my brow, but it could not calm me. I saw explosions. I clenched my eyes tight.

I got up and began pacing the living room. I stopped in front of a photograph hanging on the wall. Jim and Abe smiled at me, each holding a trout, framed against the glory of Cathedral Lake. I took the picture off the wall, lay back on the couch, and stared into it. Why hadn't Jim called?

CHAPTER 1

CATHEDRAL LAKE SITS in a bend of the Penobscot River. A short walk north or east brings you to some of the best landlocked salmon fishing in the state of Maine. The only drawback is that it is hard to get to. After tedious miles of turnpike, you bounce for hours over the paper company's dirt road before walking the final mile on a trail through the woods.

You approach the lake through arches of hemlocks. The first thing you see is a granite cliff that looms over the north side of the lake. Spruce and balsam ring the water with a wall of dark spires interspersed with pale green patches of beech and maple. Birch trunks form marble columns along the sides, and in autumn, the modulating tones of green burst into a riot of gold and crimson flames.

The water is always changing color. Before sunrise, the reflected trees paint the sheltered surface of the lake a cool lime. Under the bright sky of a sunny day, the water deepens to dark olive; then as dusk settles, the surface gradually shades into blue-black. A few boulders and dead trees mar the perfection of the shoreline, accentuating the smoothness of the rest. Some trees have fallen into the water, their bleached wood and broken branches resembling the rib cages of half submerged prehistoric creatures. Looming in the distance is the gray shape of Mount Katahdin, the highest peak in Maine.

This was our family refuge, three hours north of Blainesville, the little town in central Maine where I grew up. As a child, I longed for our trips to the lake, and as a teenager, I often came on weekends to fish with friends or to be alone. On summer evenings, I would paddle to the middle of the lake, lean back in the canoe, and watch twinkling dots of light emerge as the sky deepened from indigo into ink. I was suspended between earth and heaven. I would think of my father's sermons quoting Kant about the two things that fill the soul with awe—the moral law within man and the starry heavens above him.

The north side of the lake has a small clearing with a gentle slope filled with daisies, lupin, asters, and blueberry bushes. My grandfather built a cabin at the top of that hill in a grove of white birches. From the porch, you can look down the slope to a weathered dock, then out across the water.

The cabin itself is a simple shelter made of large logs cut from old pines. A wood-burning stove and kerosene lanterns provide heat and light. Father made it a point of principle not to bring in an electric generator or even, to my mother's dismay, rugs for the floor. As he too often put it, "I'd want Thoreau to feel at home here."

Each May when the ice "went out" and the woods smelled of damp leaves warmed by the sun, we made our family pilgrimage to Cathedral Lake and the Penobscot River. Soon after ice-out, the water in the river was often too high for good fishing, and I got frustrated by our lack of success. When I complained, Father would sit me down, and I knew that a sermon was coming.

"Someday you'll learn that fly-fishing is not really about fish."

I didn't answer. Much as I respected my father, at age seven I preferred fish to philosophy.

"Just look around you," Father continued, extending his arms. "This is what it's all about."

Father always had an answer. He was a natural preacher who filled the space of our family life with his thoughts on everything from theology to Emerson's transcendentalism to the politics of Town Meeting. At breakfast, he would read the paper and then deliver a brief newscast. At dinner, I was quizzed on everything I had done at school that day.

"Why don't you start a debate club, or a chess team?" Father would ask.

"Nobody cares about those things," I said. "Besides, they already think I'm a nerd because I get good grades."

"What's wrong with that?"

"God!" I said, shaking my head in exasperation.

He looked at me sternly. "Peter, don't take the Lord's name in vain."

After college, when I announced that I was going to apply to graduate school in political science rather than law school, he again had an answer.

"Law is an honorable profession," he said. "Your grandfather was a lawyer."

"I know," I replied, "but I'm more interested in international politics. Maybe I'll become a professor or something."

"That's an odd choice." He shook his head. "We've never had a professor in the Cutler family."

On the day of the orientation party for new graduate students at Princeton, I feared he might be right. I shivered nervously as I approached the modern Greek temple of the Woodrow Wilson School. I was wearing my old blue blazer and, for comfort, a maroon L.L. Bean tie embroidered with leaping trout. Everybody else looked so put together. I felt timid and awkward. Maybe it was the portraits of famous graduates on the walls, or maybe I had always been a little shy. Big-name professors held court in different parts of the room, each surrounded by acolytes. I hung back, partly repelled, partly envious.

Leaning against a wall, I saw another outcast, one hand jammed in the pocket of his Levis, the other holding a bottle of Bud. The first thing I tend to notice about people is their size, and this guy was well over six feet. He had unruly black hair and a wide, tanned face. He was the only person dressed in a plaid shirt and jeans. Even alone, he filled the space around him. I worked my way over.

"Peter Cutler," I stuck out my hand.

"Jim Bob Childress." His grip was tight.

"That your nickname?"

"Nope, that's how they christened me."

"Where you from?"

"Wisdom, Montana. Lewis and Clark named it for Thomas Jefferson. Population 219 when I'm not there. How 'bout you?"

"Blainesville, Maine. James G. Blaine ran for president in 1884, but he was no Jefferson. You go to college out there?"

"U. of M. How 'bout you?"

"Bowdoin."

"Never heard of it."

"You haven't spent much time in the East?"

"Spent last summer in Washington. Worked for Senator Wayne Kent."

He pointed to my tie. "You a fly fisherman?"

I nodded.

His face relaxed into a broad grin. "Bet none of those turkeys can cast ten feet." He shrugged toward a cluster of students knotted around a professor. A muffled laugh started low in his throat, at first like a cough and then breaking into clear bass notes. It was contagious, and I found myself laughing for the first time that evening.

From then on, Jim and I sat together in all the first-year courses—political theory, comparative politics, international relations. Together, we suffered seminars where students skewered each other to impress the professors and exchanged glances after classmates made particularly fatuous remarks. We helped each other endure the pressure of having to read a thousand pages a week.

After Firestone Library closed, we sometimes went to the Taproom at the Nassau Inn for a couple of beers. The Nass was a picture of a privileged undergraduate world with its Ivy League shields, leaded glass windows, and white ceiling crossed by dark beams. Jim and I sat in a recessed booth under photographs of former Princeton athletes, while students milled around a bar that throbbed to the Rolling Stones.

When I ordered two beers, the waitress asked to see my license. I was always young for my class because my parents pushed me ahead. Skipping grades was not hard in Blainesville, where most kids were killing time until they left to work as loggers or at the Great Northern paper mill. I hated being labeled the smart kid, and being the youngest in the class was even worse. None of the girls wanted to go with a younger guy. I grimaced as I fished for my license and showed it to the waitress.

"I've looked thirty since I was fifteen," Jim offered. "That means I'll look eighty when I'm sixty. It all comes out even in the end." His long fingers drummed the table in time with the Stones.

"Yeah," I twisted on the bench as I shoved my wallet back into my pocket, "but now's when I need a little help."

"Maybe you're lucky." His shirtsleeves were rolled up, exposing hairy, muscular forearms. "When I was playing football, married women used to come by in big cars looking for a little quick action when their husbands were away."

"No shit?" How different my life had been in Blainesville as a minister's son with my mother's instruction to always act like a gentleman around women.

His smile dimmed. "Sure gives you a different view of women."

I reached for my wallet again as the waitress returned with two sweating glasses.

Jim was quicker. "You get the next round."

I raised my beer and nodded.

"Here's to tight lines," he replied.

"How'd you get into fly-fishing?"

"Now you're talkin' serious passion." Jim grinned. "The Big Hole River runs four miles through our ranch. That's gold medal trout water. My dad taught me to fish soon as I could hold a fly rod."

"Sounds like a great guy." I sipped my beer.

Jim scowled. "Not really. He used to beat the hell out of me when he got drunk. But in the summer, after chores and dinner, he'd take me across the back pasture to the river. I loved those trips."

"He must have been a giant if he could beat you." I glanced at the Montana football ring on his huge fist.

"He quit trying when I turned sixteen, but he still beat my mother. He never finished tenth grade, and she was a schoolteacher. Made him feel inferior."

"What's he think about a son in graduate school?" I watched the drops of moisture wend their way down the sides of my glass.

"Thinks I'm crazy as hell. Can't understand why I don't come back and run the ranch." Jim smiled. "Or take up the offer I had to play pro ball."

"What about your mom?"

"Died last year," Jim looked down. "Probably because of her that I'm here. But who knows. Maybe it's just to thumb my nose at the old man."

"Were you tempted to go pro?"

Jim shook his head. "Scratch the surface, and we're all animals. That's why I refused. I had enough of that mindless shit."

"Grad students just cut each other's throats more politely," I laughed. "You've gone from the frying pan into the fire."

"All animals have a pecking order," Jim said. "The only choice we have in life is to find the pecking order that bothers us least."

"Maybe," I smiled as I turned the glass around in my hands.

LATER IN THE YEAR, Abe Klein joined our sessions at the Taproom. Abe was one of the first people I met at Princeton. I was sitting on the mattress in my new dorm room when a thin guy with a rusty beard and protruding ears walked through the door. He was tall, but with a slightly stooped posture. We hadn't said thirty words before Abe brought up the subject of religion.

"Where'd you go to college?" I asked.

"City College. Before that, I was a yeshiva student. I was studying to be a rabbi, but I lost it."

"Lost what?"

"My faith. That's why I decided to go to graduate school in politics. I'm going to write my thesis on Kant and the moral life of modern democracies."

I was floored. The idea of a thesis seemed incredibly remote on the first day of graduate school. And while I often brooded about religion, I rarely spoke about it. I could not believe that this strange-looking man with the New York accent was also a first-year student.

At first I disliked Abe. His intensity made me uncomfortable. Being with him was like trying to go to sleep with all the lights on. Abe clung to me, turning up in my room just before meals to walk over to the dining hall. Initially I viewed him as something to tolerate, but as I got to know him, toleration evolved into friendship. He told me he had been born in Morocco, and when his family moved to America, they spoke only French. His father had a store in Brooklyn and his mother taught French in the New York school system. They wanted the boys to become rabbis, but Abe's older brother moved onto a kibbutz in Israel, and his younger brother dropped out of school to sell real estate in Southern California. When Abe left the yeshiva for graduate school, his parents reluctantly admitted that becoming a professor was next best.

I was surprised when Abe asked if he could join Jim and me on our midnight trips to the Nass.

"I thought you didn't approve of Jimbo."

"He intrigues me. I'd like to get to know him better."

Later I asked Jim if he could come along.

"You mean Dumbo with the big ears?"

"Yeah." I laughed at the caricature in spite of myself.

Jim made a mocking gesture by rapidly opening and closing his fingers against his thumb. "That guy talks too much. All that crap about how to lead a good life." Jim frowned.

"Let's give him a try," I said. "I think you'll get to like him."

Abe came, and his questions gave us something new to talk about— whether politicians can be moral, whether President Reagan was more than an actor, how long the Republicans would be able to stay in power—leavened by a wry New York sense of humor. In the pecking order of graduate students, Abe and I clearly ranked near the top while Jim did not. Jim respected Abe's success but liked even more the fact that Abe was not what Jim called "one of those phony intellectuals." Jim loved baiting Abe but was secretly flattered that one of the smartest members of the class enjoyed his company. Abe, in turn, was openly intrigued by the rough man of the West who spoke so knowledgeably about practical American politics. Here was someone who might actually enter government someday.

When exams were finally over, I was only partly surprised that Abe asked if he could come on our fishing trip to celebrate the end of the academic year. Jim and I had been planning on going to Maine for months. I had a hard time envisaging Abe in white sneakers and an I Luv New York sweatshirt in the woods. We called him "Bear Bait." But Abe took the teasing well, and he had become so much a part of our trio that of course we had to include him on the trip.

WE LEFT PRINCETON at six in the morning, heading out Kingston Road in the battered old Ford pickup that Jim had driven east from Montana. I sat in the middle with Jim and Abe as my bookends. The fishing rods were cradled in the gun rack hanging in the back of the cab. We talked a mile a minute, criticizing fellow students, laughing at some of the professors, chewing over our first year of graduate school. When we got tired of talking, Jim suggested we listen to the news.

I fiddled with the radio and found an all-news station. An announcer reported that President Reagan had made another speech about ridding the world of nuclear weapons.

"He's such a hypocrite," Abe said, interrupting the newscast. I gave Abe an irritated look, but he kept on talking. "He should know you can't build an astrodome over the whole damn country."

"I don't agree with Reagan on many things," Jim countered, "but I'm with him on this one."

"If nuclear weapons spread, we'll need something," I said, "but I don't think the technology is ready. We're going to have to use diplomacy to stop proliferation."

We spent nearly sixty miles on that nuclear argument until a blinking red light and insistent beep burst from the small black box attached to the sun visor of the truck. Jim slammed on the brakes. "Smokey," he pointed to the state police car approaching in the opposite lane.

"What's that?" Abe asked, pointing to the box.

"Fuzzbuster," Jim replied with a grin. "High-tech that works."

"It seems wrong."

"Spoken like a political theorist," Jim chuckled, turning a knob to reduce the insistent beeping. "But it's perfectly legal."

"Suppose everyone used them," Abe asked. "What would happen to the speed laws?"

"Out west, speedin's the rule. Hell, we even have a saying: 'Speed laws are wrote to be broke.'"

The beeping stopped as the trooper passed, and Jim reached up to adjust the volume on the radar detector again. "Don't worry, little Klein, when it's your turn to drive, this knob can turn it off."

IT WAS LATE AFTERNOON by the time we pulled into the muddy parking spot where the trail to the cabin begins. When we got out of the truck and stretched, the moist scent of pine and ferns enveloped us. In the distance, I could hear the roar of the river rapids. Abe looked dubiously at the narrow trail in the woods. "Never seen so many trees."

"Or bugs." I watched him swat black flies and tossed him a spray can of Woodsman's repellent.

We divided the food and gear. My fingers lingered affectionately on the worn wicker of my grandfather's pack basket before I hoisted it onto my back and led the way down the narrow trail. The mud sucked at my boots. Whenever we came to a clearing, I pointed out the flowers—the painted trillium and the ladyslippers.

We reached the cabin and the wooden door groaned as I pushed it open. The cabin was musty and smelled of mice, but it looked the same. Mouse-proof green metal cabinets lined the far wall. In the center of the room stood a large table covered with a red checkered oilcloth. Pots and pans whose bottoms had been blackened by countless campfires hung from nails hammered into the wall behind the stove. I went to the wood box, opened the door of the cast iron stove, and stuffed in kindling and stove wood. I struck a match against the black iron, inhaled the whiff of sulfur, and watched a little yellow flame lap up the edge of the paper and eat into the wood. The pungent odor of birch filled my nostrils.

After we unpacked our gear and spread sleeping bags on the bunks, I suggested we go to the lake and catch dinner. "Come on, Abe, I'll give you a lesson in fly casting."

We strung up the rods and walked down to the dock. Rings spread out in dimples as trout broke through the mirrored surface in search of mayflies before splashing back into the depths. I drew line from the reel with my left hand while flexing the nine-foot rod in my right. The loops of line whispered through the air above my head, tracing a graceful arc against the sky. Then I brought my right hand down sharply to send the line sailing forty feet over the water. The tiny feathers of a royal coachman fell lightly onto the water. The little white speck rested on the surface in perfect stillness for a moment. Then with a splash, it vanished. The rod bowed, and the reel clicked rapidly as the fish dove for the bottom.

The rod jerked fiercely, but I recovered line and brought the fish to the dock. It was a beautiful brookie, speckled with pink dots in pale blue circles, the red and white flags of its ventral fins contrasting with its mottled green-brown back. I knelt down, grasped the slippery fish around its stomach with my left hand and inserted my right thumb into its mouth to bend the head back. Blood burst from the ruptured gills, and bright scarlet spots suddenly appeared on the weathered gray boards of the dock.

"That's my dinner. Now you try."

Abe took the long rod and started to whip it back and forth above his head. He cast, and the line fell in a tangle on the water in front of him.

"Slow down. It's all in the rhythm of the line. Wait for it to finish coiling out behind you, then let the lever of the rod bring it forward."

Abe tried again. This time he pulled forward too soon. There was a snap like a circus master cracking his whip, and the fly disappeared from the end of his line. Jim laughed from where he sat on an overturned bucket.

"Sorry," Abe apologized. "Are these things expensive?"

"No sweat," I replied. "Tonight I'll teach you how to tie a fly."

After a half hour's tutoring, Abe was able to cast without tangle and without losing the fly, but he was still unable to reach the area where the fish were feeding. I suggested we give Jim a turn.

"I had no idea it was this complicated," Abe said as he handed over the rod. "In New York, we always said that fishing is just a jerk on one end of a line waiting for a jerk on the other."

"Trouble with you, Klein," Jim laughed, "is the only fish you've ever seen is between a knife and fork in some restaurant."

We watched Jim as he curled the line out over the water. His motion was fluid. The rod seemed a natural extension of his arm. I was proud of my fly casting, but I had to admit that Jim was every bit as skilled. Jim hooked a trout and played it perfectly. Landed, it was twice the size of mine.

"Well, Peter, I guess Montana's always bigger than Maine," Abe joked.

"Beginner's luck," I told them.

THAT NIGHT I FRIED THE TROUT in a big black skillet with butter, lemon, and dill. I put the fish on the plates, poured the simple pan sauce over them, and watched with pleasure as my friends dug into the sweet pink flesh. We sat on the porch of the cabin, balancing our plates in our laps, looking out over the water.

"How's that for a three-star meal?"

"Damn good." Jim chuckled. "Almost as good as a Montana rainbow trout."

"We'll have to try a hunting trip next fall," I said.

"I don't think I'd be able to kill an animal," Abe said. He stared out over the stillness of the lake.

Jim tipped back in his chair, looked at Abe and snorted. "I don't notice you becoming a vegetarian."

Abe turned his gaze away from the lake and looked at Jim. "I mean I've never been involved in killing what I eat."

"If you will the ends, you will the means," Jim said.

"That's a lousy principle and you know it." Even in the dim light cast by the pale flames of the campfire, he seemed to be flushing.

Jim spread his arms dramatically toward the sky above us. "Typical Kantian moralist. You get lost in the stars and leave the dirty work to us utilitarians. Then you sit back and complain that we don't have clean hands."

"Doesn't it bother you to shoot a deer?" Abe asked.

"No more than slaughtering the steer that went into that Big Mac you ate for lunch."

I had been staring at the shape of Mount Katahdin in the lake. Now a slight breeze rippled the edges of the silhouette and erased the reflection from the surface of the water.

"I admit that I've had second thoughts about deer hunting," I said.

"Sometimes, after I've shot a buck, I wish for a moment I could bring it back to life. But two out of five deer starve in these woods in a hard winter. You should see 'em. Mother Nature's a lot more cruel than humans."

"But we don't have to kill," Abe said. The flames in the dying fire found an untouched pine knot. Crackling, they suddenly spurted amber and scarlet, accentuating the shadows on our faces. Abe looked serious.

"I draw a line at human life," I explained, "but animals can't escape the food chain. It's nature's substitute for birth control. They can't plan their lives like . . . "

"Like humans plan war and holocaust?" Abe asked.

"Cheap shot, Klein. Everyone's against holocaust."

"You probably believe in capital punishment," Abe snorted.

"Damn right," Jim said. He bent his beer can in two and arced it into the trash bucket at the end of the porch. "Two points," he said.

"Would you vote for a president who vowed he'd never risk a human life?" I turned toward Abe. "If a president's going to protect his people, he may have to do bad things."

Jim had been watching our exchange with mild amusement, his chair tipped back against the wall of the cabin, his hands clasped behind his head. Suddenly he leaned forward and slammed his feet against the floor of the porch. "Enough of this philosophy bullshit. We left Princeton to get away from that crap. Tell me about this river tomorrow."

I LEFT THE CABIN while the guys were still asleep to have an hour alone on the river. Wisps of mist drifted up from the cold waters. The sun had yet to reach below the fringe of spruce and fir. The waters at the head of Ledge Pool churned white from their fall over the gray granite. But here, fifty feet down the pool, the water was black with the promise of depth. A good place for fish to feed.

Bracing myself with a piece of driftwood, I eased into the belly of the pool. My feet groped for niches among the slippery stones. The current forced the Gore-Tex fabric of my waders tight against my stomach and crotch. I teetered for an instant and leaned upstream. I crept cautiously into the current.

When I was far enough from shore, I swept my arm back, flexing the long rod. I felt the weight of the line in the air, waited an instant for the loop to unfurl behind me, then thrust the line forward over the water. Not enough. I pulled back before the fly landed, stripped more line from the reel, lengthened the coil behind me, and flung it forward again. This time I let the Gray Ghost streamer sink before I pulled it back with sharp jerks, making the feathers dance under water like a wounded minnow. Again and again I cast. Up. Pause. Down. The line flickered and hovered over the water. My body rocked with the repetitive motions. Could I put the fly behind the half-submerged rock halfway across? Could I reach further with the next cast? Could I touch that promising eddy on the far side of the main current?

A sharp jolt startled me. The rod tip bent, the line surged upstream against the current, and the reel screamed as the line was stripped away. The fish turned and raced back to the center of the pool. I reeled madly to take up any slack that could allow the fish to regain its freedom. A great silver shape burst from the water, gyrated, and splashed back into the depth. I sucked in breath. This was a big salmon.

Again and again the fish shattered the surface. I reeled frantically when it swam upstream. I let it take line when it turned downstream. I reeled when it turned again. I kept the tip up, using the leverage of the rod to tire the fish without reaching the breaking point of the fragile nylon leader. Now he was waiting in the deep, refusing to move. Why hadn't I tied on a heavier leader? Still, the fish might have seen the thicker leader and would not have struck. There seemed to be no way to win when it came to the really big ones.

Suddenly the fish ran downstream. The line sliced the water toward the tail of the pool, and the rod throbbed with the added strain of the current. I had to follow it downstream or the leader would break. My feet fumbled for firmness under the current, but I could not move fast enough to save the fine line. The rod tip snapped up. Pressure gone. Slack. A void gaped where the thrill had been.

I clipped the end of the frayed leader and tied on another Gray Ghost. As I cast and recast, the image of the missing fish splashed through my mind. Finally I hooked another. My pulse leapt, but my wrist told me it was no match for the first. The new fish sped thirty feet down the pool and erupted in silver spray. Reel. Yield. Tighten. My feet searched the bottom of the pool as I slowly backed to the shore. Finally I brought the exhausted salmon into the shallow water. It lay on its side, three pounds of sleek silver beauty. I slipped my hands under it, removed the fly from its mouth, and faced it upstream in the current. Its fins began to move as the water restored oxygen through its gills. I released my grip, and the fish darted back to the depths.

Instead of returning to the river, I leaned back against a rock. The sun had begun to break through the ragged spruce curtain that framed the pool. Jagged streaks of light cut through the branches and jumped back at me from the ripples in the water. The mist was gone. A kingfisher flitted across the pool. The sunlight warmed my face. I wanted to sip it, to swill it along with the scent of fir and ferns.

The buzzing alarm on my digital wristwatch shattered the spell. I turned it off. Too late. The moment was gone. Time to return for breakfast.

AFTER BREAKFAST, Jim and I took turns on first rights to new pools. Abe watched for a while but eventually wandered back to the cabin to read. There are times in fishing when everything goes right, but there are times when nothing does. No matter how I tried, I could not catch a fish. Not even a little one.

To make matters worse, Jim began to catch fish. First in one pool and then another.

"Dumb luck, Jimbo," I joked as he held up his latest sleek silver catch for me to admire.

"Western skill," Jim shot back.

For some reason, Jim's Montana black leech pattern was proving irresistible to Maine salmon, while my trusty Gray Ghost gave up. Finally, as we reached a new pool, I smothered my pride and asked Jim what his trick was. He reached into his vest, extracted a small jar of orange salmon eggs, and slipped several onto the hook of his fly. "Drift these down along the bottom."

"That's not fly-fishing," I said, waving the jar away. My father always looked down on fishermen who used bait. "Better to have an empty creel than to lower your standards."

"It's not for purists," Jim chuckled, "but when all else fails, this works."

I vowed to show Jim that I could do as well without bending the rules. I moved ahead to be first in a new pool, but it did not help. I pushed myself, tried longer casts, went out deeper. I began to take risks, to ignore the strain of the current and the slippery rock bottom.

Then I saw a fish rise to catch a mayfly behind a rock near the other bank. My best casts fell a few feet short. The current was strong, but the water was still ten inches below the top of my chest-high waders. With another few steps, I could just reach the fish. I edged out further, slipped, caught myself. Fear set in. I began to breathe deeply. All I needed was one more step.

I moved forward. My feet groped for a grasp on a round rock. As I pressed down, my right foot slipped. I lurched sideways, leaned upstream, teetering, wobbling, fighting for balance on one leg, but lost it. The current swept my left leg out from under me. Suddenly I was submerged and choking in icy water. I kicked and fought to get my head above water, gasping. I was being carried down the center of the pool toward the rapids at its end. I still clung to my rod in one hand, but I felt the water seeping below the safety belt into my waders. My feet were becoming too heavy to kick. Dragging me down. I let go of my rod and tried to thrash toward shore with my arms. The bank of the pool was quickly slipping by.

The current hurled me against the first rock in the rapids, then into the foaming white torrent below it. I flailed with my arms and tried to move my legs. My shoulder hit a rock and my head went under. I gulped for air but swallowed water. My head bobbed up but was pulled under again by my waders. I was choking, sinking, swallowing water, seeing black.

At first I was not aware of Jim's grasp. The pressure on my shoulder was just another rock. It became a pull, then an arm wrapped around me. We bobbed wildly down the rapids until we reached a calm eddy in the next pool. Jim gripped me around the chest as he tugged toward shore with a flailing sidestroke. He pulled me up on the side and unhooked my waders. I lay gasping on the flat pebbles. When I had caught enough breath to focus, I noticed Jim wringing out his shirt.

Jim looked down and grinned. "Little cold for swimming, ain't it Cutler?"

"Shit. That was awful." I sat up, pulled down my waders, and watched the water gush out onto the rocks. My chest convulsed with dry heaves. I was still shaking.

"Couldn't miss a catch that big." Jim chuckled. "I saw you bobbing toward me like a little ball. What the hell, I thought, I haven't caught one that size. So I jumped in."

"I owe you one, Jimbo," I replied, wanting to say more.

Jim walked over and clapped me on the shoulder. "Hell, you're lucky I didn't know how cold that water is. I might have waved you by." He chuckled at his humor. I simply shivered.

"Let's go back to the cabin and dry out," Jim said. "We'll look for your rod later."

CHAPTER 2

I T WAS DARK WHEN I WOKE UP. I had no idea where I was or what day it was. Gradually I recognized my living room. I was sprawled on the sofa, and the picture of Cathedral Lake had fallen from my lap to the floor. My head ached. My throat was scratchy and dry. I felt spineless, like a jellyfish stranded on a beach. Finally, one flaccid limb at a time, I forced myself to move. I sat on the edge of the couch, elbows to knees, head in hands. I still had a fever.

I stumbled into the hall and flipped on the lights. A square of white paper lay on the floor. Someone had slipped a note through the mail slot. A reporter. She had left her office and home phone numbers and an invitation to tell my side of the story. But what could I say? What was my side of the story? Did it matter that I had acted out of good intentions? Why would she care? She wasn't interested in helping me. She just wanted to get access to me. I was a story, a notch on her gun, a step in her career.

I fell back into a chair and stared at the bare walls of the living room. An unbroken desert of white. Framed reproductions of French paintings leaned against one wall, still wrapped in the brown paper of the Georgetown gallery where I had purchased them six months ago. My wife was supposed to hang them.

I had moved from my cramped apartment in Georgetown to this empty house in Virginia in hopes of luring Kate down here. She sometimes came on weekends but refused to leave Princeton permanently. Still, I did not give up hope. I desperately wanted her to share my Washington world.

"Just try it," I said. "Maybe you'll like it."

"Like a horse comes to like a halter?" she asked quietly.

"That's a crappy remark."

"You just don't get it, do you?"

"You're the one who refuses to try."

She looked at me intently. "I'd suffocate down there."

"In Washington?" My voice was scornful. "It's the most exciting place in the world."

"If power is your drug of preference."

"Cheap shot."

She took my hand and looked into my eyes. "Come home, Peter. Washington is changing you. Those people have lost touch with what really matters in life."

"Nuclear weapons aren't real? Or war? Or terrorism?"

"You know that's not what I meant."

I shook off her hand and turned away angrily. I thought I remembered her crying, though I was not sure of my memories any more.

I put on a disc of Glenn Gould playing the Goldberg variations. As a child I used to listen to my mother practice them for hours, my mind wandering up and down the spiral staircases of their arpeggios. She had been studying piano at the New England Conservatory when my father was at Harvard Divinity School. She gave up her career as a soloist to accompany him in his church work. For two years, she tried to teach me the piano, but I resisted fiercely. For a boy in Blainesville, piano lessons were about as attractive as wearing a skirt, particularly if you were already teased for being the "preacher's kid." But she did leave me with a deep love of music.

With her black hair pulled back in a bun and her pale skin, Mother never looked like a happy person. She had firm rules for our home: no television, grace before every meal, and prayers every night. She insisted that I use my full name and would not tolerate the nickname "Pete."

"They all call me Pete."

"Don't pay any attention. Tell them Peter is a very significant name. It means the rock on which the Church is founded."

"But they'll think I'm stuck up if I tell them not to call me Pete."

"It's more important to stick up for what's right than to be popular. Always be a leader. If you are known as someone who does the right thing, others will look up to you."

Tonight Bach sounded hollow. My headache pulsed. I could not stop the questions. What was happening in Pakistan? Who had control of the weapons? Could the president change his mind? Was he thinking about me in his inner rooms? Was I vindicated?

I looked at my watch: 8:00 P.M. Suddenly I felt very hungry. I went to the kitchen, took the phone receiver from under a pile of newspapers, and placed it back on the hook. I opened the refrigerator. The stale hot dogs were covered in scabrous pale patches. I threw them in the garbage. I would have to go into Alexandria to find something to eat.

I found a parking spot easily and went into my favorite little restaurant, the one where Alexa and I had last dined. I remembered the look of hurt and anger on her flushed face. I did not want to hurt her. Who betrayed whom? Could she be playing a part in Jim's refusal to talk to me?

I remembered so clearly the day I met her at Princeton. I was stretching on the lawn near the boathouse before jogging around Lake Carnegie. A crew shell shot like a tan arrow from under the stone arch of the Washington Street bridge, shattering the mirror and scattering a pair of mallards.

She sat on the grass a few yards away, tanned legs extended, gracefully stretching first one arm and then the other to touch her toes. The muscles of her back were visible through her shirt, and her blond ponytail swayed back and forth. I pretended to concentrate on stretching, prolonging my usual routine, watching, hoping to time my conclusion with hers. She noticed me staring, and stood up.

"You're a second-year, aren't you?"

I blushed. I introduced myself and groped for an opening line.

"Did you go to Harvard?" I nodded at her T-shirt.

"I graduated two years ago, but I spent last year in Washington working for Senator Kent."

"Then you must know Jim Childress."

"We overlapped for a couple of weeks." Her tone was noncommittal, but I thought I detected the hint of a frown.

"How'd you like . . . "

"Washington is fabulous."

She started jogging and I quickly fell in step.

"How so?"

"Everything's happening there."

"Then why are you here?"

"I'm going back when I finish my master's."

The chase was on.

What drew me to Alexa was not just her perfect figure or the blond hair and striking blue eyes. It was the way she carried herself. She seemed to know something special, to be the arbiter of what was acceptable. She was not haughty, just completely self-composed.

One day, old Professor Grosz commented in our political theory seminar that women could not understand Nietzsche's concept of the superman. Most of us were used to his chauvinist comments and pompous airs. Students joked that he always spoke with a German accent in America and an American accent in Germany. We paid little heed to his obiter dicta. Not Alexa. Her hand shot up.

"That kind of remark is offensive to women."

Grosz looked stunned, as though someone had rapped his balding pate with a ruler. Twenty-three students inhaled at once. I half expected the pictures of Plato and Aristotle to fall off the dusty wall behind his desk. His chair spring shrieked as he sat back, one hand nervously straightening his bow tie.

"Well, no one else has ever complained." He sounded more puzzled than apologetic.

Alexa smiled with exaggerated sweetness. "I just thought you might like to know."

After the class, she was surrounded in the hall by the other women students.

"Nice job," I said as I brushed past.

When I met Jim and Abe for our beer after the library closed that night, I was still thinking about the incident.

"What did you think of Alexa Byrnes today? Wasn't she great?"

"Watch out for that one," Jim said. "I heard about her from some of the guys I used to work with in Kent's office."

I looked puzzled. "What the hell's that supposed to mean?"

"She's a user," Jim replied.

"Do I detect a note of jealousy?"

"No way," Jim replied. "She's the type that uses her looks to jerk guys around."

"I went running with her. She seemed nice."

"Just stay out of her bed," Jim responded with his throaty laugh.

The next day, Alexa was outside the graduate dorm as I was getting ready to run. She was stripping off her Harvard sweatshirt.

"Thanks for yesterday," she said.

"For what?"

"For understanding." She smiled. "You were the only man who mentioned it. Some of our other classmates still act like boys when it comes to women. Want to run?"

I smiled and took off after her without stretching. A bad decision. At first I thrilled at her ponytail swaying with each stride and her firm legs moving under the smooth nylon. But then a stitch began to spread through my side. I fell behind.

Alexa turned her head and called back, "Come on, catch me."

I pushed to catch up, but that made the stitch worse. I began to lose my breath. Agony was eating my ribs. "Wait," I called.

Alexa broke stride, slowed, and stopped. She turned, frowning, hands on hips. Little beads of perspiration stood out on her upper lip. "What's the problem?"

"Stitch."

We walked for a few yards while I caught my breath and rubbed my side.

Alexa broke the silence.

"They call you guys the three musketeers."

"Yeah, but we're different too." I was still rubbing my side, "Anyway, I'm more like Jim than Abe."

"Do you really think so?" She tilted her head. "I would have said just the opposite. You and Abe seem more sensitive."

"Maybe I've got some of each," I backtracked. "What I meant is Jim's more, uh, charismatic. You know, a leader."

"Charisma's relative to the situation," she said. "Jim's hardly a leader in the classroom. People pay much more attention when you speak."

I was surprised but didn't have a chance to respond.

"You ready?" She cocked her head impatiently. "I've got to get back."

From then on, I adjusted my jogging schedule to Alexa's. If she was there first, I shortened my warm-up. If she arrived late, I lengthened it until she was ready. When she did not appear, I was crushed.

A few days later, Alexa surprised me again. "I need a date for a party in New York this weekend. Want to come?"

"Yes," I said too quickly. "I'd love to go."

SATURDAY AFTERNOON, we took the train to New York. After I stowed our bags in the rack above, I settled into the seat next to Alexa. At first we both took out books and pretended to read. I was rereading a paperback copy of *War and Peace*; she appeared immersed in a book about modern jazz. I glanced sideways at the window, where her profile was reflected lightly in front of passing Jersey cornfields and hedgerows. She closed her book.

"We go quite near my home in Plainfield."

"Do your parents still live there?" I asked above the clacking wheels.

"My mother," she said. "My father moved to California with another woman when I was twelve." She turned toward the window.

"Did your mother ever remarry?"

"No," Alexa said, still looking away.

"Do you ever see your dad?"

"No. He hurt us too much." She shook her head.

I did not know what to say. We sat silently for a few minutes, looking out the window, watching the tan stubble of recently harvested cornfields pass by.

Alexa turned back to me. "I don't plan to marry."

"Ah, it's just a question of the right man."

"That's a typical male view." She frowned. "You can have your cake and eat it. But if a woman wants a real career, she has to choose."

"Lots of women have both."

She spoke slowly for emphasis. "If I have my own career first, nobody can do to me what my father did to my mother."

I picked up my book and pretended to read.

We took a cab from Penn Station to Fifth Avenue and 71st Street, the home of Alexa's friends Joan and Lenny Wasserman. Alexa had known Joan at Harvard. Lenny was older, worked on Wall Street, and was close to Wayne Kent, the rising young senator from Montana.

A doorman ushered us into the lobby. Not even my Cutler cousins in Boston had a doorman. A uniformed elevator operator whisked us to the forty-third floor penthouse, where a maid in a black-and-white uniform answered the door and took our overnight bags. I felt a little stiff in my gray suit, the only one I owned, but I did not want to look like a graduate student. Alexa was sleek in a black sheath and gold hoop earrings, her hair pulled back by a black velvet band. She was immediately engulfed by a tall woman in a red dress who rushed down the hallway to embrace her. They gushed greetings. Finally Joan extricated herself and noticed me.

"Oh," she said, extending a thin hand with long polished nails. "You must be Juan."

Alexa blushed. "This is my friend Peter Cutler."

"Wonderful," Joan replied without skipping a beat. "You two will want to run up to your rooms on the next floor and freshen up. People will begin arriving soon. Lenny will be down in a minute."

Lenny wore a smoking jacket and cravat. He had graying hair at the temples and little interest in a male graduate student. He kissed Alexa slowly on both cheeks. After a few pleasantries, he turned away and invested his attention more profitably in the other guests. Most seemed closer to his age than Joan's, and after a few rounds of introduction I found myself trapped in a corner trying to explain what I did to an overstuffed woman with bleached helmet hair as she looked over my shoulder to keep track of guests entering the room. Finally Joan came to my rescue.

"Alexa is looking for you in the solarium."

Actually, Alexa had not been looking for me, but the band began to play, and I asked her to dance. The graze of her hair against my cheek, the pressure of her breasts against my chest was triumphal.

I pressed her close and thought of what she had told me on the train, of her mother's ambition for her. She had trained as a gymnast at Plainfield High, practicing for hours after school and on weekends. She was at the top of her class and won a full scholarship to Harvard. Now she was determined to have a career of her own. Alexa had come a long way from the Irish lower middle class. She fit in with this rich New York bunch far more easily than I did. Even with my WASP pedigree, I felt like a country bumpkin. But who cared as long as I was the one holding her.

My trance was interrupted as the band switched to a song that was too fast for me. There were no dancing schools in Blainesville, and Mother had taught me only the foxtrot and waltz and that at arm's length, tracing little patterns on the linoleum kitchen floor with her thin feet encased in black shoes.

Lenny asked Alexa to dance, and they were off in an exotic display of limbs. Alexa kicked off her shoes and seemed to vibrate with the music. I watched the shimmer of her black dress over her hips. She never once glanced in my direction.

The evening became a roller coaster of slow and fast dances. I watched the fast ones from the sideline but returned for the slow, and Alexa always seemed glad to have me back. The band finally quit, and the last guests left around 1:30. Lenny plopped down on the couch next to Alexa ready to sit and talk.

"Gonna work for Wayne again this summer? They say he's gonna chair an appropriations subcommittee soon."

Fortunately Joan walked over, picked up his hand, and announced that they were going to bed. "Turn off the lights when you come up."

Alexa leaned back on the soft white couch, feet stretched out on the glass coffee table, the dress pulled halfway up her thighs. She patted the cushion next to her and clasped her hands behind her head, her breasts stretching the black crepe.

"Wasn't it fabulous?" she declared. "Aren't they wonderful people? Those were some of the senator's biggest donors."

I lay back against the cushion next to her, thought about the guests, and grunted noncommittally.

"Oh, Mr. Superior." She leaned over, kissed me quickly on the lips, then pulled back and laughed.

"Careful," I said. "You'll give me ideas."

I leaned over and put my arm around her shoulder. She moved toward me, head tilted back and lips slightly parted. As our lips touched, her tongue darted out quickly, then retreated. I ran my hand up her arm and over the dress to her breast. Our lips met again, and her mouth opened to my tongue as we stretched out on the couch. I began to fumble with the zipper on the back of the dress, but she stopped me.

"Not here. Upstairs."

Hand in hand, we stumbled up the spiral stairs to my room. I stood transfixed as Alexa wriggled slightly to shed her dress. It dropped to the floor. She reached back and with one deft motion unfastened her bra. She began to undress me, unbuttoning my shirt, running her fingers over my skin. As she stretched out her arms and folded them around my neck, I felt as if I should step back, look carefully, assure myself that this was real. She pulled me down on the bed and wrapped her legs around me. I finished too fast, as though afraid I might awaken.

Afterward I felt exhilarated but also outside myself, watching, testing reality. What should have been the most tender moment was spoiled by incessant questions. Was this real? Did she feel as strongly as I did?

"I've loved you since the first day," I said. I lay back on the tangled covers next to Alexa, one arm draped across her breast, not as much a gesture of possession as a quest for reassurance.

"You're sweet," Alexa said, and pressed a finger to my lips to stop me from talking. "Let's rest now."

We woke up to daylight painting contrasting shadows across the room. We made love again, this time more slowly, more successfully. Alexa slipped out of bed and began to gather up her clothes.

"Stay," I pleaded.

She shook her head and smiled. "Never neglect appearances."

BACK AT PRINCETON, I spent little time with my friends and started a steady diet of Alexa. I ate, drank, breathed, slept, and dreamt Alexa. I was besotted with her. We ran together, studied together, sat together and whispered together in the back of class. It was like nothing I had ever known. I was enlarged in a way I had never been in my few modest romances in high school and at Bowdoin. Yet I was also diminished in a new way, shriveled by insecurity. I became insanely jealous when I saw Alexa talking to other men.

One morning I saw Alexa with Jim in the McCosh courtyard. It was one of those perfect Princeton days. The great elms carved graceful shadows on the gray stones of the chapel. The air was crisp and the autumn sun lit their faces. They looked cleanly scrubbed, a perfect couple. Jim stood on the first step of the pedestal of the tall white sundial. Alexa was on the grass, looking up at him. Was she attracted to him?

That night, Alexa and I were studying together on the B floor of Firestone Library. I read the same page of Tocqueville three times, but it bounced off my eyes without a word reaching my brain. Instead, I saw Alexa smiling up at Jim on the white pedestal of the sundial. I kept glancing across the table at her. She was taking notes on Durkheim without apparent difficulty. Her concentration irked me.

"Hey," I finally said. "How about a coffee break?"

She looked at her watch. "Sure."

We held hands as we walked over to the student center in Pyne Hall and entered the cafeteria line. I tried to tempt her with a piece of cake, but as usual she refused.

Alexa was about to sit at one of the black plastic tables that filled the middle of the room. Instead, taking her elbow, I steered her to one of the more isolated wooden tables in the alcoves on the side. We sat across from each other under a large hanging plant. I leaned forward over the table, waited until she finished stirring the sweetener into her black coffee, then raised my coffee cup in a toast.

"To our anniversary."

Alexa looked puzzled.

"Two months."

She laughed casually and raised her cup.

"Now are you ready to answer my question?"

She raised her eyebrows.

"You know, about living together. We could get an apartment in town."

Alexa's expression did not change, so I plunged ahead. "I can't stand the idea of your going out with other guys."

Alexa's smile vanished and she looked down at the table. I barely breathed as I waited for her response. Her eyes were cold as they returned to meet mine.

"Peter, you're sweet," she said slowly. "But I'm not going to give up my freedom."

"Why not?"

"Look at my mother. My father left her with three kids and never looked back."

"I'd never leave you," I protested. "Someday we'll get married and have a home full of kids."

"That's not my dream, Peter." Alexa shook her head and looked away. "I may have grown up Catholic, but I left that behind at Harvard."

"You could have a career too."

Alexa shook her head again. "I see my friends in Plainfield trying to juggle marriage and a career, raising children through nannies. They try to have it all and end up having nothing."

"But I'd help," I said.

"I'm sure you'd try, Peter." Alexa looked down at the table and mopped up coffee drops with her paper napkin. She was always meticulous. Everything in its place.

"No, really."

She shook her head slowly.

I realized that persistence would be counterproductive. I was in a hole, and the best thing I could do was stop digging. We returned to the library without touching.

When the weekend arrived, Alexa was gone. There was nothing to do. I tried to study but the pages blurred. Monday I spotted her on the walk that divides McCosh Hall from the modern art museum. Alexa was walking quickly to avoid conversation. I finally caught up with her at Cannon Green. I seized the elbow of her coat and spun her toward me.

"Why didn't you tell me," I shouted. "Are you seeing someone else?"

A number of students in the flow that divided around us turned their heads to look back.

Alexa dug her fingernails into my hand. "Lower your voice," she hissed. "You don't own me." Her breath made little puffs of frost in the December air.

"Tell me," I insisted, still grasping her coat.

"I'll discuss it at lunch if you want," she said firmly, "but I'm not going to be late to class."

"Well, I'm going to cut it."

"Suit yourself," she said icily, turning and breaking out of my grip.

I watched Alexa's blue coat meld into the stream of students on the walk. I decided I really would skip class. I wouldn't be able to concentrate. Who cared anyway? I wandered into the gardens behind Prospect House, where the lawn was covered with frost. I needed to be alone, to think of what I was going to say.

WE MET AT THE STUDENT CENTER, where we settled into one of the alcoves. Anxiety strangled my appetite, and I left my roast beef sandwich untouched on the table. I waited for Alexa to eat a few bites of her salad and take a sip from her Diet Coke.

"Well?"

Alexa put down her fork and reached over to touch my hand. "Peter, you're a handsome man, a sweet and wonderful person. I don't want to hurt you."

"Did you see someone in New York?" I asked recklessly, afraid of the answer but unable to help myself.

"It's none of your business." Alexa looked defiant. Then she continued. "So what if I did. We're not married, you know."

"But that's the point," I pleaded. "I want us to be together forever. I don't want you seeing other men."

Alexa's defiant look softened. "Peter, you don't understand that we want different things from life. I need freedom. I want to take what I'm learning here to Washington. I'd suffocate as a housewife."

I took her hand in both of mine. "I won't cramp you," I said. "We'll be different."

"You still don't understand." Her blue eyes began to moisten. "If we continue, I'll be trapped."

"But Alexa, I love you," I blurted out.

She looked down at the table. "That's exactly the problem, Peter. Now's the time to stop, before we both get badly hurt."

"Christ," I said. "How do you think I feel right now?"

She pulled her hand back. "I want to be friends."

"Can't we go back to your room?"

"No," she said, wiping her mouth with the corner of her paper napkin. "I'm leaving now, and when I get up from this table we'll be friends. Don't follow me."

Alexa slipped out from behind the table, picked up her coat, leaned over, and kissed me lightly on the cheek. She walked toward the door. I half expected her to turn, but she never looked back.

As I entered the little restaurant in Alexandria, I recognized a reporter sitting at the bar. He was from the *Washington Post*. Ordinarily I would walk right up to him. He would probe for gossip and repay me with publicity. But tonight he was the last person I wanted to see.

I turned tail before he spotted me. I knew I couldn't fend off the questions about the weapons, the CIA operations, the battle between Pentagon and State, the White House intrigue. I was no longer hungry.

Home again, I poured myself a large bourbon and sat on the couch in the living room. I started to munch the stale saltines but they had no flavor. Might as well be chewing on the box they came in.

I rarely watched television, but I turned it on and stared numbly at a drama for a few minutes. Two policemen were questioning a small man. They pushed him against a wall, and one of the policemen punched him in the stomach. So much for justice. Just like Jack Reese. Kick 'em when they're down, that's his motto. Only he calls it protecting the president. What was it Reese used to say? "If you want a friend in this town, buy a dog."

I changed the channel. PBS had a special on nuclear terrorism. Some expert from Harvard's Kennedy School was droning on about how it would overshadow anything we had seen in the past. They cut to a picture of the World Trade Center towers collapsing. I clicked off.

Should I call Jim? Would he talk to me? He had always come to my rescue in the past. Like our trip to Maine after Alexa dumped me. We decided to splurge and flew from Newark to Bangor. Jim's seat was tilted back, and his big arms were clasped behind his head. I pushed the seat button and reclined to his level. A flight attendant handed us little paper napkins with the Delta logo and asked what we wanted to drink. She was not very pretty, but as she turned and flounced her long blond hair, Alexa flooded my mind so powerfully that I had to face the window and swallow hard.

"Ya know, Cutler, you've had your head up your ass for three months."

"You already told me that."

In fact, it was the first thing Jim had said after he barged into my room and virtually invited himself to Maine for Christmas. I had been planning to stay in Princeton ostensibly to study, but really in hopes that Alexa would come back from vacation early.

FATHER MET US AT BANGOR AIRPORT. I volunteered to drive.

"Peter tells me you're quite a fisherman."

"Now and then," Jim replied. "He casts a pretty fine line himself. Says he learned it all from you."

"I've always wanted to fish Montana. Have you ever read Norman McLean's book?"

"Great yarn," Jim said. "I like his opener about there being only a fine line between fly-fishing and religion."

"That one even appeals to our agnostic friend." Father nodded toward me but winked at Jim.

I shifted in my seat, tightened my lips, and kept my eyes on the road. I was struck by the way these two people, both so important to me, physically as disparate as Mutt and Jeff, hit it off so quickly.

"What happened to the young lady you said might visit us?" Father asked.

"She stayed in New Jersey," I said tersely.

"Everything going all right?"

I did not reply.

Jim broke the silence. "Peter finally saw the light."

I braced myself for my father's next question, but Jim deftly changed the subject back to trout.

"You should come try our Montana rainbows, Reverend Cutler."

"Do they fight as well as our brook trout?"

"Your brookies are pretty," Jim said, "but they don't jump the way our 'bows do."

Mother also liked Jim. I could see it in her smiles and her insistence on second helpings as we sat round the dining room table in the old manse in Blainesville.

"Best apple pie I've ever tasted, Mrs. Cutler."

Jim's accent had thickened. Even my puritan mother was vulnerable to the power of flattery.

"Oh, I'm sure your mother's was just as good." Mother blushed slightly.

"Yes, she was good at everything. She was a social studies teacher before she married." Jim said.

"I hear Montana's very beautiful."

"I can see sixty miles of the Bitteroot Range from our back porch," Jim said, sitting back in his chair. "Sometimes I watch the sunset over those snowy peaks and want to howl with the coyotes." Jim looked down at his plate, slightly embarrassed at his unaccustomed eloquence.

"If it's that beautiful, why study politics? Why not go back and ranch?" Father asked.

"I guess the short answer is my mother always told me to do more with my life. She wanted me to get out of Montana."

"Government service can be a noble calling," Father said. "Peter's great-grandfather was a senator. That's his portrait behind you."

Jim twisted in his chair to face a large man with a white beard and sharp blue eyes staring from a gilded frame. As a child, I had stared at that picture for hours, thinking how much I would like to become a senator.

"He was a great man," Father said. "My father tried to follow his footsteps, but he lost in the dirty election of '36. That was a bad year for us Republicans. Watching his defeat convinced me that politics is too brutal for my taste."

"It can get nasty," Jim said. "But it's hard to think of a more exciting game." He paused, then added for my father's benefit, "It's also a way to do good on a large scale."

Father smiled. "I've only got the stomach for small-scale good. There's plenty of that to be done right here in Blainesville."

"Harry Truman got politics right," Jim continued. "If you don't like the heat, you'd better stay out of the kitchen."

I was pleased that Jim was such a hit with my parents. I was almost beginning to enjoy myself when I suddenly remembered that Jim was not the guest I had intended to bring to their table. My involuntary sigh of deflation was so noticeable that Mother looked at me quizzically. Father put down his spoon. "You haven't said much all day."

Jim jumped in. "They been working him pretty hard down there. I'll fix him up in the woods tomorrow."

THE NEXT MORNING we drove north. After we parked, we skied the last few miles to Cathedral Lake. A light snow had fallen. Rough gray maple trunks were plastered on one side, their long limbs iced, as were the dark green boughs of balsam and hemlock. Chef's hats had been issued to the rocks and stumps. Powder snapped from branches brushed by our sleeves. The skis hissed through the snow, slim red tips diving in and out of white.

Sharp cracks came from branches as the remaining sap froze and split them. Cold bit our cheeks, and crystals of our breath hung in the air in puffy bursts. Without breaking stride, I mopped a drop hanging from the tip of my nose with my deerskin mitten. The straps of my pack basket pulled against my shoulders, but the rhythmic movement felt deeply satisfying.

In winter the Maine woods looked different, revealing splendid vistas as well as unknown rocks and stumps. I thought of running with Alexa, of watching the muscles in her legs. So far away. Yet everything here was so immediate. Katahdin stood even more majestic than in summer. I could almost reach across the lake and touch it. There was a stark beauty in the cold absence of leafy dress.

When we reached the cabin, it was roofed in white, and the first two steps to the porch had vanished. We leaned our skis against the wall, thunked the snow off our boots onto the weathered boards of the porch, and pushed open the heavy wooden door. The dark interior smelled musty.

"Let's start a fire, then go for grouse." I began to pile kindling in the stove. "It'll take a couple of hours for this place to warm up anyway."

"Lead the way, Peter." Jim said. "You're the king here."

Shotguns in hand, we trudged across the lake on snowshoes, etching a webbed trail of human purpose on its pristine surface. Clouds spread across the horizon, and the lowering sun purpled their edges. High above, contrails from a distant jet sketched faint white lines on the wintry sky.

"The birds sometimes sit in that spruce thicket," I said, as we reached the far side of the lake. "Walk a few steps, wait, then take a few more steps. They can flush in any direction."

I cradled my grandfather's old Winchester twenty gauge in my left arm, right hand ready to flick off the safety at any time. I ducked under a spruce branch, dislodging a tiny avalanche of icy crystals that burned their way down the back of my neck. With my gun barrel, I nudged aside the frail skeleton of a dead spruce that had lost the competition for summer sun. I took three steps, waited, listened. I twisted around fallen trunks. A branch stung my face. Occasionally I called to Jim to check location in the thick cover.

The whirring wings of a grouse exploded from a small spruce not fifteen yards to my left. Startled, I jerked the gun to my shoulder, trying to follow the bird's dodging path between the trees. I squeezed the trigger, shattering the silence of the woods. Needles fell, the grouse veered to the left. Missed. My heart was pounding. Surprised, I had not led it properly.

"Coming your way, Jimbo," I yelled a moment before the loud report of his twelve gauge.

"Shit! These little buggers don't fly straight."

I laughed out loud for the first time in a long while.

After several more spruce thickets and a cedar swamp, Jim missed another bird and I finally made a nice shot. By then it was getting dark, and we headed back. I had left a kerosene lantern in the window of the cabin, and the flickering light guided us across the frozen lake. In the west, the low clouds still glowed faintly pink. Above them, a band of blue faded smoothly but quickly upward into deepening ink. We stopped in the middle of the lake and looked up at the first stars that pierced the blue-black ceiling. I inhaled a deep breath of cold air. I finally felt full again.

I pointed toward the stars with my grandfather's shotgun. "There's ten to the twentieth power of those things up there. That number's too big for me to fathom."

Jim came up beside me and rested his right arm on the back of my down parka.

"Don't count 'em, Cutler. Just soak in 'em."

LATER, IN THE CABIN, Jim took a sip from the bottle of Jack Daniels and passed it to me. We tilted back in the straight wooden chairs, pushed away the dirty dinner dishes, and put our feet up on the table. The floor was still cold, but the air was now warm enough that we rolled up the sleeves of our checkered wool shirts. The fire popped and crackled in the black iron stove, and above it the stovepipe glowed a rusty red.

"You got a nice family, Peter."

I looked away from Jim. Amber light from the kerosene lanterns reflected off the frosted windows. "I love my father, but sometimes he drives me crazy."

"How so?" Jim tilted his head.

"He's so damn sure of everything." I hesitated, then had an urge to say more. "I mean, he tries to run my life, my mother's life, the church. If he wanted power, why didn't he do what my grandfather did? Instead, he tries to micromanage his tiny kingdom."

"Aren't you being a little too hard on him?" Jim asked. "You oughta meet my old man."

I nodded. "I know he loves me. I know he's been the strongest influence in my life. But I need more space. He crowds me."

"That's normal," Jim shrugged. "But what I see is two good people who showed you good values. That's why you talk about marriage and family so much."

The word "marriage" brought Alexa rushing back. I winced. Jim had been watching me closely.

"She wasn't right for you," he said, shaking his head.

"We'll never know," I avoided Jim's eyes, "I pushed her too fast, mentioned marriage too soon."

Jim snorted. "Cutler, it's too bad self-deception isn't an Olympic event. You're world-class."

I shrugged. "You never understood her."

Jim touched my arm, beckoning for the Jack Daniels. "Wrong, Peter. I know her too well. That gal ain't the marryin' type. I heard stories about her when she worked in Kent's office last summer. She loves power. She knew you were the smartest guy in our class. She loved bustin' your balls."

"It could've been different." I shook my head. "I would've met her halfway."

"Shit," Jim drawled the word into two syllables, "she-it." He drank from the bottle and handed it back. "She doesn't know what halfway means."

I pushed my chair back from the table and away from Jim, not yet ready to confess fully to myself, much less to Jim, something I was beginning to suspect. Alexa never really loved me, at least not in the desperate way I loved her. Even when we made love, she always held something back, always controlled the relationship.

"You don't really know her," I tried again.

"Don't kid yourself, Peter. Alexa hides things well. As she says, she never neglects appearances."

I looked sharply at Jim. Where had he heard that? That was one of her intimate expressions. Jim and Alexa couldn't have gotten together. They didn't really like each other. In a way, they were rivals. Jim returned my look without averting his eyes. There was no sign of the throaty chuckle that usually accompanied his tales of conquest. I should just drop it.

I walked over to the wood box, picked up a log, and kicked open the stove door with my boot. The inferno inside the black iron spewed out a wall of heat. I shoved in the log and kicked the door shut with a clang. I stood and listened to the crackling, inhaling the intense odor of burning birch bark. My face glowed and my head buzzed with bourbon.

I stood by the stove, hands extended to capture the rising warmth, my back to Jim. I could not look at him right then. Occasional drops of water from the wet mittens drying on hangars above the stove fell down, emitting little hisses that punctuated his continuing sermon.

"You know, Cutler, it's hard to blend two lives. There's always a struggle for power, and someone comes out second. I saw it with my parents. I hated to watch 'em fight."

"Mine never fight," I said, turning now to face him and reaching out to grab the bottle, "but sometimes I wish my mother would stand up to my father more."

"You can't have two number ones," Jim said, "And that broad would've kept you in second place."

"That why you can't stick to one woman?" I retorted. "Afraid she'd get too much power over you?"

"You got it," Jim gave his deep throaty chuckle. "I'm too selfish for marriage. At least I know it. But so does Alexa."

I felt flushed and slightly dizzy. Had Alexa been toying with me? Did she care? Would she ever come back? I was in no shape to fit the pieces of the puzzle together. I stumbled out on the porch to pee. Icy air stung my cheeks. I soaked in silence so deep that it rang in my ears.

When I returned to the warmth of the cabin, Jim was already snoring on the bunk. I crawled into my sleeping bag, snuggled deep into the down, and gradually succumbed to the narcotic of sleep.

JIM HAD ALWAYS talked me through tough times. Couldn't I count on him now when I really needed him? Alexa gone. Kate gone. Only Jim. I would try him again. For a little extra courage, I went into the kitchen, brought out the bottle of bourbon, and filled my glass. I twisted the glass, watching the streaks that the amber fluid left on the side of the clear crystal. These glasses had been a wedding present. I finished the drink and felt the liquor burn its way down my throat. Relief for my headache. I filled the glass and drained it again. I waited while a warm, furry sensation brushed the length of my spine and warmed my head.

I picked up the phone and dialed Jim's number at the White House. He always worked late. I would explain everything and ask him to intercede with the president. If Jim heard me out, he would understand. He could persuade the president to change his mind. The president always listened to him. I reached an operator. There was a long pause. Then she said Mr. Childress was not available.

"Tell him Peter Cutler called," I said, slightly slurring my name.

The operator asked me how to spell it.

"He'll know," I said, and hung up.

Now I felt dizzy. The alcohol had deceived me, like an importunate child that begins with smiles but slides into a tantrum when its demands are not met. It was now tapping the interior of my skull with a thousand little hammer blows. I started to get up but bumped the coffee table. The bottle tipped over and the whiskey reached the edge of the table and began to drip onto the white rug. I should go to the kitchen and get a sponge, but why? I sat back in the couch, holding the bottle firmly in both hands to steady it, watching a brown splotch expand into the white rug. I was fascinated by the spreading stain.

I rested my head on the back of the couch, but the room was spinning too fast to allow me sleep. I staggered to my feet and went to the bathroom. I reached for the medicine cabinet and grabbed hold of the mirrored door. Two bloodshot blue eyes stared back at me. I opened the cabinet to find the little plastic bottle of sleeping pills that the State Department doctor had prescribed for jet lag. Escape.

CHAPTER 3

I FIRST NOTICED ALI AZIZ because he sat alone in the dining hall and stood out among the American faces and button-down shirts. With straight black hair swept back from a long brown face and a neatly trimmed mustache, Ali struck me as the embodiment of a Pashtun warrior straight out of Kipling. He seemed aloof, but his severe look vanished when he unleashed his charming smile. As a shy foreign engineer, however, he had few friends on whom to lavish it.

One evening, I persuaded Abe and Jim to join me in sitting down next to him, and we introduced ourselves. Ali was born in Islamabad, son of a minor civil servant who had fled from India and just escaped with his life. His father had invested his hopes for Pakistan in Ali's success. All his life, Ali had done well in school, and now he had a government scholarship to study nuclear engineering at Princeton. He said he liked America but could never feel at home here.

We got into the habit of eating together. We often lingered over coffee in the cavernous dining hall. Ali could be puzzling, but he was never boring. He was a unique combination of Western scientist and Muslim mystic. He drank whiskey but would not eat pork. He went out of his way to drop the names of the many Western writers he had read but swore that all wisdom was captured in the Qur'an. He loved American technology and gadgets and was sometimes critical of his country's government, but he turned defensive when others criticized Pakistan.

Ali was a genius at math. When we had problems with our quantitative methods course, he gave us free tutorials. Struggling over an algorithm at one session, I asked Ali what had attracted him to engineering.

"I love the purity of problems with a logical solution," he replied. "Ever since I was a small boy, it was a way to escape the world around me. I always did my math homework first."

"I always did it last," I laughed, "until it was too late to concentrate. And my father was no help."

"Nor mine," Ali frowned. "He had little education. He pressed me very hard to succeed in school. If I got a bad mark, he beat me, but I never had a bad mark in math or science."

While Ali did nothing to hide the differences in our backgrounds and disciplines, he seemed to crave our acceptance.

"I like you three," he said one night after dinner. "It's nice to see such friends."

"Now it's four," I smiled.

Ali glanced down. "Only for a little while."

"Hell," Jim said. "You'll meet some gal, and she'll make an American out of you. That's how it happens."

Ali shook his head. "American women are impossible."

"What's that mean?" Abe asked.

"They don't understand that men and women are equal but in different spheres." Ali looked pensive. "In sport, man is stronger, but in nobility woman is stronger. She is equal when we pay her respect. But when she takes her clothes off in Western pornography, she loses respect and loses equality."

"You're taking an extreme case," Abe objected.

"Allah created two sexes for a purpose," Ali replied. "Procreation. Some day after I return, I will have a wife and many children."

"You're gonna miss a lot of fun if you keep believing that stuff," Jim said with a chuckle.

Ali smiled. "Be glad He did not create five sexes, Jim. Think how that would complicate your life."

"Amen to that," Abe said.

"The fact is, I have to go back because they've paid for my scholarship. I've signed papers promising to return."

"This is a free country," Jim said. "You can make enough money to buy them out."

"Well it's more than that, you see." Ali looked pensive. "I want to serve my country. My father would never forgive me if I stayed here. And if I go home, I can work to make Pakistan democratic. That is what our history requires. Here I'm just another exile."

"Is Islamic democracy possible?" Abe asked.

"I'll bet my life on it."

"But how can you accept a religious basis for the state in Pakistan and not in Israel?"

"Pakistan is founded on the Qur'an, and I accept the Qur'an."

"But physics isn't based on the Qur'an," Abe replied. "And you're committed to science."

"Ah," Ali said, warming to the subject, "but that's different. We live to learn and there are two types of certainties, science and religion. Natural knowledge can take you only so far. After that, knowledge is spiritual, and it's all in the Qur'an."

We also argued about Pakistan's efforts to develop nuclear weapons, a subject often in the news. "If you develop a nuclear arsenal," I said, "you may jeopardize the lives of millions of people in South Asia."

"We have no choice," Ali replied, "since India exploded its nuclear test in 1974. As Ali Bhutto said, we'll eat grass if that's necessary. India has already dismembered our country twice. We can't let them have power over us."

"There has to be a better way," Abe objected. "Nuclear weapons are too risky."

"We have no intention of spreading it," Ali replied. "This talk of an Islamic bomb is nonsense. We'll never spread the bomb. I'll give you my word on that. All we need is to be able to stand up to India as an equal. It's as simple as that."

It was through Ali that I met Kate. Once he became more comfortable at Princeton and began to expand his circle of friends, Ali threw a party in his room; like all dorm parties it quickly became overcrowded. People jostled between a keg and a small area cleared for dancing. I lingered near the keg talking to Ali. Some drunk bumped my arm, and beer spilled down the back of a woman with long black hair. She wheeled around and glared at me.

"Juvenile trick," she spat out.

"I'm sorry, but . . . "

Ali came to the rescue. "It wasn't his fault; Kate, this is Peter Bradford Cutler; Peter, this is Kate Ling Chen, my date for this lovely evening. Now you nice Americans make up."

When she smiled, I realized what an attractive woman she was. She was a good head shorter than me and slim. She had intense eyes, high cheekbones, and delicate features. Her skin was flawless. When I asked her to dance, I discovered that Kate had grown up in Princeton, graduated from Wellesley, and returned to get a Ph.D. in American literature with the intention of teaching. Her father had come from Hong Kong to study engineering at Princeton and stayed on to start a successful software company. Kate had grown up in a big house on Prospect Street and graduated from Princeton High School.

I first asked her out because she was attractive, and I needed a woman to distract me from Alexa. At best, I expected a brief diversion. After all, Kate was indifferent to politics. While I reached for the op-eds when opening the *New York Times*, she turned first to the crossword puzzle. On our first date, we went to a movie and then to the taproom at the Nassau Inn where we joined Jim and his woman of the moment. I mainly wanted to show Jim that I was dating again. But we laughed so hard and had such a good time that I could not wait to call Kate the next morning.

Alexa and Kate were near opposites. I remembered Alexa telling me she thought Ali a bore with his strange preoccupations. When I asked Kate whether there was anything between her and Ali, she laughed and said, "I love him, but not in the way you think. He's a perfect gentleman. Besides, I can't imagine living as a woman in an Islamic country."

What captivated me more than anything was the way Kate laughed.

She loved silly jokes, and her sparkling laughter infected everyone around her. Talking to Kate was like opening a bottle of champagne. It wasn't until Kate that I realized how rarely Alexa had laughed.

Kate introduced me to things I had not focused on in Princeton. I had ignored the university art museum until Kate took me there and explained the intricate geometry and color of the Frank Stella canvases. Trips to New York with Kate were totally different from those with Alexa. Instead of beautiful people, we visited beautiful places.

When the New York Ballet came to McCarter Theater in Princeton, Kate bought tickets for me and Ali to accompany her. I had little experience with ballet in Blainesville, and Ali teased her about "a bunch of scantily clad ladies jumping about."

"It's so fleeting," I said as we walked back from the theater. "It's beautiful but it's gone after the performance. At least books last."

"But that's the point," Kate replied. "Each detail is perfect while it lasts. Focus on the moment."

Kate was absolutely sure of her tastes. She knew what she liked and what she wanted, and was happy to leave the rest to others. Literature and art were her world. Her approach to life was summed up in a passage she once read me from Samuel Johnson: "It is by studying little things that we attain the great art of having as little misery and as much happiness as possible."

Kate loved long walks rather than running. "You notice more when you walk," she said. We often strolled along the canal or around Lake Carnegie, watching the crew shells spurt along the silvery surface like eight-legged water spiders. Kate could name the calls of birds. I found myself discussing novels and poetry, subjects I once neglected as insufficiently practical. Kate was writing her thesis on Emily Dickinson, and she often quoted the Belle of Amherst. Sometimes she tested me by slipping in a verse of her own.

When we made love, it was like the ballet we had watched, not just in the beauty and movement of her lithe body, but the gentleness of her gestures afterward. She blended passion with tenderness. She would rub my back and massage my neck.

"I love you," she would whisper over and over as she nuzzled my ear.

"I love you too," I replied, stroking her arm.

AFTER WE HAD DATED for a few months, Kate invited me to dinner at her parents' house. As I stood on the large porch and nervously rang the doorbell, I was reminded of my Cutler cousins' house in Chestnut Hill outside of Boston. It had the same feel of a comfortable, well-ordered world.

When Kate opened the door, however, I was ushered into bedlam. As I entered the large hall, I was attacked at the knees by a four-year-old while another fired a toy gun at me from behind the banister of the grand staircase.

"Got him," yelled the one who had wrapped his arms around my knees.

"Bang, bang. You're dead, Kate's new boyfriend," screamed the sharpshooter from his ambush on the stairs.

Kate dropped my hand, picked the attacker off my knees, held him to her chest, and twirled around laughing. She waltzed him down the hall singing, "You—promised—not—to—do—that" The little bandit was giggling and slapping her back. She deposited him on the second stair and slapped his bottom lightly. Along with his sharpshooter twin, he scurried up the stairs.

Kate turned, smoothed her angora sweater, and smiled at me. "Don't mind them. They love to embarrass their sisters, and I'm the only one living at home now. Come into the library and meet my parents."

Dr. Chen was a man my size with slate gray hair and horn-rimmed glasses. He extended his hand. "It sounds like you met the twins." Mrs. Chen, a handsome graying version of Kate, seemed unfazed by the recent commotion. "We call them God's blessing because they came so late in life, but sometimes they act like God's plague." She smiled. "Harold, I think Peter deserves a drink."

At dinner, Mrs. Chen quizzed me about Blainesville, Bowdoin, and graduate school. She looked puzzled when I tried to explain my interest in political science.

"I'm so disappointed with our politicians today," Mr. Chen said. "Where are the leaders we had in the past?"

"Some of them weren't so great," I hesitated, unsure whether I should argue with Kate's dad. "One of my professors says the only difference between a politician and a statesman is the passage of time.

Politicians are the glue that holds our democracy together. We need their power."

"I thought Lord Acton said that power corrupts," Mr. Chen interjected. "And absolute power corrupts absolutely." He sat back with a satisfied look.

"There's a new twist on Acton," I replied, nervous but unable to keep my mouth shut. "Lack of power can also corrupt absolutely."

Kate quickly jumped in to change the subject. "Has anyone seen the new exhibit at the rare books collection in Firestone?"

THE NIGHT BEFORE OUR WEDDING, Jim, Abe, and Ali insisted on a bachelor's last drink at the Nassau Taproom.

Ali proposed the first toast. "My people," he said, holding up his glass and flashing his perfect smile, "say you're not a man until you're married."

"What's that make you," I joked, "a little boy?"

"No, but these chaps are," Ali laughed, indicating Jim and Abe with a sweeping gesture. "My marriage has already been arranged."

"You mean you didn't choose her?" I asked incredulously.

"No, our parents arranged it."

"Do you know her?" Abe asked.

"Not yet," Ali said. "But there'll be time."

"That's unbelievable." I looked puzzled.

"No," Ali smiled, "that's life."

"I can't imagine not choosing Kate."

Jim leaned over and cuffed me on the shoulder. "You got a short memory, Cutler," he chuckled. "Here's to Peter the slow learner," as the three laughed and clinked their glasses. "It took awhile, but he's finally made the right choice."

"Peter's so smart he can rationalize anything," Abe said, looking at me with a broad grin. "So why face tough choices, Peter? Let Ali convert you to Islam. The Qur'an allows four wives. You can have Kate and Alexa too."

"Yes," Ali said, "but the realities of life permit only one."

"Whatever my past faults," I said with mock humility, "Kate is all I want for the rest of my life." Then, raising my glass and looking around the table, I added, "And my three best friends."

KATE AND I SPENT the next few years preoccupied with our theses: mine on controlling the spread of nuclear weapons and Kate's on Emily Dickinson. One night, Kate announced she had decided to give up her thesis and would take an editorial job that had been offered to her at the Princeton University Press.

"We can't afford two of us in school," she said, "and two jobs in one town are hard to find."

"You don't have to quit," I said. "We'll live on love and spaghetti."

Kate smiled. "One makes you too fat and the other too thin."

"What about Emily?"

"I can love her without deconstructing her," Kate laughed. "Besides, my thesis is not going well. It doesn't fit the current fads. I might not find a job in any good English department."

"I'll make it up to you later," I said, taking her in my arms.

"Don't forget," she said as she kissed me.

I SAW LESS OF MY FRIENDS. Jim went to Washington to work for Senator Kent, and Abe was buried in the depths of a thesis on the European origins of American democratic thought. We held a special dinner to celebrate Ali's completion of his doctorate in nuclear engineering. Kate put two card tables together in the living room of our little apartment, spread a white cloth, and put vases of fresh daisies on the table. Abe was there, and Jim came up from Washington.

Ali arrived in a long white tunic, buttoned closely at the neck. He brought Kate two dozen red roses. His smile was as enchanting as ever, but he seemed subdued.

Abe toasted Ali. "Here's to Dr. Aziz."

"Thank you," he said, raising his glass and looking intently toward each of us in turn. "I'll never forget you."

We put down our glasses, and Abe turned to Jim with a smile. "Next year, you'll have to toast Dr. Cutler and Dr. Klein."

Jim snorted. "You guys may become doctors, but you'll never be the useful kind."

"Very funny," Abe said, "but at least we won't be surrounded by puffed-up politicians."

"Who're you kidding?" Jim growled. "Academic politics is worse because it's so petty. Wake up and smell the real world."

Kate turned the focus back to Ali. "I think all politicians are the same whether they're learned or not. They should all study English or engineering. Right, Ali?"

We laughed and toasted Ali's future again. He seemed touched.

"I'll miss you beautiful people," Ali said after the toasts were finished. He had refused champagne, asking for fruit juice as he prepared himself for life in Pakistan. "You know," he said, looking down at the half-empty glass of juice, "sometimes I'm almost reluctant to return home."

"Stay," Jim said. "America needs people like you."

"Pakistan needs me more," Ali looked away toward the window. Then he flashed his bright smile at Kate. "Besides, how could I bring up children in this country? Your women are too liberated."

Kate laughed. "I have friends who could turn you into a good American husband."

"That's what I'm afraid of, my dear," Ali replied, still smiling. "I would have to work too hard."

"You could always be a free spirit like Jim," I said, turning toward Childress. "Found any marriage prospects down there, Jimbo?"

"Still a confirmed bachelor," Jim replied with a grin. "In Washington, there's time for women but not for wives."

"Do you see much of Alexa Byrnes?" Abe asked with a malicious smile.

"Every day. She's on Kent's committee staff." Then he added with that deep chuckle that seemed to come up from his knees, "But never at night, if that's what you mean."

"Now there's a woman for you if you stay." Abe looked at Ali with a smile.

Ali laughed. "Not my type, I'm afraid. Now if Kate were still available, I might have to reconsider." He picked a daisy from the vase and extended it toward Kate with a slight bow.

Kate blew him a kiss from across the table. "If only American men were so gallant . . . "

"But then we wouldn't do the dishes," Abe interrupted with a laugh. "Life is full of hard choices, Katie."

Ali lingered after Abe and Jim left. He was clearly reluctant to go. He and I stood in the doorway of our little apartment.

"You are my brother, Peter," Ali said, his voice becoming soft. "You'll always have a home here."

"I know that. You and Kate have been . . . "

"Stay," I said, reaching out to touch Ali's arm.

Ali shook his head and looked away. Finally he turned back and smiled.

"I've written down your birthday. Every year I will send you a card to prove that I remember."

He reached into his jacket and took a slender silver cigarette case from the pocket.

"Here," he said, thrusting the case into my hand. I saw that it was engraved with a crescent and initials. "This was my father's. I know you don't smoke, but I'd like you to have something from my family."

"That was a lovely gesture," Kate said later when I showed her the box.

"Yes," I replied, running my thumb over the worn silver surface of the case. "Totally useless and perfectly beautiful."

WHEN I COMPLETED MY THESIS, the Politics Department voted to make me an assistant professor. Kate was delighted that we would not have to search for new jobs in another city, especially since we had learned that she was pregnant a few weeks earlier. Two of her poems had been published in a small magazine, and she was doing well at the Press.

Things got more complicated as our daughter and son grew. There were times when I feared I was falling behind in the rigid race on the tenure track. My first book was easy because it was based on my thesis, but the second book on foreign policy went slowly, in part because I often took care of the kids. I felt like a passenger standing on the dock, watching my ship depart, wanting to jump. I found it difficult to concentrate on my work when interrupted constantly by smelly diaper changes and pushing spoonfuls of mushy baby food into resistant mouths.

One day, when Kate was in New York at a meeting of university presses, the kids fought constantly. I could not interest them in anything. Each demanded my full attention. While I tried to focus on my computer, I heard a crash. Jimmy had pulled a whole case of books to the floor. I picked him up roughly and sent both of them to their rooms. I looked at the mess they had made of Kate's poetry books. For a moment, I was tempted to leave the pile where it lay. Frustration festered as I slowly picked her books off the floor and rearranged them on the shelf. I was a sour stew by the time Kate returned a few hours later.

"You realize we're risking our future," I said irritably as she walked across the room to give me a kiss.

"What's that supposed to mean?" she asked, stopping short.

"Haven't you heard of publish or perish? I'm now six months behind schedule."

"And why is that my fault?" She stood rigidly in the center of the room, dark eyes flashing.

"Have you ever tried to write in midst of screaming brats?"

Kate looked at me icily. "All the time, Peter. I have a career too, you know."

"But you don't have a guillotine hanging over your head," I knew that I was being small.

"I hate it when you play martyr." She turned and walked out of the room.

AFTER SEVEN YEARS OF PINS AND NEEDLES, I learned that the Politics Department had voted to promote me to tenure. Liberation! For the rest of my life, I would be master of my own fate. The dean approved my promotion the day after Clinton won a second term. That night, I celebrated with Kate at Lahiere's, the best restaurant in town. We sat at a little table by the window. The flicker of a candle reflected in the glass, and I glowed with wine, soft light, and success. I reached across the table, picked up Kate's hand with its long, delicate fingers, and kissed them one by one.

"I love you so much," I said, watching her eyes moisten as she smiled and nodded.

"I'm so glad the struggle for tenure is over," she said. "Now I can have you to myself."

CHAPTER 4

IT ALL BEGAN WITH A PHONE CALL. I was in my office grading freshman midterm exams. Much as I loved teaching, grading papers was like paying taxes. Several piles of academic articles littered my desk, and a small stack of books sat on the floor waiting for me to find space on the overcrowded bookshelves. My computer screen was jammed with unanswered e-mail, and student recommendation forms filled my gray metal in box. Outside the window, slushy piles of dirty snow chilled the stone buildings; the sun had not shone all week. March was always a bad month. When the phone rang, I lunged for it, ripe for interruption.

"We're going for it," Jimbo declared. "Wanna help?"

"Going for what?" I struggled to shift gears from freshman misunderstandings of the nineteen-century balance of power to current Washington power politics.

"The big enchilada," Jim said. "All the way to the Casa Blanca."

I hesitated for a moment. While Jim had mentioned Wayne Kent's ambitions to me before, Kent had never struck me as an ideal candidate for president. True, he was the scion of a western political dynasty, handsome and charismatic in a Clintonesque manner. The conventional wisdom said the Democrats needed a southerner or a westerner to break the Republican grip on the heartland, and Kent was touted in the press as an important fresh face. On the other hand, Montana commanded only three pitiful electoral college votes. Then again, Jim always said that in Washington "every politician looks in the mirror and sees a president."

Over the last two years, at Jim's request, I had briefed the senator several times on foreign policy. Kent wanted advice on the situation in Pakistan and I was becoming something of an expert on the proliferation of nuclear weapons and how to slow it down. I would take the train from Princeton, rehearsing what I would say. As I waited in Kent's outer office in the ornate Russell Building, I studied the pictures of Montana, a portrait of his bleached-looking wife, and endless photographs of Wayne Kent shaking hands with famous people: Clinton, Gore, Blair, Bush.

Like Clinton, Kent always kept people waiting. Was it to make them more appreciative when they were finally admitted into his presence? Or just carelessness about his schedule? It certainly kept me on edge.

When I was ushered into his office, Kent thanked me warmly for coming and got right to the point. I noticed that four television monitors, temporarily mute, flickered with images from different networks.

"So where do we stand with Pakistan? Is this new general as bad as they say?"

"He is certainly worse than President Musharraf was," I replied, "and the Islamists were important in planning his coup. But we still don't know if he is in their pocket or if he just used them to gain power."

"What's it mean for the war on terrorism?" Kent leaned forward in his chair.

"Bad news. The Islamists have infiltrated both the army and the intelligence services, and many of them are sympathetic to the Taliban and Al Qaeda. It will make things worse in Afghanistan."

"And the nukes?"

"They keep them under tight control. General Ziad sees them as his trump card. There is no evidence that he would transfer them to the terrorists. But if Pakistan fell apart, we could have a lethal mixture of loose nukes and wild mullahs. It would make Iraq look like a cakewalk."

"Could we preempt?" Kent looked at me intently. "Iraq as a precedent?"

"Pretty hard," I replied. "They already have nuclear weapons, and their conventional forces are much better than Iraq's were. Besides, there is the danger that if we use force, it may play into the hands of the Islamists."

"Yeah," Kent replied. "But it doesn't hurt to put them on notice. The administration has gone too quiet this time."

Kent had a good mind and asked intelligent questions. But we were constantly interrupted by phone calls on local subjects that I considered trivial compared to what we were discussing. I was also disturbed by the way he raised his eyes to glance over my head at the television monitors. Occasionally he reached for the remote control on his desk, saying, "Let's check this out." The sound of the broadcast would suddenly fill the room.

I was also a little uneasy about Kent's cowboy boots and the exaggerated twang of his populist rhetoric. As Abe said, Kent tended to make the world clearer than reality. I knew that Wayne Kent had graduated from Harvard Law before returning to practice in Helena. He had made a fortune as counsel to a software start-up and spoke eloquently about the need to bring government into the digital age. There was something incongruous about cowboy boots and Harvard, but the press pundits proclaimed him the Democrats' best hope, a combination that could win both coasts and some of the heartland by overcoming old divisions and appealing to the wired generation. That was important, since the Republicans had a firm lock on the South. Kent had cultivated a western conservative edge and was trying to move the Democratic party in new directions. Since I had always considered myself a moderate and sometimes crossed party lines in my voting, I found his positions attractive.

Kent played both outsider and insider. Even though he was a senator, his Montana base allowed him to rail against Washington and call for bringing government into the age of the Internet. Kent's championship of environmental causes and campaign finance reform threw the Republicans off balance, and the combination made him "green and clean." On foreign policy, his tough Senate speeches against the proliferation of nuclear weapons had earned him frequent appearances on the Sunday morning shows. The environmental organizations were behind him, and Mervin Field's poll showed he had major name recognition in California. The big money in Silicon Valley and Hollywood loved him.

When Kent spoke at Princeton, I was impressed. He sketched a six-point plan to revive the economy, preserve the environment, protect us against terrorism, promote family values, heal racial wounds at home, and restore America's reputation abroad. He faulted the administration for failing on both the domestic and foreign fronts. At home, tax cuts favored the rich and serious campaign finance reform languished. Abroad, polls showed a decline in support from America's allies. Kent criticized the administration for failing to put an end to terrorism, and he denounced their appeasement of the new Islamist government in Pakistan. He also condemned Pakistan's abuse of human rights through the cruel application of Sharia law.

Kent's voice was melodic when he spoke about family values. But when he turned to American military strength and terrorism, his voice became harsh and angry.

"The place we need affirmative action," he said, stabbing the air with his right hand, "is in our nonproliferation policy. We must not tolerate threats to Israel, the one viable democracy in the Middle East."

His voice deepened when he described race relations. "Don't let cynical politicians play white against black. We are one people. Cut us, and we all bleed red. Take our bread, and we all starve. Divide us, and we all fail." His arms were now spread wide. "It's time for change. I'm running for president to pull this great nation back together. With your help, we can renew the American dream."

The crowd rose to its feet and applause surged over him like a wave. Kent held his pose, arms outstretched to embrace the welcome sound. I was swept along, less by the content of his generalities than the power of the emotions he aroused. He made me want his vision of America. He exuded leadership.

Afterward, at Jim's suggestion, Kate and I hosted a small reception for Senator and Mrs. Kent to meet some Princeton faculty members. I was curious about how Kate would react to this gale force in her home. But in that intimate setting, Kent became pastor rather than preacher. His voice modulated to fit our living room, and his answers conveyed friendliness and concern. As people clustered around him, he made each one the center of his world, shaking hands, fixing his eyes on them, patting shoulders, squeezing elbows, pressing flesh. When Kate, at the fringe of a group, turned to leave rather than push forward for her turn, Kent called out, "Here, don't go away." Kate turned back with a slight frown.

Evelyn Kent also shook hands and smiled a lot but said very little of substance. She seemed distracted, distant behind the fixed smile. I wondered how she coped with the rumors of her husband's various affairs. She had once been a pretty woman, but now her beauty had been stretched thin by face lifts and her hair bleached to a pale yellow. Although they had been high school classmates, Kent seemed younger, more vibrant, invigorated by the same limelight that sapped her strength.

After an hour, Kent's staff whisked him off to a fund-raiser hosted by a wealthy real estate developer in Trenton. Jim stayed on for a drink and post mortem. He sat back on the couch and stretched his legs out on the polished maple coffee table. Kate forbade me to do that because it scratched the surface, but tonight she didn't say anything.

"How'd ya like my man?"

"Great job," I replied. "Had 'em eating out of his hand."

Jim turned to Kate. "How 'bout you, Katie?"

"I don't know," she said, knitting her brow, "he seems so, uh . . . I don't know . . . "

"You mean smooth," Jim said with his throaty chuckle.

"I just wasn't sure . . ." Kate continued to frown. "I mean, what does he really believe?"

"Honey, he believes everything he says when he's in front of a crowd," Jim laughed.

"Does he really have to pander so much on protecting the textile and steel industries?" I asked.

"That's the price you have to pay in our party," Jim replied, "but he won't do much about it."

"What about his wife? She didn't look very happy," Kate said. "Her smile looks pasted on."

"Are the rumors true about their marriage?" I asked.

"Let's say it's a good thing he isn't running for pope," Jim grinned.

"Won't that hurt?" Kate asked. "What about the family values he keeps talking about?"

"Naw, look at Clinton," Jim said. "She's a trooper. Besides, she wants to live in the Casa Blanca."

"That seems so cynical," Kate said. "How can they be happy like that?"

"Maybe you have to be a little unhappy to run for president," Jim said, his tone more serious. "If his life were full of bliss like yours, why would he put up with all the hassle?"

I laughed. "Maybe we should never vote for anyone who's willing to run."

"Politicos ain't angels," Jim said, "but don't knock 'em. Somebody's got to do the hard work of putting a coalition together. Otherwise there'd be anarchy. Like the Balkans or the Middle East. Be glad that everybody's not as happy as you and Katie. Who would run for office?"

"But why don't they just give us straight talk?" Kate asked. "Tell the public the truth."

"The truth is that there isn't one public," Jim said. "Straight talk that pleases one group scares the hell out of another. We need politicians who can blur people's differences if we're going to get anything done."

"That seems like such a cynical view of democracy," Kate said. "What about principles?"

"Katie, you sound like Abe—or Ali. I gotta tell you what I told them. Different groups have different principles. If people stood only on principles, we'd wind up killing each other. Remember Bosnia? Democracy only works where there's politicians who can overcome our differences."

I nodded. "But there ought to be some limit on the pandering these guys do."

"There is," Jim said. "If they go too far, they lose the average voter."

"But that's still a practical answer," Kate said. "Isn't there a role for principles just because they're right?"

"Sure, but deep down, not on your sleeve," Jim said. "First ya gotta put together a coalition and win power. Then your principles tell you what to do with it."

"You make it sound so easy," Kate smiled.

"That it ain't."

Kate leaned over to kiss Jim on the cheek. "You're impossible, but I'd vote for you anyway."

"See what I mean?" Jim said with a laugh.

"What's he like when you're alone with him?" I interjected.

"Good man. Great with his staff. Wants to make this country a better place. Really believes that stuff about overcoming racial differences. But down deep, I don't think anyone really knows him. For all their surface friendliness, politicos are lonely people. He keeps a big part of himself fenced off. Working for him is like being invited onto the front porch for a drink, but never into the house."

He smiled. "But let's keep this to ourselves. After all, his house is where I've made my political home."

NOW, A YEAR LATER, Jim was calling about the White House, and I realized that it didn't matter what I thought of Wayne Kent as a candidate. If Jim asked for help, I had no choice.

"So what do you want me to do?"

"Feed us ideas on foreign policy," Jim said, "You know, speech drafts, position papers. It shouldn't take too much time."

"Okay, where do I send them?"

"Send 'em to me or to Joe Locara, the staff guy I introduced you to last year."

I had an indelible image of Locara etched in my memory. A dark, handsome Californian with a winning smile and a year-round suntan. He usually had his jacket off, revealing red suspenders and rolled-up shirt sleeves. He always wore a bow tie and loafers with tassels. Coming from Blainesville, I never understood why people wanted tassels on their shoes, but he was friendly enough and I took a liking to him. We lunched at a French restaurant, and Locara ordered a very expensive wine. But he also ordered a Coke and drank the two beverages interchangeably. He told me he had grown up in Hollywood and studied film at USC. His father was a script writer and his mother acted in soaps. I had never heard of the programs he mentioned, but I nodded as if they meant something to me. He said he preferred politics to theater because it was a bigger stage. Bill Clinton was his hero. He did most of the talking. But the real reason I remembered Locara so well was because someone told me afterward that he and Alexa Byrnes were "an item."

I had felt curious, not jealous. I had been completely faithful to Kate for two decades. I had neither seen nor thought much about Alexa, though I knew she had left Kent's office to work on the staff of the Senate Armed Services Committee. Still, the passing comment served to lock Locara firmly in my mind.

"And by the way," Jim said, "we want to identify Kent's brain trust soon as he announces. The names will help show he's got support in the universities as well as business. Don't worry about the other names. Some of 'em may turn your stomach, but each one's nailing down a different piece of real estate. You know, women, ethnics, regionals, small colleges, and big universities. Any problem with being listed?"

"I'll be happy to be your token eastern WASP." I was slightly bemused by the prospect of how my academic colleagues would react. Most wouldn't care, but some would probably feign indifference while secretly stewing in envy.

After Jim hung up, I went down the hall to Abe's office and told him about the call. Abe had been appointed a professor of political science at Princeton the year after I had. We often lunched together at the Faculty Club and compared notes about politics. Abe had met Kent at my house, but he was less favorably impressed than I.

"He says the right things but something's missing," Abe said, putting down the paper he was grading. "He makes everything too simple."

"Think small," I said. "Television ideas only take eight seconds."

Abe grimaced. "That's why I don't watch it."

"Don't be such an academic snob," I said. "TV is the mother's milk of modern politics. If you can't reduce your idea to a bumper sticker, you can't sell it."

Abe sat silent for a moment. "What about his foreign policy? Do you think Kent is right to confront the Pakistanis? The editorial in yesterday's *Times* says the administration is right to try to win over the new government."

"I'd like to influence the decision."

"Think Kent can win?" Abe asked. "The polls don't look good."

"Who knows, it's still early, and we could still see a recession. In any case, it shouldn't take too much time to write a few speeches and position papers. And maybe I can help on Pakistan."

Pakistan was one of my main academic focuses, but it was also important to me for personal reasons. I had been worried about Ali. He was running a nuclear research lab in Pakistan and had to be careful about what he wrote in his letters to me. But he clearly felt uneasy with the new radical Islamist government. Some of his friends had been arrested, and the government cancelled his plans to travel to the United States. I was not only concerned for him but also disappointed that I hadn't been able to see him. We had a wonderful visit just before the coup when he came back for a conference. He stayed with us in Princeton and seemed completely unchanged. Kate loved having him around, and he spoiled the kids like a doting uncle. Abe came for dinner, and we argued and bantered like old times. Now there was an ominous tone in his recent letter.

My dear Peter,

I hope all is well with you, Kate, and the children. I thoroughly enjoyed my visit. You have such a wonderful family. Fatima joins me in sending her greetings.

I must report that things are now somewhat unsettled in our country. The recent change of government has many people concerned. While some reckless elements are now near the seat of power, I pray that General Ziad will continue to see the importance of following the main lines of his predecessor's foreign policy. But frankly it is too soon to be sure.

If you do not hear from me as often as in the past, have no concern. There will be times when it may not be opportune to commit words to paper. But I shall always be thinking of you and I will be sure to communicate on your birthday.

May Allah bless you, and may He continue to bless our beloved country.

Your eternal friend,
   Ali

The recent news reports heightened my concern, as they reported that General Ziad had come to power in a coup backed by fundamentalist elements in the army and was beholden to them. Liberal Pakistanis had been arrested, and some executed. I was sure that there was much unsaid in Ali's letter.

I HAD NEVER BEEN to the National Press Club. As I left the elevator, a receptionist pointed me down a long hall. The East Room was fifth on the left, but I didn't have to count. People were clustered in the corridor around a desk with a large red Educators for Kent sign. A campaign worker gave me a name badge, a Kent button, and a folder of Kent position papers, and then told me to sit near the front.

I entered a long room that had been narrowed by movable partitions. At the far end, a podium with the shield of the National Press Club presided over a table with a Kent banner and five black microphones. Two American flags hung limply from staffs at either end of the table. Workers were still arranging folding chairs in rows. Since the cameramen were just setting up, the light was dim, and I slipped anonymously into one of the front rows. In a few minutes, Jim moved to the podium and tapped the mike.

"Glad to have y'all here. Thanks for coming. The reporters will be here in a few minutes. I want to remind you what we're doing. We'll have three people talk about Kent's positions. You all have the papers; the press has your names. They'll ask you questions. Anything tricky, let me answer. Don't try to answer charges that his positions don't add up. You're here to represent your community, not the campaign. Only answer questions about why you support Senator Kent. Any questions? Okay. Our guests are about to arrive."

I thought I saw Jim wink at me, but I couldn't be sure because at that moment, television lights transformed the shabby room into a blazing arena. I listened to a graying man with beady eyes, identified as the issues director, explain Kent's policy positions. After a few questions of substance, a reporter from the *Times* switched to the New York primary and whether rumors about Kent's marital problems were likely to hurt him there. At the end, the reporters jockeyed to interview Jack Reese, the campaign manager, a large man with bushy eyebrows who stood in the back of the room. To my disappointment, there were no questions for the notables who had assembled from the four corners of the academic world.

Nonetheless the story ran, and my father was the first to call when the article on Wayne Kent's foreign policy team appeared in *Time*. He had seen it at the Florida retirement home where my parents now lived. His voice sounded weak as he told me how proud he and Mother were. I tried to dismiss the story as unimportant, but secretly I was pleased to see my picture in a major magazine for the first time.

My father was the first of many callers. People I had not heard from in years suddenly felt a need to reach out and get in touch. Long lost friends, including some I did not remember meeting, offered their services, sending résumés and articles with notes saying "you might like to pass along to the senator."

A week later CBS called and asked if Lisa Volpe could come to my office to film a nightly news story about Kent's foreign policy. She turned out to be older under her heavy makeup than she appeared on-screen, and I was distracted by the bright lights, umbrella reflectors, and the snare of wires on my office floor threatening to trip the unwary.

"How will Senator Kent stop the spread of nuclear weapons?"

"He'll call a special session of the UN Security Council to ask for sanctions against the next country that tries to go nuclear."

"What if it's one of our friends? Like Israel?"

"In that case, we'll have to use bilateral diplomacy."

"And if Pakistan or Iran were involved, should we be willing to use military force?"

"Only if all else fails."

"Even against a friendly country?" She leaned forward, smiling, nodding, enticing me to indiscretion.

"We would hope that wouldn't be necessary."

She looked disappointed and tried a few more times without any better results. As soon as the TV crew packed up their electronic trapping gear, I called my parents to tell them to watch the *CBS Nightly News*. I also called Kate so she could make sure the kids saw it.

Kate was supportive in the beginning. I suppose she enjoyed having a slightly famous husband almost as much as I enjoyed being one. I was not away all that much; the speech drafts did not take a lot of time, and the attention was flattering. Although I sometimes wondered about a post in Washington, the polls did not place high odds on Kent winning. So I enjoyed the ride without worrying overly about the destination.

Everything changed after California. Kent's victory in that primary not only clinched the nomination, but the decisiveness of his win provided a new momentum that made the political soothsayers reassess his chances. John Tillot, the Republican candidate, was a popular governor of Ohio, but polls showed the public responding favorably to Kent's attack on the administration's do-nothing policies on the environment and the economy at home and the growing spread of nuclear weapons abroad. Most important, the leading indicators for the second quarter showed the economy turning down, and that would hurt Tillot. The Kent campaign began to reorganize for the main event. As they prepared to take on the administration directly, they needed more help on foreign policy. Jim pleaded on the phone.

"Take a leave, Peter. We really need you."

"I can't; I've already planned my courses for next fall."

"Screw the courses, Cutler. This is the biggest fish I've ever hooked. You've gotta help me land it."

I thought about the dean. He would certainly grant leave. I should probably ask Kate first, but she was always supportive. The promise of increased involvement was exciting. Besides, Jimbo was asking for help.

"Okay," I said. "As soon as I grade my final exams."

I broke the news at dinner. We almost always ate with the kids. Particularly as Jimmy and Monica grew older, Kate was adamant about having dinner together. That night, we talked about Monica's ever changing group of friends in junior high and about Jimmy's Little League team, and then about the Yankees.

"I hear they lost this afternoon," I said. "That puts my Red Sox in first place."

"I'm not worried about your Red Sox," Jimmy said with all the confidence that a nine-year-old can muster. "Everybody knows the Sox will fold."

"Just you wait," I said. "This year we'll surprise you."

"Wanna bet?"

"Okay, as long as it's not more than a dollar."

"Chicken?"

"No," I laughed. "Realist."

I had never cared much about baseball growing up, but I now cultivated the taste because of Jimmy. The hours of playing catch and occasional trips to Yankee Stadium were the equivalent of the hours my father spent taking me fishing.

Normally, after the children went upstairs for homework, Kate and I lingered over coffee and compared our days. Those were the moments when we knit our daily lives together, inspecting the separate threads, casting some aside, weaving others into a common fabric. We shared gossip about the faculty and the university press. Sometimes she described a manuscript she was editing; occasionally she read me her latest poem.

When I had announced my news, the children were initially excited but quickly drifted to other topics. Kate was silent. After the kids went upstairs and I settled back in my chair with my coffee, Kate returned to the subject.

"What about us?"

"Nothing will change"

"Don't you think we should've talked it over before you accepted?"

"It's not that big a deal," I said defensively, knowing she was right. "And Jimbo really needs help."

"You're not married to Jim," she said quietly.

"But this is a chance to elect somebody who'll deal with the issues I believe in."

"Why can't you help from here?"

"I'll commute, and it might only be for a few months. That way you can keep your job at the Press. The kids don't have to change schools."

"You were against the idea of commuting when I had the offer from Yale Press. You said it would disrupt our family life."

"I'll come home every weekend."

"It's not that simple." Kate looked at me intently.

I slowly returned my cup to the saucer. "Katie, I can't pass up an opportunity like this. It's once in a lifetime."

Tears were starting in the corners of her eyes. "I keep thinking about what Jim said, you know, everyone having her legs in the air in the back of the campaign bus."

I pushed my chair beside hers and leaned over to kiss her forehead. Kate pressed her head hard against my chest, closing her eyes. "Stop worrying," I said. "You know it's not really like that."

FINDING A MODERATELY PRICED one-room apartment in Georgetown was difficult, but it was easy compared to trying to squeeze into a campaign organization already in full swing. Nobody wanted to surrender his turf, particularly not Joe Locara. As a consultant from Princeton, I had posed no threat. Joe had been cordial, even friendly, during my occasional visits to Washington. He had taken me to lunch again, flattered me about my writing, given me his unlisted number as well as his cell phone, and told me to call at any time. Peter Cutler in Princeton had been an asset rather than a competitor. But Peter Cutler at campaign headquarters was an entirely different situation.

My first problem was getting a desk. The campaign headquarters occupied the low-rent space of the first floor of a former furniture store. The cherry suites and recliner sofa sets were long gone, replaced by gray metal desks and folding chairs crammed into every square foot. Telephone and computer wires were taped to the floor like emergency life support systems. The din was terrible as people called across rows of desks, held conferences in the aisles, and answered the continually ringing phones. Recent polls showed Kent gaining ground, and the large room hummed with the high voltage of anticipated victory.

Jim was traveling with Reese and Kent when I arrived in Washington. Locara was supposed to help me get set up. I arrived in coat and tie, briefcase in hand, my mind brimming with ideas. I had new material for speeches that would expose how sloppy the administration had been on export controls as well on homeland defense. And I would tone down the rhetoric on Pakistan. I could barely wait to sit down and start typing. Joe greeted me cordially and showed me around headquarters.

"How do you think in a place like this?" I asked, raising my voice to be heard above the clamor.

Joe hooked his thumbs behind his suspenders and smiled. "Campaigns aren't for thinking."

"What're the chances of a private office?" I asked.

Joe laughed. "Only the campaign manager and the regional directors," he said. "Frankly, until we get more space, we can't even give you a private desk out here. You'll have to share one of these issues-staff desks."

"Any secretarial help?"

"One secretary for six of you. And all the college volunteers you want, if you can figure out what the hell to do with 'em."

"Shall I start drafting the speech on new dimensions of national security?"

"No," Joe said, turning to leave. "Just do some background papers on globalization and the debt problem."

When Jim and Reese got back from the road, my complaints produced a private desk in a corner of the big room. But that rise in status also produced a noticeable coolness in Locara's greeting the next morning.

THE SHOWDOWN with Locara came over Kent's trip to Milwaukee. I had worked hard on the draft of a speech on Middle East security, producing example after example of where the administration had caved in to business interests and allowed the export of advanced technologies to ruthless regimes. I carefully excluded any military threats against Pakistan.

I expected to accompany Kent on the plane and brief him before the delivery. When the trip itinerary reached my desk, I eagerly scanned the passenger roster. My stomach twisted as I realized that my name was not there. I looked again. No name. Then after a third, more careful reading, I spotted "Locara, J." I felt sick. I grabbed the phone and dialed the chief scheduler.

"Why am I not on the trip to Milwaukee?" I demanded, trying to speak slowly to contain my anger.

"Locara said he'd do the foreign policy briefing."

"Bullshit," I shouted into the phone. "I wrote the goddamn speech."

"That's your problem, buddy. You gotta sort that out inside the issues staff."

"Who spoke to you about this?" I demanded.

"Locara," the scheduler replied. "I just take instructions."

My next call was to Jim. As the deputy campaign manager, Jim overruled the schedulers. In the end, I rode on the plane instead of Locara. From then on Joe's attitude was downright icy.

The trip was worth it. The back of the chartered 737 was filled with reporters and assorted staff. The forward compartment held the fax machine, the bank of phones, and the few coveted seats near the candidate. Kent was seated by the window in the front row. I hesitated for a moment as I entered the plane, but Kent beckoned and I felt all eyes on me as I settled nervously into the big seat. I had never been nervous around Kent in his office or when he visited Princeton. Quite the contrary, I had kept a certain psychological distance, reserving judgment and openly expressing some differences. But now that Kent was the nominee and polls showed him capable of victory, I felt a new awkwardness in his presence. Some journalists wrote about charisma, but I suspected it was the aura of power. Odd. I hadn't felt it before.

As the plane reached cruising altitude and we reclined our seats, Kent stretched his arms behind his head. I started awkwardly with small talk about the campaign, trying to recapture a natural repartee.

"You must get pretty tired of six cities a day."

"It's a road show," Kent said. "No time to think."

"Their negative ads are outrageous. How do you keep so cool?"

"They want me to get mad." Kent's laugh was more like a snort. "Every time I start to burn, I tell myself it's better to get even."

"Why do they make it so personal?"

"In this game, if somebody tells you it's nothing personal, they're fixin' to stick it to you."

"But they're appealing to the electorate's worst instincts." After I said it, I regretted it. I knew I sounded naive.

"That's politics. Unfortunately self-interest is stronger than love. People ask what you'll do for 'em or to 'em."

"Does it have to be so negative?"

"That's what works. Drive up the other guy's negatives. Define him before he can define himself. Remember what Bush did to Dukakis back in '88? Or Clinton did to Dole? Or George W?"

"Couldn't we refuse to lower ourselves to that level?"

Kent shook his head. "If you don't fight fire with fire, you're dead meat. But I'll tell you one thing those guys are doing wrong. Appeal to the public's fears but also throw 'em scraps of hope. Keep your personal image positive. The economy has got them scared. They've gone too negative; Tillot's handlers have forgotten to include enough sweeteners."

"But in the meantime, you've got to listen to that abuse."

Kent shrugged again. "It's a hard business. Everything's fair game from your economic plan to your mother's sex life."

"Then why do it?"

Kent laughed. "If I don't, somebody else will, who'll be worse. I like to think I can make a difference. That's part of it."

"But you lose all your privacy," I said, warming to the topic. "The press pries into your private life, and everywhere you go people recognize you."

Kent looked over at me with a puzzled smile. "I'd worry a helluva lot more if they didn't. That's the other part of the answer. Now tell me what to look out for when I deliver this speech."

"First part outlines the worsening situation in the Middle East and South Asia," I said. "Syria has chemical weapons but has eased off somewhat on support for terrorism. CIA reckons another eight years to effective biological weapons."

"Eight years is two elections from now," Kent replied with a shrug. "Eight days is a lifetime in politics. What do you have that's more immediate?"

"There's a lot about Iran," I said. "Their nuclear program is making progress, and they are getting missile technology from the Russians and the North Koreans.

"They already have intermediate range ballistic missiles. CIA thinks Saudi Arabia may try to buy a bomb somewhere to keep Iran from dominating the Persian Gulf. And there's always the danger of leakage to terrorists."

"Where could they buy something like that?"

"There's a black market in stuff stolen from Russia. Or another country might help them."

"Is that really an option?"

"There's a saying in the nonproliferation business," I replied. "Every country that gets the bomb spreads the disease once before they get religion and rediscover nuclear chastity. We helped Britain, the French helped Israel, the Soviets helped China, China helped Pakistan. But China seems to have cleaned up its act."

"So now the problem is Pakistan?"

"It's possible," I said. "We know that A. Q. Khan sold sensitive technology to Libya, Iran, and North Korea a decade ago. So far as we know, they never sold the bomb itself, but the new Islamist government is getting more involved in the Middle East."

Kent shook his head. "So we hit 'em for being soft on Pakistan?"

"No. I took out the hard line on Pakistan. It would be counterproductive. The administration is right to try conciliation for now. That may be the only way to get some leverage with the new government. But we can hit 'em hard on export controls."

"That in the speech?" Kent raised his eyebrows.

"The second part gives chapter and verse on the failings of the administration's policy. They're too close to the big businesses that supported them. I've dug up several examples of sloppy export control. They're letting our companies sell the rope to hang us. That's one of the lines I put in the speech."

"Give me some examples," Kent said.

"They allowed General Data to sell massive parallel processing machines to Pakistan, and they didn't complain when the Russians sent Iran maraging steel that could be used in gas centrifuges."

"Those bastards," Kent said, shaking his head. "They're such goddamn hypocrites. Didn't they deny everything last week?"

I nodded. "We can prove they're liars. We got back channel info from a guy in Commerce who sits on the export licensing committee."

Kent leaned forward and put a hand on my arm. "That's why this is worth it," he said, lifting his hand and gesturing toward the back of the plane. "I know I can make a difference."

Before I could reply, I felt a tap on my shoulder. The head scheduler had arrived to take my seat. As I rose, Kent said, "Thanks, Peter. Nice job."

I walked back glowing. I was putting my words into the mouth of the man who might soon be able to do something about the greatest problem of our time. I exhaled loudly as I settled into the empty seat next to Jim. He looked up from his papers.

"Jimbo," I said, "this is really worth it."

"Look out, Cutler," Jim laughed. "You're gonna catch the disease."

My sense of euphoria continued as Kent's motorcade wove its way through the streets of Milwaukee. The advance men had done their job well. Banners hung from the windows of office buildings. People waved from the sidewalk. Twice the caravan stopped so the senator could jump out and "press flesh" with the crowds. People loved him.

At the entrance to the auditorium, I trailed after Kent through a storm of flashbulbs. I sat next to Jim under the blinding television lights in the row reserved for top staff and local dignitaries. I squinted up at the art deco podium with red, white, and blue bunting. In front of a huge blue velvet curtain, three chairs sat between two large white buckets, each holding a bouquet of ten American flags. The news photographers hobbled forward on their knees. When they reached their positions in front of the podium, they held their cameras in front of their faces and flashed away. Behind me, people were clapping and stomping their feet.

Finally the mayor of Milwaukee silenced the crowd until the only sound left was a chorus of clicks, flashes, and whirs of camera autowinds. He introduced the governor of Wisconsin, who in turn introduced Kent as the next president of the United States. Jim nudged me with his elbow and leaned over to whisper in my ear.

"Clinton used to say, always be introduced by somebody you've appointed to high office or who wants to be."

Then the purported next president was speaking the words of warning that I had put in his mouth. My chest swelled when Kent's mellifluous voice pronounced the words "selling the rope." At one point, the TV cameras turned from the podium and panned the front row. I hoped Kate and my parents would see the news that night.

After the speech, while Kent and Jim took a limo to Chicago to attend a fund-raiser, my job was to ride the press bus and make sure that the speech had been properly understood. Spin control.

I edged my way to the back of the bus. Reporters leaned over seats, pads in hand, firing questions and scribbling furiously. I crafted cautious answers. Before each sentence, I had to think how it would appear in print, weighing words, imagining their impact when they were twisted and truncated into headlines. My mind split in two, with one half talking and the other half warning about the words that came out of my mouth. A photographer from *Newsweek* took pictures.

"How're you gonna stop North Korea selling missiles?

"We'll take a stronger stand than the administration, threaten to cut off trade. Impose sanctions, Get Beijing to help."

"Would Kent bomb the chemical plants in Syria?"

"We won't do anything rash, but no option is ruled out."

"Do you think the new government in Pakistan will continue to co-operate with us?"

"That's what we have to hope."

"Will they spread the bomb to other Islamic countries?"

"We wouldn't allow it."

"How would you stop 'em?"

"Do you expect a crisis over oil in . . . "

"What about Israel?"

"Did you write the speech?" a woman from the *Journal* interrupted.

"I helped," I said, relieved not to have to answer the hard substantive questions. Thank God for reporters' fascination with the trivia of bureaucratic infighting. "Everything is a team effort."

"How do you and Mr. Locara divide up foreign policy?"

"We work very closely together."

"We hear there's division in the staff over Middle East policy," someone said from the back of the group.

"News to me."

"What job will you get in a Kent administration?"

I smiled. "Only the senator can answer that."

When they finally returned to their places to write their stories, I slumped back and closed my eyes. The bus hummed on the highway. My mind jumped back and forth between instant replay and fast-forward. I was tired but not sleepy. I felt the way I did after winning a hard set of tennis.

THE TRIP TO MILWAUKEE was an unqualified success. Things only got rocky when I was sent to Europe. The campaign staff had begun to worry about foreign reactions to Kent's tough rhetoric. It had been one thing to stake out an extreme position on foreign policy in the primaries, but now it was time to move back to the center. We had to show we were tough on foreign policy, while not letting the administration paint us into a corner.

It was agreed that I would accept an invitation to speak at the Royal Institute for International Affairs in London and then go to the Continent and privately reassure officials there that a Kent administration would not mean a radical break in policy. I had cleared my speech with the issues staff at campaign headquarters, and it had been well received in London. Those headlines came out just right.

The problem came in Paris. I was met by a French government car at Charles DeGaulle Airport and whisked to the Elysee Palace. We sped through the streets and with only a rare touch of the siren; my driver ignored red lights and whizzed through intersections. I smiled as I thought of how I would describe this reckless ride to Monica and Jimmy.

The car turned through wrought iron gates into a cobbled courtyard off the Rue de Rivoli. A huge glass entry broke the smooth stone facade of the Elysee Palace. Two guards in plumed silver helmets stood at attention as I was ushered up a broad staircase and down tapestried halls to the office of Marcel LaTour, the president's assistant for security affairs. LaTour rose from behind a gilded Louis XV desk, greeted me in French, and then switched to English. He nodded toward an upholstered chair. My eyes traveled up the brocade walls to the high ceiling and ornate chandelier before returning to the desk and the task at hand.

LaTour listened attentively as I explained Senator Kent's desire for continuity in foreign policy. "Our party has a fine tradition in this area."

He raised one eyebrow.

"President Kent would certainly consult with our European allies before making any radical changes."

"Of course we are glad to hear that," LaTour replied. "But am I to understand that major changes are intended?"

"Not necessarily," I said, "but we're determined to stem the spread of weapons of mass destruction, particularly in the Middle East. And we're worried about the new Islamist government of Pakistan meddling in the region. Given Europe's dependence on Gulf oil, I'm sure you would agree."

The floor-length windows behind LaTour's desk were open. I could see the June sun playing on the white flowers and green leaves of the chestnut trees in the palace park. I wanted to pinch myself. But I had to pay full attention to the purpose of my visit. LaTour began a small lecture.

"France will not support the use of force against Pakistan or Iran," he said. "We supported you in '91, but that was different. Iraq's aggression was clear. We supported you again on Afghanistan a decade later. But you acted too hastily in 2003, and as a result you inflamed the Islamists, diminished your own popularity, and made the terrorism problem worse. Today, France has friendly relations with all the states in the Gulf and even the new regime in Islamabad. So far, Pakistan's bark has been worse than its bite. Your senator's threats will not produce oil or peace; they will only aggravate Islamic fundamentalism. He will increase the religious backlash in the region and help the terrorists with their recruiting campaign. We regard such open threats of force as misguided and dangerous."

"That's not our intent either," I replied. "But Senator Kent is determined to stem the spread of nuclear weapons. We have to warn the new government in Pakistan that we will not tolerate any transfer of weapons to Iran or to terrorists. And the senator is also worried about European nations trading civilian nuclear technology to Iran for access to its oil."

LaTour picked a pencil off his desk. "Our policy has three points: nuclear is the energy of the future, peaceful nuclear trade is a global necessity, and France will live up to her obligations as a responsible supplier. Our sales to the region are completely consistent with those principles, and we have seen no evidence to the contrary." He punctuated each point with a sharp tap of his pencil against the desk.

"I am sure the senator would agree," I said, "so long as we have a common understanding of what 'responsible' means in the context of the Middle East."

"Ahh . . ." LaTour lingered over the expression. "Then we will have to consult." He paused, pursed his thin lips in the semblance of a smile, and added almost as an afterthought, "If your senator wins."

The surprise came after I was ushered down the staircase, past the guards, and back out to the limousine. Several reporters had been admitted to the courtyard and stood between me and the car. I had intended to keep my visit a secret, but it seemed at the time that a few innocuous remarks would help spread the senator's message of moderation. And I was flattered by all the clicking cameras and people waiting to jot down my words.

"What did you discuss?" asked a man thrusting a microphone in my face.

"Our desire for close relations with France when Senator Kent becomes president," I replied, pushing toward the car.

"Will you try to block French exports to Middle East?" a woman asked.

"I can't comment," I said, inching forward to where the driver was holding the door open.

"Did you rule out the use of force against the new government in Pakistan?" shouted a third reporter, from the rear of the pack.

"No," I said, proud of my developing skill at handling the press. I escaped with relief into the plush interior of the limousine. The door thunked shut. As the wheels crunched on the gravel and the guards saluted at the gate, I felt a solid sense of accomplishment.

Little did I expect the next day's headline. "Kent Adviser to Elysee; Veiled Threat of Conflict." It seemed so absurd that I laughed at first. I had not ruled out the use of force, but I had certainly not threatened it.

Had they misunderstood me? No, this was being blown out of proportion by someone who wanted to hurt Kent. Probably a French official acting at the behest of someone in the administration.

When the American reporters called, I tried to explain that my remarks had been taken out of context. But the damage was done. Two days later the *New York Times* and *Wall Street Journal* ran stories on European anxieties about Kent's bellicose foreign policy pronouncements. Editorialists worried about whether Kent had a firm grasp on the international situation. Several pontificated about the dangers of further alienating the new Islamist government of Pakistan.

I returned home dejected. There were no limos, no chariots of fire, no plumed guards. Not even a private car awaited me. I took the bus from Dulles Airport into Washington. Here I was not the emissary of the next president of the United States. I was just Peter Bradford Cutler, one of a number of advisers swarming around a handsome senator from Montana who wanted to be president. And I had screwed up.

As I entered Kent headquarters on Wisconsin Avenue and pushed past the reception area with its crowds of hangers-on and stacks of posters and press releases, I thought I noticed several people giving me strange looks. Ron Krause, one of the volunteers who manned the desk in my absence, greeted me with a face fit for a funeral.

"Reese wants to see you right away."

I made my way through the maze of desks. At the back of the open area was the private office of the campaign manager. "Go on in," said the tight-lipped receptionist at the desk guarding the door. "He's expecting you."

Reese was tipped back in his chair, feet on a metal desk, phone to his ear, necktie at half-mast, chewing out someone about a scheduling snafu in Florida.

"You're fuckin' hired to make sure that doesn't fuckin' happen."

Smoke from a cigar curled up from the ashtray on his desk. Reese nodded for me to take a seat without interrupting his harangue.

"I don't care whose fuckin' fault it is. All I care is who wins Florida. Fire anybody you want. Cut their balls off. But straighten it out by tomorrow morning or you're fired. Do I make myself clear?"

Joe Locara and several other staffers were already seated around a table across the room. They pretended to ignore the verbal violence occurring a few feet from them, but none dared speak. Somebody muttered, "Welcome back." Nobody smiled. Behind Reese was a huge red, white, and blue poster with Wayne Kent smiling broadly above his slogan "ReNew America."

Reese simultaneously slammed the phone into the receiver and his feet onto the floor. "Bunch of fuckin' idiots down there," he said to no one in particular, shaking his head. He was a heavy man with bushy eyebrows and thick gray hair. His shirt was open and gray hair peeked above the neck of his collar. His shirt sleeves were rolled up, exposing large arms that looked like they belonged to a boilermaker rather than a campaign mastermind. As a lifelong political pro from Chicago, Reese made no effort to disguise his disdain for intellectuals and other amateurs who dabbled in his sport.

"What the hell'd you do over there, Cutler?" he greeted me.

"I was misquoted."

"It's a hell of a mess, these stories. Joe had to background some of the columnists. Said you weren't speaking for the senator."

My face felt hot. I saw Locara trying to suppress a smile. "But Jack," I said, "you approved the trip yourself, and I cleared the speech with Joe and other members of the issues staff."

"That's irrelevant now," Reese said. "We gotta think damage control. We told people you were on your own. Joe told 'em you were freelancing."

I winced at the idea of Locara telling reporters that I had been out of control.

Reese paused, scowled, puffed on his cigar. I hated the smell of cigars, but under the circumstances I couldn't object. The smoke spiraled slowly toward the grimy ceiling.

"Another thing," Reese continued. "Lay low for a week. Do me a draft on defense spending. By Wednesday." I started to speak but Reese did not wait for a reply. He dismissed me with a backhanded gesture and started talking to the table of staffers.

As I walked out of Reese's office toward the corner of the big room where the issues desks were clustered, I felt a number of eyes following me. I smiled and pretended to be oblivious, studying a piece of paper I was carrying in my hand. One thing Alexa had taught me: Appearances matter.

THE NEXT STEP was the convention. I had never been to Atlanta, much less a national convention. At first I felt disoriented. I stood for a moment staring over the chaotic scene in the Atlanta Hyatt. Clear Plexiglas elevators with tiny lights twinkling on their chrome ribs slid up and down rails to the top of the cavernous atrium. Gigantic brass chandeliers dangled under an enormous skylight, and row upon row of balconies trailed green plastic vines. Babble rose from the swarms of people buttonholing each other among the potted palms and ficus trees. A piano at the cocktail bar added an ignored obbligato.

I found it hard to keep track of what was happening. I decided to head up to campaign headquarters on the top floor, but as my elevator ascended, Kent's passed me going down. He was flanked by blank-faced secret service men, wires dangling from their ears. Next to the candidate, whispering in his ear, was Joe Locara.

I felt hot as I tried to shove through the crowd in my elevator. "Push three," I yelled from behind a TV crew, struggling through their electronic spaghetti. I got out but had to wait forever for a descending elevator. When it finally reached the ground, the crowd swept me out into the lobby. Kent was nowhere to be seen.

"That bastard," I said out loud, knowing that no one would hear or care. Locara had told me that the six o'clock meeting was in the convention command post on the top floor. It would be just like him to send me to the wrong place. Yesterday we had quarreled openly at the staff meeting. Locara wanted the acceptance speech to promise that in the first year of his new administration, President Kent would threaten to bomb Pakistan if it transferred nuclear weapons to other Islamic countries or failed to take measures to protect nuclear materials from terrorists. I thought of the letter I had recently received from Ali.

"We can't threaten Pakistan in the speech," I said to the advisers at campaign headquarters. We sat around a table littered with papers and Styrofoam coffee cups. The room was warm. Most of us had our shirt-sleeves rolled up, and I was beginning to sweat. "Only a few years ago, they helped us against the Taliban and Al Qaeda in Afghanistan. Even though Ziad's coup has brought in a fundamentalist group, the situation is not yet beyond repair. What's more, publicly threatening the new Islamist government will just provide ammunition for the anti-American terrorists in the region. Besides, the allies will object and the administration will call us reckless."

"Nonsense," Locara shot back. "Kent said it in the Dallas speech. Look." Locara jabbed a finger at a piece of paper like a preacher pointing to a Bible. He read with an unctuous tone. "In this era of terrorism, the spread of nuclear weapons is the greatest threat to our vital interests. I promise to take stronger action to stop this menace."

"That doesn't say bomb Pakistan," I countered.

"But it follows logically from vital interests," Locara smirked. "You should know that. You're the professor."

"We'll never get a U.N. resolution allowing us to bomb Pakistan's nuclear facilities. China would veto it. And we don't have proof that they are planning to spread the bomb." I felt the tightening in my chest that always accompanied my arguments with Locara. Beads of perspiration dotted my forehead and my muscles were tense.

"That's a crock of crap," Joe said, spreading his hands in an appeal to the circle around the table. "Are we the world's only superpower or not? Kent has to show he is tougher on terrorism and tougher on proliferation. Pakistan is our best chance to outflank them. The public thinks the administration's been coddling Pakistan. It's their weakest point on foreign policy. It's the one place where we can get 'em by the balls."

"But we won't be able to deliver if we win," I replied. "It's a false promise."

"When we win, not if," another staff member corrected. There were nods around the table. I felt like an acolyte who had been caught questioning the virgin birth.

"This isn't a seminar, Cutler," Locara sneered. "Winning is the name of the game. I don't give a shit about Pakistan. This is about Florida and West Virginia." The others agreed, and Locara's paragraphs on Pakistan were approved for inclusion in the draft of Kent's speech.

I left the meeting feeling sick. I had lost, but I knew I was right. And it was not just my friendship with Ali. It was wrong to pretend to the

American people there was an easy answer to the nuclear proliferation problem. This was not like Afghanistan or Iraq. We could not bomb every country that obtained nuclear weapons. We had to use diplomacy because we needed other countries to help. Didn't they understand that? Putting false promises in Kent's speech would come back to haunt him when he was president. Who could reverse that decision? I rushed over to the convention hall to find Jim.

At first the guards would not let me onto the floor of the convention. I brandished the credentials dangling from a chain around my neck.

"It's urgent," I said.

"Sorry, fire laws," the police officer replied.

I thrust my badge in his face. "Look, I'm on Kent's personal staff."

"I don't care if you're Noah," the policeman said. "That ark's full."

I paced impatiently until three delegates came out and I was permitted to enter. The cop was right, but the convention was more a zoo than an ark. There might be no issues at our newfangled conventions, but there was no shortage of people and noise. The vast hall was flooded with light and festooned with banners. Nets pregnant with balloons hung from the ceiling. Signs identifying the state delegations stood above the crowd. Nevada delegates vigorously pumped their signs up and down. I deduced that their governor must be the one on the podium. He was making a futile effort to attract the attention of the unruly crowd or, more likely, the TV cameras for the folks back home.

I finally spotted the New York sign that marked where Jim would be reassuring the delegation on the Israel plank in the platform. Getting there was another matter. The aisles were jammed with delegates cajoling and schmoozing, but the worst road blocks were the mobile TV cameras. Wherever they stopped to interview a notable, scores of delegates jockeyed to get into the background of the picture. Wannabes jostled into a position where they could accidentally run into Diane Sawyer or Lesley Stahl. I pushed through a CNN crew and finally found Jim in the middle of New York. When I described the showdown with Locara, Jim nodded distractedly. He promised he would call staff headquarters and tell them to hold all decisions on the acceptance speech until the next day's staff meeting. I felt relieved by the minor victory.

But now I was in the hotel lobby and could not find the goddamn meeting. I pulled out my cell phone only to find that the battery was dead, so I pushed across the lobby to the public phones. The line was three deep. A young volunteer was busy impressing his girlfriend: "I was within six feet of Senator Kent, close enough to touch him."

I coughed loudly.

"Yeah, he's a cool guy," the volunteer confided into the receiver.

I glanced at my watch, grimaced, glared, but the kid was oblivious. I suppressed an urge to simply grab the phone from him.

A heavily made up woman with a big Kent button on her tight tank top came up and smiled. "Aren't you Peter Cutler, the foreign policy adviser?

I nodded.

"You're as cute as your pictures."

I gave her a tight smile.

"Buy me a drink?

I shook my head and turned away from her, immune to her come-on. Henry Kissinger supposedly said that power is the ultimate aphrodisiac. Not now.

I looked at my watch and held it out toward the volunteer tying up the phone. He finally hung up. I dialed headquarters but no one answered. The empty ring ricocheted back through the wire. At last there was a voice on the other end.

"Where's the six o'clock meeting?" I tried to control the sense of urgency in my voice.

"Nobody here now," the voice replied.

"But where's the meeting?" I asked, my voice rising slightly in pitch.

"Don't know 'bout no meetin," the voice said. "I'm cleanin."

Next I tried Kent's room.

"Kent for president," a woman's voice chirped.

"Where is he?"

"I'm sorry," the voice responded, "We're not authorized to disclose his locations."

"This is Peter Cutler, his foreign policy adviser. Where's the meeting on the acceptance speech?"

"We have nothing on it here."

I slammed the receiver back into its cradle, lifted it, and frantically dialed again.

An incessant, mocking buzz at Jim's number. Stymied. This was a matter of national significance, but all I could get was an earful of static.

I surrendered the phone to the heavyset man glowering in the line behind me. A rustle in the lobby caught my eye. Waves of people swept forward and then parted as a small, gray-haired woman made her way across the lobby, surrounded by a reporter with a microphone, a camera man, and a technician carrying a TV light that shone brightly above her silver hair. Kent's mother. I turned away from the spectacle in disgust. I may not have known where Wayne Kent was, but at least I knew he was not with his mother.

A reporter from the *Atlanta Constitution* approached, notepad in hand. "Hey Cutler," he called across several people. "Anything on the Middle East in his acceptance speech?"

I edged away. "Sorry," I yelled back. "I have to meet about the speech right now."

I fled toward the elevators. The last thing I needed was another headline. Locara had already zapped me on that. The best I could do now was to retreat to my room and wait for a call.

I threw my jacket over a chair and flopped down on the couch. Hotel modern. Who designed these things? Recessed lighting glowed artificially. The air conditioning whirred, the minibar hummed, but the phone sat dumb as a stone. I opened the minibar, took out a Diet Coke, and clicked on the television: Kent speaking to the California delegation earlier in the day. The anchorman speculated about how far Kent would go in breaking with the administration's foreign policy while the screen showed scenes of ships loading oil in the Persian Gulf. Then a picture of General Ziad, and speculation about whether the new Islamic government of Pakistan would follow through on its threats to defend fellow Muslims in the Middle East. A picture of Paris and speculation about the European reaction to Kent's approach. I wasn't in a mood to watch. I clicked off in disgust.

Was Reese punishing me by shutting me out of the meeting on Kent's acceptance speech? They were all out there strategizing and here I was alone in a damn hotel room. I was trapped. If there were a meeting, it would be a mistake to be seen in the lobby. Then the press and the rest of the staff would know I had lost influence. At least by hiding away, I wouldn't tip them off. I had learned quickly that a reputation for power is almost as good as the real thing.

I looked out the window at the reflections in the silver tinted glass of the adjoining building. The white railings of the Hyatt's balconies curved like shark's teeth, and the glare of reflected light echoed back across the empty space. I needed air.

I opened the door and stepped out on the balcony. The heat of Atlanta in July was oppressive, and the cacophony of downtown traffic swelled up through the haze. I looked down and saw a caravan of black limousines snaking toward the hotel, escorted by several motorcycle policemen. There he was! Now I remembered. Kent must have gone out to make that appearance at the Illinois reception. I hadn't been shut out after all. I grabbed my jacket and rushed down to the lobby.

AFTER LABOR DAY, the pace became even more frenzied. Polls showed Kent moving slightly ahead, but the Republican campaign had moved into high gear. I divided my time between headquarters and the traveling circus. Home was a Holiday Inn that recreated itself no matter what city we were in. I spent almost no time in my Georgetown apartment and too little in Princeton. I subsisted on junk food, adrenaline, and gossip about the tracking polls. Our campaign staff was on high voltage. We were often exhausted, but the excitement of the contest energized us and substituted for sleep. Although I had no time to exercise, I found myself losing weight because of the meals I missed. For three weekends in a row, campaign emergencies and flaps forced me to cancel my trip home. I called Kate from San Francisco on a Friday night. I woke her up.

"You won't like this, Katie, but Kent wants me to go to LA with him tomorrow."

Silence.

"Katie?"

"We're having a dinner party for the Kleins tomorrow night. You've known about it for weeks."

"I'm sorry sweetie, but if I don't go to LA, he'll use Locara."

"I don't care if he uses the pope."

"It's not a joking matter, Kate."

"Peter, seven people are coming here for dinner tomorrow night. You'd better be one of them. The Kleins are counting on it. And I've invited Robert Carney."

"Katieeee."

"You go right ahead, Peter." Her voice choked. "Go to LA. But if you do, don't come home. Just keep flying." The phone clicked.

I started to dial again, then slowly put my phone back in my pocket. What a mess. If I didn't go to LA, Locara would get Kent to take too extreme a position on Pakistan. It would play well in domestic politics, but it would foment such strong reactions in Europe and the Gulf that we would never get the cooperation we would need to deal with the problem after the election. It would be a disaster. I had to go to LA.

I sat on the corner of the bed and held my head in my hands. I ran my fingers through my hair and pressed my knuckles against closed eyes. When I picked up the phone, I was not sure who I would call. Finally I dialed American Airlines to get a seat on the red-eye to Newark.

THE PARTY STARTED WELL. Abe and his new wife, Rachel, were the guests of honor. Rachel worked with Kate at the Press; in fact Kate had introduced them. Bill Stevenson, chair of the Politics Department, was there with his wife, Jenny, a somewhat tedious woman whose conversation was restricted to the four Stevenson children. Kate's boss, Robert Carney, the handsome young director of the Press, sat on her left.

The assembled guests plied me with questions about the campaign. I continued to gush answers long after I had slaked their thirst. Actually, I found it impossible to stop.

"California looks okay," I said, "though their negative ads about Kent's record with Montana ranchers is hurting a bit with the environmentalists around San Francisco. But we're doing okay in LA."

"What about Florida?" Abe asked.

"We're going gangbusters in Miami. Even cutting into the bubbas in the panhandle. But we're still uncertain about New York."

"Speaking of New York," Kate said, "I hear the new show at the Whitney is fabulous. Have you seen it, Robert?"

"The problem with New York," I continued, "is that the party organization is so fragmented. That state is worse than the UN. Kent says they're hopeless."

Kate glared at me from the length of the table.

My cell phone interrupted. It was Jim in Los Angeles. I left the table to take the call, and we went over the way Kent should play the question of force. I told him not to mention Pakistan and warned him not to let Kent be swayed by Locara.

When I returned to the table, I noticed that the others had finished dessert while my roast beef remained half eaten on my plate. Kate's mouth was compressed and her eyes were icy. Embarrassed, I mumbled an apology. Kate interrupted to announce that we would take coffee in the living room.

I sat on the sofa between Jenny Stevenson and Robert Carney, exhausted. After hearing about three of the four Stevenson children in excruciating detail, I turned desperately to Carney and asked about the fall list at the Press. Carney described several new authors at some length. I nodded politely while thinking *here's a guy you ask the time and he reads you the timetable.* Carney's rich voice overwhelmed my ears. I had trouble concentrating. My mind was in Los Angeles and my batteries were running down. I felt myself nod as my overnight flight caught up with me. I nodded again to keep up the pretext of listening. The next thing, someone was touching my shoulder. I opened my eyes and found Kate shaking me. She was crying.

"You self-centered boor," she choked out between sobs.

"Where is everyone?" I asked, raising my head from the back of the sofa.

"They left early," she says. "They didn't want to disturb the great man." She slumped down in the chair by the fireplace, wiping her eyes with her fingertips. "How could you do that, Peter? Don't you know how important Robert Carney is to my future? Don't you respect my world at all?"

I pulled myself off the couch and walked over to her chair. I got down on my knees and put my head in her lap. "I'm sorry, Katie. I do respect your world. That's why I came home."

"I wish I could believe you."

"Trust me," I said. "Six more weeks and this will be over."

CHAPTER 5

THE LAST DAYS of the presidential campaign were nail biters. Tempers flared, voices cracked, orders were shouted and ignored. But Wayne Kent remained composed. The dark circles below his eyes deepened and his usually square shoulders began to droop. But the reassuring voice remained unchanged both on the public platform and in private with his staff. When he walked into the crowded headquarters, we felt a surge of electricity. He was our leader. If he wavered under the strain, we might crack. But he held firm. His stamina was our steel.

Every night, the opposition ran ads accusing Kent of various evils—selling out the environment for the sake of Montana cattle ranchers, taking campaign money from a convicted drug pusher, pandering to special interests in his Senate votes, being dangerously naive on foreign affairs. The tabloids continued to print stories about his marriage being shaky. One woman claimed he was the father of her child, but the majors did not pick up the story. A Web site reported rumors about visits to a psychiatrist.

Kent did not break stride. He stressed his message of ecological balance, reviving the economy, racial healing, improving homeland defense, and stemming the spread of nuclear weapons. No accusation went unanswered, and when he complained about the Republicans' negative campaign, he managed to do so without whining. When he hit back, he did it without sounding mean. He had, as Jim put it, "perfect political pitch."

The polls showed Kent slightly ahead as we traveled to the final presidential debate in Durham. If Kent could hold his own in this one, we would probably win. The danger was a visible slip before a national television audience. No one wanted to mention it openly at the interminable meetings and debate rehearsals for fear of spooking the candidate. There was an artificial calm in the studio in the afternoon while Kent rehearsed his answers.

The night of the debate, the field house at Duke University was as packed and feverish as at a Final Four basketball game. Red, white, and blue banners hung from the rafters. The stage was bathed in hot lights and surrounded by TV cameras poised to shoot both candidates from several angles. Governor Tillot's supporters crammed the left side of the aisle; ours filled the right. I glanced over the competition and recognized one of their advisers as a former student of mine at Princeton. I nodded. He smiled weakly. I looked up at the stage. The moderator sat in the middle of a horseshoe panel of journalists with their backs to us. The two candidates stood stiffly behind their podiums, trying to look relaxed but wary of cameras catching an inadvertent move.

The moderator instructed the audience to hold their applause and refrain from interruptions. He might as well have asked a flock of gulls to refrain from attacking a pile of fresh fish. Kent handled a question about his inexperience in foreign affairs by referring to the number of foreign leaders he had met. Staged laughs and loud snickers erupted from the other side of the aisle. I burned with indignation. After the second question, when Tillot referred to his record on education, hoots came from our side of the auditorium. At first I tried to be fair, but I was soon swept along by my crowd.

In response to a question from the third journalist on the panel, Kent promised he would double expenditures on cleaning up toxic waste sites. "There's no issue more important in this election than the quality of the world we hand on to our children." He knit his brow and jabbed his hand in the direction of the camera whose little red light showed it was active.

"My opponent vetoed two environmental bills during his period as governor and appointed party hacks to the Ohio Environment Agency." Kent's voice took on a note of earnestness. "One of my first acts as president will be to double the EPA budget to fulfill this sacred trust to the next generation." Loud applause. I was on my feet cheering.

Tillot quickly rebutted. "Ohio has saved thousands of acres of wetlands during my administration, while Senator Kent has voted for bills that allow overgrazing of federal Forest Service lands. My opponent voted to open those lands for the large ranchers who back him. The green he's interested in is dollars, not grasslands. I shudder to think what kind of appointees he will make in the environmental area. Just look at his campaign contributors." Cheers from the other side.

Style dominated content. As an academic, I should have been appalled, but I had the thrill of watching an all-star game. The debate had the white-knuckle, sweaty-palm tension of a close ball game. Impartiality was out of the question. I held my breath before Kent tackled a difficult question, cheered loudly when he cut off Tillot's attempt to paint him as weak on defense, rose to my feet in exhilaration when Kent exposed the administration's duplicitous record on trade in sensitive materials.

Afterward, when the candidates were whisked away by the secret service, I joined the crowd in the basement of the student center. The tables had been pushed back against the walls. Rival staffers and reporters milled about in clusters trying to shape the follow-up stories. Reporters sought staff to interview as eagerly as interviewees sought reporters to spin. It reminded me of freshman mixers at Bowdoin.

"Any surprises?" asked a reporter from *USA Today*, half looking at me, half looking over my shoulder for a larger catch.

"I was surprised at how poorly the governor answered the questions on the environment," I said.

The journalist shrugged off my comment. Too obvious. "What about foreign policy?"

"I think we showed that the Republicans have dropped the ball on sensitive exports. They just don't get it."

"What job will you get?"

That question alone told me who won the debate. Clearly it was Kent, and already the reporters were less interested in our spin on the issues than in speculating about who would receive which plums in a Kent administration.

That question consumed me as well. Any lingering doubts I had about going to Washington evaporated in the white heat of the TV lights. I had entered this chase on a lark, as a favor to Jim. Now I had bitten the apple of power and my appetite grew with the eating.

Sitting in my room at the Indianapolis Holiday Inn the day before the election, I realized that I had not been home in ten days. Kate's voice sounded clipped when I called. I offered to come home. I could skip the election night bash in Washington. Nothing special would happen there anyway, and I could watch the results with Kate and the Kleins. I half dreaded the evening, fearing an onslaught of negative numbers pasted on the national map. The polls were favorable, but polls could be wrong. I didn't dare talk about the election for fear of jinxing the outcome. Throughout election day, I was underwater holding my breath.

When the exit polls and early precincts showed Kent surging better than expected, I finally exhaled. At first I was light-headed, unable to comprehend the import of what I was watching. I floated in midair, disembodied. It all felt unreal. I laughed too loudly at Abe's wisecrack when Dan Rather made an obvious comment. I clapped when favorable new returns were posted for the western states. I talked loudly during the commercials. Until Rachel's question.

"Does this mean you'll be going to Washington?"

"No, Abe and I'll be lecturing to Princeton freshmen, not a freshman president." My humor fell flat.

"But won't he need your help?" Rachel continued innocently.

"He'll manage."

"I'm sure he'll want you."

"We'll see."

Kate was giving me a hard look. That night, neither of us mentioned my future, but I was sure we were both thinking about the same question. Would Kent want me in Washington?

THE NEXT DAY Jim called and asked me to join Kent's transition team for the State Department. Before I could get too excited, Jim added that Jack Reese had chosen Joe Locara to chair it.

"Oh shit," I said. "That bastard's out to get me."

Jim laughed. "Relax Cutler, it's mostly a payoff to campaign loyalists. Transition teams are like steers. No balls. They're made to slaughter. Even so," he said, "it's always better to be inside a tent peeing out than outside peeing in."

I wasn't so sure. Even if Jim was right about transition teams, didn't Locara's selection mean that he had a leg up? Could he use his new position to hold me back? When I told Kate about the offer, she wasn't entirely happy with it but agreed that I should try it for a while and we would discuss it later. The next morning I left for Washington again with a suitcase full of shirts and a mind full of worries.

THE TRANSITION TEAM SAT in an unadorned suite on the ground floor of the State Department. After being photographed for my department pass, I called on Locara who was using the spacious office reserved for the secretary of state-designate. Jacket off, he was tilted back in a swivel chair, Gucci loafers up on the big desk.

"Welcome aboard, Pete." Joe smiled without rising. "Those bureaucrats upstairs are drowning us in paper. I need people like you that I can trust. We're going to work well together."

I was pleased that he was willing to bury the past. "That's great," I said. "Sorry for any sharp elbows during the campaign."

"No problem, Pete." He flashed his handsome smile. "We all got a little excited in the heat of battle. That's to be expected."

"How can I help?"

"You're going to be a key player on our team," Joe rocked his chair and clasped his arms behind his head.

"Great," I said. "But what exactly do you want me to do?"

"I'd like you to oversee the Latin American, African, and economic bureaus. Check the paper the bureaucrats send down. Rewrite whatever you want to put our twist on it."

I wrinkled my nose. "I'd rather do security. You know, alliances, export controls, the Persian Gulf, Pakistan, terrorism."

When Locara frowned, I added, "Well, at least the proliferation of nuclear and biological weapons?" Joe took his feet off the desk, sat forward in his chair, and leaned over the desk. The smile had vanished. He spread his hands out on the expanse of polished wood. "I'm handling those," he said icily. "And no calls to Childress this time. Jack Reese gave me carte blanche."

"Fine," I said, and silently to myself, *so much for the nanosecond of friendship.*

I consoled myself with Jim's advice about not taking the transition too seriously. I would enjoy being a viceroy even if it wasn't the empire I wanted. I met with outgoing officials and drew up plans for the bureaus that were in my jurisdiction. I also perused classified papers related to the areas of greater interest such as Pakistan and the Middle East.

Ali wrote me a note of congratulations right after Kent's victory. He had seen my picture in *Newsweek International.* But his note was brief and said nothing about his personal situation; the silences worried me. I sought out cables and intelligence to discover what was really happening in Pakistan.

By keeping my head down, working hard, avoiding reporters, and going home to Princeton on weekends, I was able to manage my anxiety. Occasionally, while taking a shower or sipping my coffee, stress would suddenly break through, throwing me off balance. Why hadn't I heard anything? Would Locara try to block an appointment? When would they decide?

This fragile equilibrium was destroyed by the news that Kent had decided to appoint Tom Kovic as secretary of state. Kovic was popular with the labor unions and had nailed down a good chunk of the blue-collar Catholic vote. As a governor of Iowa, Kovic made one inspired decision—backing Wayne Kent before the state caucuses. But he was not a great choice for secretary of state. Kovic saw foreign policy through the lens of grain sales. He knew little about how world politics really worked. Even worse, he knew little about Peter Cutler. I had met Kovic briefly at a fund-raiser in Des Moines and at the Atlanta convention, but I doubted he would remember me.

Kovic moved into transition headquarters, greeted the transition team perfunctorily, and vanished behind closed doors with his own staff imported from Iowa. I spent two days in purgatory, not knowing whether he would keep me or not. I phoned friends, gleaning what I could about Kovic. I also began to inquire about jobs elsewhere in the government. After coming this close, I could not bear the idea of returning to Princeton empty-handed.

My worries deepened when Kovic called in two members of the transition team, thanked them for their services, and dismissed them. He's started slaughtering the steers, I thought, remembering Jim's remark. On Friday morning when Rab White, Kovic's special assistant, called to invite me down the hall, my hand trembled as I put down the receiver.

Kovic nodded when I entered his big office. While I waited for him to finish a call, I studied him surreptitiously, catching snatches of his side of the conversation.

"You betcha. . . . No three dollar bills in my shop . . . That's the way we do things in Des Moines. . . . Anything the president wants."

Kovic was strikingly handsome with a broad, ruddy face and hair that started white at the temples before it swept back to join the carefully trimmed black back of his head. He had thick dark eyebrows and a large mouth. He looked strong. Finally he put down the phone, tipped back in his chair, and crossed his arms across his broad chest. He did not invite me to sit.

"I took this job on condition I could choose my own people," Kovic announced. "You were their one exception, but of course I'd be delighted to have you on my new team in any case."

He paused and studied my face for reaction.

I nodded silently, afraid to say the wrong thing.

"Gotta have team players."

I nodded again.

"They tell me you've got a quick hand on the pen."

"I write easily."

"Well, I'll make you part of my bullpen."

I smiled nervously, not certain whether I had just heard a joke or whether people from Iowa really talked this way.

"I'm offering you undersecretary for security affairs. I assume you'll take it?"

"I'm flattered," I gulped. "I mean, of course, I'd love any chance to work with you and your new team."

"Good. Draw up a plan for how to organize the department and the interagency process for security affairs."

"Okay."

"Give it to me by Monday. We're gonna hit the ground running." Kovic pointed toward his assistant. "Rab will start the paperwork."

Kovic turned abruptly toward the phone and picked up the receiver. Before dialing, he looked at me over his shoulder. "Glad to have ya on board, Pete."

Before I could respond, Kovic continued. "And in case you're interested, the White House made clear that I have the right to dismiss the people I appoint."

I was out in the hall before I realized what had happened. Slightly dazed, I walked back to my office and shut the door. I guess I had expected a more elaborate invitation. Instead, it had been like watching a courtship scene in fast-forward. Shouldn't there be more pomp and circumstance?

On second thought, who cared. I had what I wanted: a position of power and a chance to make a difference in our nation's future. What will they think when they read about this in Blainesville? I was following in my great-grandfather's footsteps. Won't my father be proud! And what about Kate? At least we can move to Washington and be together again. Elated, I inhaled deeply and broke into a broad smile. I would jump on the early train to Princeton and surprise her. Then I would tell Abe. Maybe he would come to Washington too.

"I'M GLAD YOU'RE HAPPY, DARLING." Kate reached across the dining room table and took my hand. Her face was grave. "But Washington is your world, not mine."

"That's crazy," I said. "There must be editorial jobs in Washington. I'm sure you could find something."

"Peter, it's taken me ten years to establish an identity in Princeton as more than just a professor's wife. Robert says I have a real future with the Press. I don't want to go back to the beginning in a city that only cares about what position my husband holds."

"Screw Robert," I said, pulling my hand away. "This is our big opportunity. Why are you always talking about Robert?"

Kate arched her eyebrows and smiled. "Do I detect a little note of pettiness in the great man?"

I could not maintain my pique in the face of her mockery. She always knew how to handle me. "Just try it for a while," I pleaded.

She raised her wine glass and took a long sip. A frown replaced the smile. "Imagine what it will be like for me with people constantly looking over my shoulder to find someone more important to talk to? Or being obsequious because I'm the big man's wife?"

"It won't be like that," I said. Then meeting her eyes, "Well, not exactly."

"Here I have an important job and my own identity. I would lose both there."

"You could try it for a while," I said.

She brushed off the suggestion. "The children don't want to leave their friends," she continued. "Jimmy is having enough trouble without changing schools."

"They'll make new friends," I said, "and so will you."

"People will seek me out because of you," she replied. "I'll know that and I'll never be able to be open with them. I'm not made for that kind of world."

"You could learn."

Kate shook her head. "I don't want to learn, Peter. What you married is what you've got. Remember the Dickinson line? 'The soul selects her own society, then shuts the door.'"

"Okay," I said, realizing that I was not going to change her mind. Whenever Kate quoted her favorite poet, I knew the discussion was over. "It's only two and a half hours by train. I'll come up some weekends, you come down on others."

"That's not my idea of an ideal marriage either," she said. "Are you sure about this job? What's wrong with being a professor?"

"Come on, Kate," I said, shaking my head in disbelief. "It's only for a few years."

Kate shrugged. "Tomorrow we'll go to Brooks Brothers and buy you some new suits. If you insist on going to Washington, we can't have you looking like a professor."

I HAD NO BETTER LUCK with Abe. We lunched at the Faculty Club, seated by a window looking out over the wintry garden with its few tufts of frozen chrysanthemums. I looked around with satisfaction. The large dining room was mostly deserted because of Christmas vacation, but a few tables were occupied, and someone waved from across the room. When I entered, several colleagues greeted me warmly as they looked up from their papers in the outer lounge. The waitress said she had seen my picture in the paper. She brought me a beer I had not ordered. Said it was on the house.

"I'll make you my deputy," I said, even before Abe started his tomato soup. "We'll make a terrific team."

"I'm not cut out for it, Peter."

"Nonsense, Abe." I talked with my mouth full of tuna sandwich. "You've got the best mind in the Politics Department."

"Studying fire is different from playing with it." Abe laughed. "I learned my lesson watching you in the campaign."

"What's that supposed to mean?" I frowned.

"It's a comment about me, not you," Abe said, reading my face. "I know my limits."

"You'll do fine," I replied, leaning forward and resting my elbows on the checkered tablecloth. "Give it a try."

Abe smiled and shook his head. "I know myself pretty well," he said. "You and I share an interest in the study of power, and how to couple it with values. But you're also interested in the exercise of power. I'm not. Sure, I'm not immune to temptation, but I know I'm not cut out for those struggles."

I looked at Abe carefully and realized he was serious despite the lingering smile. He was probably right.

"Well, I'll make you a consultant," I said. "You'll enjoy peeking at classified material, and I'll get the benefit of your wisdom."

"I think I can handle that." Abe smiled again. "What about you? Any qualms."

"Why do you ask?"

"I know you pretty well too," Abe said, looking directly at me. "You're your father's son. Think you can keep hold of those values in DC?"

"Are you saying it's impossible to do good and be good at the same time?"

"No, but it's not easy."

"Well, I guess we'll find out soon enough."

"And I'll make sure you speak truth to power." Abe raised his glass of beer in a mocking toast.

"I know I can count on you." I clicked my glass against Abe's. "But remember in politics there's a thing called 'applied truth.'"

JIM CALLED from Florida with congratulations. "Got some more news for ya, Cutler. Kent's gonna make Jane Garcia the national security adviser. It's a brilliant political stroke," Jim said, "putting a Latina in that position. And she's immensely popular on the Hill. You'll want to call to congratulate her."

I knew of Jane Garcia as a popular congresswoman from Florida, but I wondered whether she knew enough about foreign affairs. On the other hand, maybe this meant I would have a relatively free hand without the White House holding my elbow.

Before I could articulate my question, Jim anticipated it. "She'll have four strong deputies. Locara will be her deputy for security."

And before I could absorb that shock, Jim added another. "Your old friend Alexa Byrnes is gonna be undersecretary of defense."

"Oh shit," I said, already imagining the tight connection those two would make between the White House and the Pentagon. What would that mean for my chances to move forward on the Middle East issues? Alexa had spent most of the campaign managing California. I had seen little of her, and when she came to headquarters, I kept my distance. She was clearly in Locara's camp.

"I'll be Reese's deputy chief of staff," Jim added.

"Great, sounds like I'll need your help to combat the Locara-Byrnes team."

"I won't have much time for foreign policy," Jim said. "But I'll look in on you from time to time."

"Promise to return my calls?"

"Promise," Jim said. "But you'll have to work with Garcia and Locara most of the time. I'll help when I can, but try not to step on their corns too much."

When I returned to Washington on Monday, I made an appointment to show Kovic a suggested plan for organizing security affairs. He seem distracted. Rab White took notes on the conversation.

"In terms of budgets, Defense is a giant, and State's a pygmy. Since money talks on Capitol Hill, and since the National Security Council staff has the president's ear," I explained, "they're both better placed than we are to promote their own agenda."

"Sounds like I've gotta play this course with a nine iron," Kovic said with a grimace. "So what do you recommend?"

"If State's going to be a player on security issues, we have to chair the interagency committees. Otherwise, we're just diplomatic messenger boys in no position to shape the president's programs."

"What's Jane Garcia think of that?" Kovic asked, turning a pencil over in his hands. "Why is she gonna hand me a driver?"

"Maybe she won't," I said. "You'll have to sell it to the president."

Kovic snapped the pencil and threw the two halves into the waste basket. "Everyone's got something they wanna sell the president," he growled, "and I've got more than one fish I want him to fry. I'll mention your scheme to him, but you'll have to work it out with Garcia."

Two days later, I called on Jane Garcia in her temporary office in the Old Executive Office Building, once the home of the State Department but now an annex to the White House. With its high ceilings, huge rooms, and stone fireplaces, it reflected a day when State nestled closer to the presidential center of power. Now it represented the growing power of the White House staff.

Jane Garcia greeted me cordially. She was an attractive woman with a gray frost on curly brown hair, an open face with prominent cheeks and dark brown eyes. The deep creases at the edges of her mouth and the corners of her eyes gave her a solemn appearance, but her frequent smile was charming. It was hard not to like her at first sight. I spread out my papers and seemed to be making good progress explaining my plan when Garcia interrupted.

"Do you mind if I ask my deputy to join us?"

She pressed a button and within a minute, Locara entered the room. For once he was wearing a jacket, but little else had changed. Bow tie. I looked down. Sure enough, the tasseled loafers. He acted as though we were great friends, calling me Pete and clapping me on the shoulder. He listened politely while I repeated what I had outlined to Garcia. Then he launched a barrage of objections.

"State can't chair these meetings," Joe said. "Those bureaucrats have their own agenda, and it's not always the president's agenda."

I was tempted to point out that Kovic had not offered Locara a job even though he had been dying to land a job at State. Instead, I bit my tongue. I had to sell, not score, points. I needed to convince Jane Garcia. Fighting with Locara would not advance that cause.

"I'll be in the chair," I said, turning toward Garcia, smiling, "and I'm a presidential appointee, not a career bureaucrat."

"The other agencies will never tolerate being directed by State," Locara replied. "Only the National Security Council staff stands above all agencies because we're part of the White House."

"Does that really make it impartial?" I asked, unable to suppress an acerbic reply, "or does it just cover its own special pleading?" I knew I should try to be ingratiating, but Locara was such a shit.

"It gives us the presidential perspective," Locara said, haughtily.

We continued to spar until Garcia stopped us. "I'll discuss it with the president. Thanks for coming over, Mr. Cutler."

On that note, I returned to Princeton. I had convinced Kate to come to the Inaugural festivities, and had promised to come back and drive the family down to Washington. I hoped that by exposing them to some of the excitement, I might gradually break down their resistance to moving. But I found it hard to concentrate on celebrating when I was so uncertain about the arrangements that would decide whether my job was meaningful or not. I had the title, but would I have the substance?

As we drove down the Jersey Turnpike, Kate joked with the kids.

"Isn't it wonderful? Now that he's forty-five, Daddy's finally getting out of college."

Monica and Jimmy giggled. "Forty-five is pretty old, Dad," Monica teased. "Soon you'll have to lie about your age."

"Yeah," Jimmy chimed in from the backseat, "I can see through your hair in the back."

"Guess I'm over the hill," I laughed. "Think Mom should start looking for a younger man? I think she's got her eye on Mr. Carney."

"Peter, that's terrible," Kate said.

"Don't worry, Dad," Monica said, patting me on the shoulder. "Mr. Carney's nice, but we still love you."

I managed to join their laughter, but I still felt unsettled. When I tried to phone Rab White, I found that my battery had died. I pulled into the next service area and stood shivering at an outside pay phone. Around me, the dirty snow formed a tattered gray blanket over dead grass.

"Has Kent decided on my role as coordinator for security affairs?

"I haven't heard anything," Rab replied.

"I hope you're keeping on top of it," I shivered. "It's critical to Kovic's ability to be a strong secretary of state."

"I read you," Rab said. "Let me see what I can find out."

"I'll stop and call again in an hour."

Rab did not know the answer when I phoned from Delaware. Only in Maryland did he have the answer. Kent had avoided a clear decision and split the difference. In normal times, the State Department would chair the committees under the National Security Council structure, but NSC staff would take the chair in times of emergency. With at least some of my worries gone, I could now try to enjoy the Inaugural celebrations.

INAUGURATION DAY was one of those clear, cold January days that make Washington appear majestic. The white dome of the Capitol stood solidly against a royal blue sky, and flags snapped briskly around the towering obelisk of the Washington Monument. Our little family joined the crowd that surged toward Capitol Hill. Jimmy and Monica wore big green Kent buttons. They darted in and out among strangers in the crowd. Kate smiled as we walked hand in hand.

Our seats were in the second row on the ground, just in front of the platform where Congress and cabinet sat. I looked up at the little figures of the two presidents and the chief justice dwarfed by the Capitol dome. I heard Wayne Kent's mellifluous appeal for "a strong, vital, caring America—a beacon of leadership for the world."

There was a momentary crackling in the loudspeakers. "Rich and poor, black and white, women and men: together we will heal this nation."

I knew his speech had been written by several people. After all, I had helped write such speeches. Nonetheless, a tear came to my eye, perhaps from the cold, perhaps from my fervent hope for the future that Kent promised my children. Somehow, above the messiness of the political process, it was important to have someone who could articulate a larger vision that would bring the nation together. This was what leaders were for. This justified the indignity of the process. Public service was noble. We would protect the people from the dangers that were mounting in the world.

I feared that the prospects of disaster in the Middle East were rising. And I knew we would suffer more terrorist attacks. If the terrorists got their hands on nuclear weapons, the results would be catastrophic. Yet despite my fears and what I knew about Kent's limitations, I suddenly felt that he would turn the situation around and that I was called to play a role in that noble task.

My euphoria survived the parades, cocktail parties, and Inaugural ball, where Kent shook our hands. The ballroom was jammed with little people trying to meet bigger people. Cameras flashed and a rustle went through the crowd whenever some new cabinet member entered the room. I knew I should be making contacts, but the band was playing and Kate wanted to dance. She looked magnificent. Her body pressed against mine, hair brushing lightly against my cheek. I had not enjoyed dancing so much since our wedding.

After we sank into bed in my bare little Georgetown basement apartment, I held Kate in my arms. The kids were already conked out on cushions spread on the floor.

"I love you all so much," I whispered.

"I love you too."

"And you're going to love this new adventure."

Kate squeezed my hand.

DAY ONE in the State Department started out all right. I was able to get a department car to take my family to Union Station. I liked my paneled office with its splendid view out over the marble memorials. Julie Smith, my new secretary, and Tony DiNatale, the young foreign service officer assigned as my special assistant, seemed bright and efficient. Kovic's first staff meeting in the secretary's conference room on the seventh floor just down the hall from my office was a friendly round robin of introductions. But when I returned to my office, Julie handed me a list of two dozen calls, and my e-mail inbox was a mess. Before I could begin to tackle it, John Marcus of the *Post* was on the line.

"I hear Iran is offering to sell chemical weapons to Pakistan. What's the administration plan to do about it?"

"It's news to me."

"Rumor has it that they want nuclear technology in return."

"No comment."

"Off the record?"

"If Pakistan were to sell or trade nuclear weapons to Iran, it would be to this administration what the Cuban missile crisis was to Kennedy. But I don't know anything about it."

"You sure there's nothing to the rumors? Folks in Defense think something's going on. They've been leaking it to the *Washington Times*."

"I really don't know."

"I'm not usually in the business of offering advice," Marcus said. "But you'd better get your act together fast. Senator Peary plans hearings on the issue next week."

"Thanks."

I buzzed for Tony.

"What's all this about Pakistan and Iran?"

"The rumors have been around for a while," Tony replied earnestly. "It's one you'll have to watch closely."

"You can say that again. How good's the evidence?"

"So far, it's based on unconfirmed intelligence reports. DIA thinks its real, but CIA doubts that the Sunni Islamist regime in Pakistan would do a deal with Shiite heretics in Iran. I'll dig out the files for you."

"But what do I tell the press?"

"Nothing," Tony said. "Just tell the political-military bureau to prepare press guidance for the spokesman's office in case any questions come up at the morning press briefing."

"Okay, the press guidance should say that we know nothing about any Pakistani nuclear transfers to Iran, but it would be a matter of utmost concern to the Kent administration if there were anything to it."

Then I called the undersecretary for management to complain that I was short three foreign service officers and one secretary.

"How can I do my job without troops?" I complained. "The press is already beating on my door."

"It's routine to rotate foreign service officers to other offices with the change of administration," the Management man replied.

"How about rotating some in my direction?"

"We hope to have some candidates for you to look at within the next few weeks."

"Thanks, but see if you can't speed that up."

Tony knocked and came in with an armload of documents, which he placed in two piles on my desk. I had not yet gone through the rows of papers already crowding the polished surface. Now the mahogany had nearly vanished; I had barely started and I was already falling behind.

"What are those?"

"You wanted the background on Pakistan and Iran," Tony said. "That's the pile on the left. Also, I think you will want to look at the files on chemical and biological weapons verification problems. There's a meeting on it tomorrow."

After he left, I picked up the top file on Pakistan and started reading an intelligence cable. I inhaled and frowned. Maybe there was something to this. I looked back at the front page of the report. It referred to "humint"—a human intelligence source with the code word name

HANDY. It described the source as being new and having good access but no proven track record. On the other hand, there was insufficient corroboration in the older reports.

Julie buzzed. "The White House is on the phone." I picked up and heard Joe Locara.

"Cutler, we're getting quite a few inquiries about biological and nuclear weapons in the Middle East. Mrs. Garcia wants you to organize an interagency policy review. We're looking for a presidential decision in three weeks."

"Isn't that an awfully short deadline?"

"If you can't handle it, we can always organize it over here," Locara replied acidly. "If I remember correctly, you're the one who insisted that State be the lead agency on these studies."

"Okay, I'll get right on it."

I put down the phone and Julie buzzed again. "Mr. Vole would like you to come to his office as soon as you're free."

George Vole was the undersecretary for political affairs, a career man with a reputation as a tough bureaucratic infighter. It would have been more courteous for him to call on me as the newcomer, but he slightly outranked me and pecking order is everything in Washington. I headed toward his office down the long inner hallway that links the principal officers on the seventh floor. When I entered, I noticed that his office was not only larger but more elegantly decorated than mine. He had an oriental rug, an antique desk, and numerous oil portraits.

"Welcome to the department," Vole said, pointing to a brown leather chair next to his desk. "I'd like to be helpful in any way I can."

"I need it," I sighed.

"Good," Vole replied, leaning forward to hand me a paper with diagrams, names of bureaus, and dotted lines connecting the boxes. His eyebrows were so blond that they virtually vanished, leaving icy blue eyes that never blinked. It made me uncomfortable.

"I know you're shorthanded," Vole said, "and I thought it might help if the political-military and nonproliferation bureaus reported to me in the first instance. When your interests were involved, my people could inform yours and bring you in. I've checked this with Management and the secretary. They think it makes sense."

The ploy was so blatant that I was nearly speechless. "Thanks," I said, "but I'm planning to add staff."

"That's fine," Vole said. "But it takes time. And in any case, since the regional bureaus already report to this office, this arrangement will make coordination easier."

"I'll get back to you," I said, "but we'll leave things as they are for now."

"Well, I know you'll want to discuss this again. Why don't we plan to meet tomorrow after you've given it a little thought?"

THE NEXT BLOW came as soon as I returned to the office. As Julie handed me yet another list of calls to be returned, Tony asked if he could come in. He closed the door and sat on the arm of the big leather chair by my desk.

"Aren't you going to chair our delegation to the terrorism consultations with the Germans next month?"

"Far as I know."

"Funny," Tony says, "but a friend at the German embassy just called and asked who would be heading the American side. Apparently Mr. Locara told the German ambassador that he'll head the delegation under the new administration."

"Must be a misunderstanding," I said. "I'll straighten it out with the White House."

When the door closed, I rested my elbows on the desk and my head in my hands. A sense of panic, almost nausea, threatened to choke me. My heart was beating rapidly. I was drinking from a fire hose. Was it possible that I could fail in this job? I thought of my father teaching me to swim. He was in water up to his waist with his hands under my stomach. Suddenly he let go and moved back three steps. I screamed, water filled my mouth, and I thrashed wildly toward my father. I never thought I would repeat the experience, but here I was in the Department of State, drowning.

I rang Julie and asked her to make excuses to the Belgian ambassador and cancel lunch. Instead I ate a candy bar. Later I skipped a reception at the Nigerian embassy and read through the new batch of papers and cables that arrived for clearance at the close of the day. Despite my efforts, the pile on the desk continued to grow. Dinner was a quick hamburger in the downstairs cafeteria, and then back to the office to plow through the classified files that Tony dumped on my desk in preparation for tomorrow's meetings. I got back to my apartment at 11:30, too late and too exhausted to call Kate. I fell asleep on top of the covers with all my clothes on.

SLOWLY I BEGAN TO NAVIGATE the bureaucratic swamp, learning to jump between solid hummocks and avoid getting sucked into muck holes. I learned which meetings to skip and which people were a waste of time. I became less intimidated when everyone else cited details from classified reports that never reached the newspapers. I realized that there was only so much I could read in what was basically an oral culture. The bureaucratic machine produced mountains of paper, but the communications that really counted were short and spoken. I learned to make the Pentagon briefers turn off their PowerPoint presentations and tell me their ideas in a few sentences. It was amazing how brief their briefings became.

One morning I learned that despite our conversation, Vole had convinced the secretary to have the military and proliferation bureaus report first to the political rather than the security undersecretary. I demanded a meeting with Kovic. The secretary was seated near the fireplace in his large paneled office. The windows displayed a panoramic view out over the Potomac. As I walked across the room, I braced for confrontation. Kovic looked up, puzzled.

"What's so urgent?" He did not invite me to sit.

I fired both barrels at once. "If you approve Vole's plan, I'll resign." My hands clenched together behind my back. I felt the blood flushing my face. "I have a perfectly good job waiting for me at Princeton."

Kovic seemed taken aback. "Now don't do anything hasty," he said. "Nothing is decided yet."

"I can't do my job if you approve Vole's plan." My face felt hot and my pulse throbbed.

"Well, see what you can work out with him. I won't approve anything you don't agree to."

He smiled, rose from his chair, and draped a large arm around my shoulder. He was obviously worried about how the White House would react to such an early departure of a former campaign worker with ties to the president. "You're an awfully important part of my team, Pete. Don't do anything hasty. I'd really hate to lose you." He withdrew the arm. "And by the way," he added as he ushered me toward the door, "let's keep this little issue inside this building. No need to get the White House involved."

By afternoon, I received a list of candidates to interview for the three empty slots in my office. Now I could add staff and use them to keep track of the shifting currents in the informal structures that made the State Department tick.

I HAD MORE TROUBLE, however, with the interagency process. I convened several meetings to begin the Middle East policy review, but once the work was delegated to subcommittees, it seemed to get stuck. When I asked what was happening, I was told, "Meetings are underway." I asked again about progress. "Everything is under control." But when I finally saw the first draft of the interagency report, I was appalled. If it were a student's paper, I would have given it a C minus. Banal options written in bureaucratese. I remembered joking with my Princeton students about Washington bureaucrats who prepare three options for the president: (1) declare nuclear war, (2) sign a surrender document, or (3) let the bureaucracy continue business as usual. The class had laughed but now the joke was on me. Sure enough, business as usual. No sense of urgency about the flow of weaponry that was the short fuse on the Middle East powder keg.

I had to redraft the paper. After all, it was the first paper I was going to present to the National Security Council in the White House, and I needed to make a good impression. I took out a pencil and started to edit. After twenty minutes, I had fixed the first page. Thirty to go. I glanced at my schedule and realized the futility of such an academic approach. My day was fully booked. No way I could get this done. The phone buzzed and Julie announced that the Japanese delegation was waiting in the conference room. They had come to discuss the coordination of policies on exports to the Middle East. I buzzed for Tony and quickly told him how I wanted the report rewritten. Then I hurried down the hall to the conference room.

The Japanese were seated on one side of the long table; my aides and representatives of Defense, Commerce, Energy, and the White House lined our side. I shook hands with Vice Minister Sato, the head of their delegation. The others bowed. Photos were taken, and I sat at the empty place in the middle of the American side, behind my nameplate and a little American flag. I told the assembled group how glad we were to host such a distinguished delegation and why the president felt strongly about tightening restrictions on the export of supercomputers and advanced sensors to areas of tension like the Middle East.

Sato slowly read from papers laid out on the table in front of him. The contracts for the supercomputer sales to Pakistan, Iran, and Syria had already been signed, and there had been no objections from the previous administration. Shipment was planned in three months. It would be a terrible loss of face for Japanese industry if the exports were halted at this point, particularly under American pressure. Moreover, the technical experts reported that much the same computing capability could be achieved by stringing together less powerful computers. And there was no assurance that the Europeans would hold back if Japan pulled out.

I explained the importance of supercomputers for nuclear weapons and ballistic missile tests. Powerful computers allowed designers to simulate weapons effects secretly without the embarrassment of public testing. Our experts reported that stringing together less powerful computers was possible, but not the same as having access to the most advanced supercomputers and source code. I went over the importance of Persian Gulf stability for world oil markets in general and Japan in particular. I argued that Japan and the United States shared a common interest in restricting the flow of potentially dangerous technologies to the region.

The other members of the Japanese delegation sat impassively. Some had their eyes closed. I wondered if they were pensive or jetlagged. A few took notes. When Sato spoke again, he repeated the points in his paper instead of addressing my arguments. For an hour, we played variations on our themes.

As I waited for the interpreters to finish, I considered the futility of these large formal sessions. Basically this meeting was for Sato and me to impress the people on our own side of the table with how firmly we were defending the agreed interagency positions. The real bargaining between the two countries would come later in smaller informal sessions. The morning would have been much better spent rewriting that miserable policy review. But diplomatic niceties required that I waste it repeating ritual lines in a Kabuki play.

THE REWRITTEN Middle East policy review paper was still a tangle of bureaucratic compromises. Now it was a C plus, but the elegance of the prose mattered less than the outcome of the meeting. I overruled the bureaucrats who wanted no changes and told them to incorporate more innovative options. Now I faced the opposite danger—the cabinet principals who were in too much hurry. If I were unable to stave off their rigid positions, I would fail to open up the space I needed for my diplomatic efforts.

I had never before presented a paper in such a rarefied atmosphere as the Situation Room of the White House. My stomach knotted the way it had before finals in college. I stepped down into a windowless room with a dozen chestnut leather chairs along the walls and another dozen around a polished oak table in the center. The chair at the end, higher than the rest, sat below the presidential seal. At the other end of the room, the red numerals of three digital clocks glowed faintly above the labels "President," "Zulu," and "Gulf." I was struck by how small the room was. The indirect lighting added to the illusion of intimacy. And illusion it was, for in this little room, the major cabinet officers would battle over my policy and determine its fate.

Small white cards on the table reserved places for the secretaries of state, defense, energy, homeland security, commerce, and treasury, the chairman of the joint chiefs, the director of Central Intelligence, and the national security adviser. Since the president was in California on a political trip, Vice President Alfred "Bud" Robin sat in the big chair. Kovic was on his right, Garcia on his left. The second echelon filled the chairs along the walls.

Alexa Byrnes sat across the room behind the secretary of defense. I had seen her a few times in the past year, but only fleetingly. Still a beautiful woman. How ironic that we met for the first time in this small room, just like a Princeton seminar. I tried to get rid of that thought. At best, the memory of past friendship could soften the hard edges of bureaucratic position. Alexa returned my smile and then looked down at the papers in front of her. I wondered if she would oppose my policy. I was less pleased to see Locara behind Jane Garcia, but that was to be expected. The National Security Council staff take the notes and draft the presidential decision memorandum after the meeting. Unfortunately that bastard would write the last word.

As chair of the interagency working group, I went first. My voice sounded strained and distant. "As you know, the president believes that the spread of nuclear, biological, and chemical weapons is the gravest threat we have faced since the end of the Cold War. Not only is there a risk of war in the region, but weak governments may allow the weapons to fall into the hands of terrorists," I heard myself say.

"The situation in the Middle East is urgent. Iran and Syria are on our near term watch list. There are unconfirmed reports about Saudi Arabia shopping for nuclear weapons, and a new intelligence source reports that Pakistan may be tempted to sell its nuclear technology." I looked up from my notes. Several people around the table nodded. The general picked up a pen and underlined something on the paper in front of him.

"On the other hand, it would do no good for the United States to restrict technology unilaterally," I continued. "We have to persuade the other suppliers to join us or our efforts will be futile." I began to warm to the argument, and my voice returned to normal. I glanced over at Alexa. She seemed attentive.

"The Defense Department wants to station a strike force in Israel and another in India, in addition to our forces in Bahrain and Qatar. State believes that will exacerbate Islamic fundamentalism in the region and complicate our problems with the Europeans. The Defense suggestion of preparing preemptive strikes against suspected chemical and nuclear weapons facilities in Pakistan can serve as a fall-back position, but State believes it needs further study."

I looked up from my paper and saw that the others were paying close attention. Locara was scowling. He would be trouble. Kovic was looking at papers in front of him. Bud Robin gazed off into some invisible space.

"State recommends that we fend off congressional pressure for unilateral export legislation. Instead, we should convene a conference of supplier countries to negotiate a tougher international agreement on restricting exports. We do not think it wise to base a rapid strike force in Israel or India at this time." Out of the corner of my eye, I saw Locara pass a note to Alexa.

"We share the same objective," I said in conclusion, "but we shouldn't let purism blind us to reality. Pursuit of the perfect must not defeat achievement of the good." I sat back in my leather chair. Although the room was air-conditioned, my armpits were damp. Under my starched shirt, sweat trickled down my chest.

Bud Robin spoke first. Behind his back, he was called the "little bird," or less charitably, "brain dead." But as a senator from Illinois, he had helped bring the Midwest to the Kent/Robin ticket. "Seems pretty far from what we were saying in the campaign." Robin turned his handsome, vacuous face first to me and then toward John Castle, secretary of defense.

"Typical State Department pablum," Castle boomed in his Texas baritone. "Either we're serious when we say this is the biggest threat of the century or we're not. Seems to me the president has been pretty clear about this. We need a policy with teeth, and the teeth we need are prepositioned strike forces in Israel and India." I groaned silently but decided not to respond.

Commerce supported me on exports, but Energy argued that Congress was going to pass tough legislation in any case. "The president may as well get the credit," said Delia Smith, the secretary of energy. "Given his campaign promises, he'll be in an untenable position if he tries to resist the legislation."

Smith was interpreting domestic politics to suit her agency's preferences. She certainly fit that adage of Washington politics: "What you see depends on where you stand, and where you stand depends on where you sit." I was tempted to blurt it out, but I coughed lightly. I needed a coalition. Couldn't afford to burn bridges now. Instead, I said, "Our congressional people think there's still room for compromise."

Treasury Secretary Pauling worried about the budgetary impact of stationing more troops overseas, but Castle retorted that the costs would be minimal. Kovic warned about the negative international reaction if word should leak that we were planning preemptive strikes without UN authorization. General Adams, the chairman of the joint chiefs of staff, argued that the latest generation of smart weapons would be surgical and involve very little collateral damage to civilians. I answered each point politely. Predictable bureaucratic arguments circled the little room like crows over a corn field. Finally Bud Robin looked at his watch.

"We've aired the options," he declared, smiling and looking around the table. "Jane will summarize and put them to the president for decision." The battle ended in stalemate, but at least my policy had survived the first round.

AFTER THE MEETING, as I rode back to the State Department in Kovic's car, I suggested that we send the president a note to reinforce State's concerns. Kovic shook me off with a toss of the head. "I trust Jane," he said. "Let the process take its course."

Major mistake. Three days later, I received a copy of the president's decisions. I looked in disbelief at the little boxes where Kent had placed a check mark and his neat initials. He had ticked the options supporting restrictive unilateral export legislation and secret preparation of preemptive strikes. Only on the question of stationing a rapid strike force in Israel and India had he held the issue for later decision. What's more, as I read the decision memo that Locara had drafted for Garcia to present to the president, I realized it was strongly biased against the State Department position. I asked for an urgent meeting with Kovic and pleaded that he appeal the decisions.

"We've got to reclama," I said, using my new bureaucratic jargon. "We need more wiggle room for negotiations."

"The president has decided," Kovic replied, "and we'll just have to live with it."

I went home that night exhausted and depressed. I slept fitfully, replaying the meeting in the Situation Room in my dreams. I explained the virtues of moderation and negotiation, but everyone laughed at me. "Sticks and stones will break their bones, but words will never hurt them," John Castle intoned with his Texas twang. He wagged a finger at me. That made Bud Robin laugh till the tears poured down his face. Joe Locara whispered something in Alexa's ear, and they both smiled knowingly. Jane Garcia shook her head. I tried to respond, but my voice vanished, and each time I opened my mouth, I made a feeble croaking noise like an immature bullfrog. That made the others laugh even harder.

I woke up with my heart pounding. The pillow was damp with sweat. I threw off a blanket and looked at my watch. It was only 2:00 A.M. I had to get back to sleep if I was going to make it through the next day.

I pulled the pillow over my head to shut off the glare from the street light outside the window. A car sped down the street, its muffler rattling as it struck the potholes. Why had Kent signed that duplicitous memo? Why had he chosen Locara's goddamn foolish policy of unilateral legislation and military force, the one I had struggled against throughout the campaign? Now I was stuck with the task of implementing it. In the public eye, I would be responsible for the policy, and I would reap the blame when it failed. Joe had laid a cuckoo's egg in my nest, and there was no way I could kick the damn thing out, at least not publicly, without seeming to be disloyal to the president. I tossed and fumed until morning.

I HAD MY FIRST BITTER TASTE of Locara's agenda when I gave a speech at the Council on Foreign Relations in New York. Even though the speech was off the record, I had to clear it through the bureaucracy. After the bureaucratic censors had mangled it, the speech had few nuances.

I had often visited the council when I taught at Princeton, and this was like a homecoming, as I caught up with old friends and acquaintances over tea before the meeting. I smiled as I walked up the marble spiral staircase and entered the great hall with its long drapes and portraits of establishment figures who had guided the council since its founding in 1922. But I seethed inwardly as I read the speech the bureaucracy had prepared for me. When giving official answers to the sensible questions, I found myself in the ironic role of playing Joe Locara to the questioners' Peter Cutler. One businessman, Dwight Carter of General Data, was particularly irate. His hand shot up as soon as I finished.

"Why does this administration support Senator Peary's export control legislation?" he asked from the middle of the great hall. "It makes no sense to prevent the American computer industry from selling to the Middle East unless other countries restrict their exports as well. This unilateral approach is simply destroying American industry."

It was all I could do to keep from nodding agreement, but I soldiered ahead as a representative of the administration. "We hope that by going first we will be better able to persuade other countries to follow our lead."

"It's idiotic," Carter shot back, his face reddening. "No other countries will go along with the approach in Peary's legislation. Most of that technology is so common you can buy it at Radio Shack."

"We're committed to getting our allies to negotiate a common set of export controls," I reiterated, afraid that a longer answer might expose the internal fissures in the administration.

"Good luck," Carter snapped. "And in the meantime, our European and Japanese competitors are going to eat our lunch. And once the American industry loses market share because we're seen as unreliable suppliers, we'll never get it back. Then where's your influence?"

"We understand the problem," I replied, "but we have to set a good example if we hope to persuade others to slow the export of the technologies that are feeding the proliferation of weapons of mass destruction."

"You'll do terrible damage to American industry and accomplish nothing at all," Carter retorted.

I defended the administration policy as best I could, but when I was leaving the building to catch a cab, Carter approached me. "You goddamn ivory tower academic," he hissed in the hallway. "I've got friends. We'll get you fired."

THE NEXT DAY was devoted to Congress. I led a group of administration officials to brief the leadership on the new policy. An informal closed session would be followed by public testimony before the Senate Foreign Relations Committee. I had set my alarm for five that morning so I could study the massive briefing book that had been assembled for my testimony. Arriving at the office to look at the overnight intelligence and press clippings before Kovic's 7:30 staff meeting, I found a nasty surprise. My picture stared out next to a front page story in the *Post* about the hostile reaction in Europe to Kent's policy. Inside was an editorial entitled "The Hell of Good Intentions."

Oh shit. Who's doing this to me? Should I call someone on the editorial staff? Would it do any good?

When I entered the ornate chamber of the Foreign Relations Committee, I found Locara already talking to several senators. I was surprised since everyone knew that congressional testimony was a State Department prerogative, not a responsibility of the NSC staff. I noticed that Alexa was there from Defense and Walt Platt from Commerce. They broke off their conversation, and Locara came over. He smiled broadly and greeted me cordially.

"They plan to sit down for the informal session at 9:30," he said. "I'll take ten minutes to introduce you and say a word or two about the policy, then turn it over to you. Your open testimony begins at 10:30."

My pulse quickened. Locara's seemingly innocent gesture was clearly a way of signaling his central role to the senators and staffers who were interested in this policy. Locara was establishing that he was in control. If I let him get away with this, I would lose all credibility on the Hill and with it, the chance to alter the policy later. I had to fight back.

"Like hell," I said. "NSC staff doesn't belong in this, and you know it. I'm perfectly capable of introducing myself and the policy."

Joe put his arm on my shoulder as if we were old friends. "Not to worry, Pete. I'll just explain the president's personal interest."

"I work for the president too, goddamit," I said, dropping the thick blue notebook on the witness table for emphasis. A few people glanced in our direction. I looked Joe in the eyes. "You try to introduce me to the senators, and I'm out of here. Then what're you going to tell 'em?"

"Relax," Locara said, wrinkling his brow. His bow tie was slightly crooked. "No problem." Then softly, almost inaudibly, "You don't have to be such a prick about it."

Locara turned back to smile at the senators and took a seat behind me. As I settled behind the witness table, I noticed that Alexa had been watching closely.

In this hearing, the criticism came in the opposite direction from Dwight Carter's the night before. Somebody must have primed Senator Peary because he immediately went on the offensive, training his guns on me. "Is the administration gonna support me on restricting computer exports to the enemies of Israel?" he asked with his Carolina drawl.

"Yes, Senator, we've agreed to work with your bill."

"Then why is the State Department tryin' to insert so many loopholes? You're makin' a Swiss cheese out of it," Peary retorted.

I was tempted to ask how he knew the position of the different executive branch agencies but responded coolly, "It's the common administration position that we need flexibility in the legislation so that our diplomatic efforts can succeed."

Senator Rodriguez, the ranking minority member, was next. "Secretary Cutler, I assume you've read the president's speeches calling proliferation the greatest danger of our age?"

Read them? I was tempted to reply that I was the one who wrote them. Instead, I nodded, "Yes, sir."

"Then why is the State Department being so spineless on this issue? That's what people ask me when I go home to New Mexico. What am I supposed to tell them?"

"I would not characterize our position that way," I said. "We live in an interdependent world. We have to use diplomacy to persuade others to go along with our positions. That takes time."

"I'm not criticizing the president," Rodriguez said. "I give him full marks for hanging tough and holding to his campaign promises. But I don't see any evidence that his State Department shares his determination to stop proliferation in the Middle East at any cost."

"The president's policy is our policy," I assured him.

They were firing warning shots across my bow. Or more accurately, across my stern, warning me not to try to change course or back up. And they probably got most of their ammunition from Locara.

That night I called Kate to tell her that I could not come home for the weekend. I wanted to use Kovic's Saturday morning staff meeting to get the secretary and the others to understand the problems we had to manage in implementing the new policy. In addition, Defense had called a meeting of the nuclear arms planning committee, and my desk was piled with papers that I needed to clear so the bureaus could proceed.

"Peter, you have to come home," Kate's voice was insistent. "Jimmy flunked math again. Last night he snuck out of the house after I thought he was in bed. Today he's come home with a note from his teacher about lying. And two nights ago, Monica made a scene about never seeing you."

I hesitated for a moment. I couldn't possibly leave Washington at a time like this. And I couldn't possibly ignore the needs of my children. Family first. "Okay," I said, drawing a deep breath. "I'll be there."

IT WAS ONE OF THOSE RAINY, FOGGY WEEKENDS in early March when the natural beauty of Princeton sinks under a sea of mud. To make matters worse, my mind was in Washington. Monica may have cried for Daddy during the week, but after she was invited to a slumber party on Saturday, Kate refused to let her go because I was coming home. When I arrived Friday night, Kate announced that Monica was sulking upstairs.

I opened the door to Monica's room. Stuffed animals sat on the pillows on her bed, and posters of rock stars decorated the walls. Monica was curled up in the big white chair, earphones on, her head moving rhythmically to the beat. When she saw me, she slipped the earphones back, two black bumps on her head.

"Oh, hi Dad," she said. "I didn't hear you." I was suddenly struck by a memory of a younger Monica jumping up to hug me when I came home. Now she was becoming a woman, and our easy physical intimacy was replaced by more awkward expressions of affection. I walked over, sat on the arm of the chair, and kissed the cheek she turned up to me. I could hear a faint throbbing from the two black dots.

"How's my little girl?"

"Dad, don't call me that," she said. "I'm almost thirteen, you know."

"Okay." I noticed that she was wearing lipstick, though Kate disapproved. I started to mention it but thought better. Instead, I asked, "What's this problem about a party?"

"Mom's being a jerk," Monica said, wrinkling up her nose. "I told her you wouldn't mind if I went. It's really important. Jenny and Pam are both going."

I must have looked hurt because Monica suddenly put her arms around my neck and kissed my cheek. "Please, Daddy. Pretty please?"

Of course I gave in. Later at dinner, Kate commented, "It must be nice to suddenly arrive from Washington and play the role of good cop."

The next day was too wet to play catch, and Jimmy treated Kate's insistence that I help with math as the equivalent of a prison sentence. I wasn't much better. I was exasperated by Jimmy's refusal to solve the most elementary equations.

"I hate stupid math," Jimmy squirmed in his chair in front of a kitchen table strewn with papers.

"I never liked math much either," I confessed, "but you can't go far in life without it."

"Baseball players don't need math," Jimmy said, petulantly, "and they make lotsa money. More than teachers who go to school half their life."

"Money isn't everything. If it were, I wouldn't have chosen to be a professor."

Jimmy shrugged. "I don't wanna be a professor, I wanna be a baseball player."

"Listen," I wrote another equation for Jimmy to solve, "if you can memorize the batting average of every Yankee player, you can remember how to do this." I pointed at the paper.

"That's different," Jimmy complained, pushing too hard on his pencil and breaking the point. He got up from the table and walked slowly across the kitchen to the pencil sharpener.

"I'll make a deal with you," I said in desperation, "if you can do all the equations in this chapter by next weekend, I'll take you to a Yankees game next month."

Jimmy looked at me levelly. "And promise to come to my Little League games?"

"You're an extortionist," I smiled, "but you've got a deal."

To Kate's irritation, I spent little time with her. I was constantly interrupted by calls from my Washington staff reporting on the meetings I had missed. The next morning I left home at 6:00 A.M. to catch the early train.

A STATE DEPARTMENT DRIVER picked me up at Union Station. As the car turned onto C Street and approached the hulking facade of the State Department building, my stomach tightened and anxiety crept up the back of my throat. What disasters would I find this time? As I entered the elevator and pushed seven, a man with press credentials dangling from his neck entered behind me and looked at me for a minute.

"You're Cutler, aren't you?"

I nodded.

"I'm John Marcus from the *Post*. We talked on the phone. I want to see you. They say you're getting control of this Middle East weapons policy."

"Okay," I said. "Call my secretary."

"I'll call today." He replied. "I've got something important to ask you about Pakistan."

CHAPTER 6

A YEAR INTO MY TENURE AT STATE, I ordered champagne with dinner at Lahiere's. I was in Princeton for the weekend, and since both kids were at parties, Kate and I decided to splurge on a rare dinner out. We sat at our favorite table near the window. "What are we celebrating?" she asked after the waiter had filled our glasses and left.

"My survival." I lifted a glass and watched the bubbles rise. "I'm not going to drown."

"I thought it might have been my new poem." She raised an eyebrow at me quizzically.

"Let's celebrate that too." I tipped my glass toward her. "To both of us."

Kate sipped tentatively.

"What I meant is that I'm a player," I continued. "I've mastered the Washington game." I downed half the glass.

"I was never worried about that," Kate said. "Just the opposite."

"Bully for you." I laughed, feeling the slight rush of alcohol. "I was scared stiff."

I emptied my glass, took the green bottle from its silver ice bucket, and filled up again. Kate's glass was barely touched.

"Peter, I'm glad you love your job," she said. "I just don't want you to love it too much."

I laughed. "Jealous?"

She nodded. "It seems to be all you think about these days."

I tried to explain to her how all-consuming Washington was. "You have to be constantly on your guard. It reminds me of the dodgeball games we used to play in elementary school. During recess, the boys would form a circle and throw a volleyball at a player in the middle. If you hit him, you took his place."

"We had that game too," Kate said. "I hated it."

"I hated it too when I got blindsided and hit in the face. It stung like a hornet. But as I got good at anticipating the passes, at jumping and darting, I loved being the survivor."

"Maybe that was my problem," Kate said. "I rarely survived. But I also didn't like hurting other girls."

"Each dodge felt like a victory." I confessed. "When I was hit and put in the outer circle, I learned to fake passes and shoot quickly to knock the new guy out of the ring."

Kate shrugged and smiled faintly.

"Washington is dodge city," I continued, "only they hurl words that sting worse than any volleyball. Same tactics of deception, passes, and evasions. But the stakes are higher."

"Doesn't that seem juvenile?" she asked.

"No," I replied. "It's serious. Political bruises are less visible, but they're more painful. You have to learn to hit more than you are hit. I've learned to survive."

I was proud of my new skills in bureaucratic politics and wanted Kate to appreciate my prowess. I resented the fact that she could not or would not grasp the pleasures of my new game. As I tried to explain by giving examples of my bureaucratic victories over dinner, her attention flagged.

"So we moved the meeting to a Friday afternoon when I knew he was leaving town early," I chuckled. "I announced that it was principals only, no deputies. We got six agencies to sign off on the paper. He bitched like hell when he got back on Monday, so we held another meeting to calm him down. But by then he was playing catch-up trying to amend our agreed interagency draft. First rule of bureaucratic politics: Make 'em work from your paper."

Kate poked at the food on her plate with a fork. "That hardly seems fair, does it?"

"He'd been doing the same things, stalling for months. I had to find a way to move the ball forward. This terrorism issue matters."

"It all seems so petty. Why not just discuss differences openly like grown men?"

"We do, and we disagree," I said. "We could talk forever, but nothing would come of it. We could appeal to our bosses, but their plates are already too full. So we try to outmaneuver each other with bureaucratic ploys. It's unavoidable. In the end, that's how you get things done at our level."

"I still think it sounds demeaning," Kate shook her head.

I frowned. "You don't make any effort to . . . "

"That's not true," she interjected. "But it's not for me."

"If you moved down there it could be."

"You see it as basking in shared glory," Kate said. "I see it as living in your shadow again."

"You could find a good job," I countered. "That would give you your own life."

"I have a good job," Kate replied. "Robert hinted that I'll be promoted again within a year."

"I can help you get something better than anything Robert has to offer."

"You're missing the point." Kate's voice was brittle. "I don't want something that you have to get for me."

"Even if it's better? Don't be foolish."

"Don't talk to me about foolish." Her voice now cracked. "I hate it when you act like this."

"I'm not trying to upset you," I replied, struggling to inject a tone of calm reason into my voice. "I'm just explaining, and you're not listening."

"I hate it when you act so superior." Kate choked out the words. Now there were tears in her eyes.

"You're not listening." I could hear my voice brim with exasperation.

"I don't want to talk about it anymore." Kate ended the conversation. I knew she was frustrated by her loss of control.

A cloud hung over the rest of the weekend, and I returned to Washington tense and angry. This was becoming a pattern. Every time I came home for the weekend, Kate nagged me to help Jimmy with his homework or repair the leaking gutters, or she told me that we really must pay a visit to my parents at their retirement home in Florida. During my first months in Washington, a weekend at home had meant a relief from Washington struggles. Now the struggles were at home. By Sunday afternoon I found myself secretly looking forward to the excitement of Washington.

I HAD GRADUALLY consolidated my position, but it had not been easy. Early on, my assistant, Tony DiNatale, found that some highly classified cables from Pakistan were routed to Vole without copies to my office. Apparently they were from the new untested but promising source. The cables were tightly held, labeled NO DISTRIBUTION CODE WORD, or NODIS for short. I called in the director of the communication center.

"Why am I no longer getting the NODIS HANDY cables from Pakistan?"

"Mr. Vole told me to restrict them to the secretary and the undersecretary for political affairs," the director replied.

"Well, now you can add me to the list."

"I'm not sure I can do that."

"Do I have to raise the issue with Kovic?" I threatened. "If so, he'll back me, and I won't let you forget it."

Within days, the pattern of cable traffic was corrected.

I remembered Jim's advice that power flows to those who are helpful, so I included a number of bureaus, even the weak ones, in my morning staff meetings. My information proved useful to the weaklings, who then wanted me to succeed. By holding my meetings right after Kovic's morning staff meeting, I could speak authoritatively about what the secretary of state had on his mind and direct the flow of work among the various bureaus. People came to me to find out what was going on. They were pleased to get a share of the tasks I assigned. In turn, their troops swelled my forces and helped me shape the implementation of the Middle East weapons policy.

When I found that the South Asia bureau was blindsiding me by sending position papers to the secretary without my clearance, I invited Walt Salmon, the assistant secretary, to lunch in the elegant executive dining room on the eighth floor. Over soup, we chatted about the president's recent trip to Asia and debated the mixed prospects for the Redskins this season. When the main course was served, I got to the point.

"You know, Walt, I always invite your deputy to my morning staff meetings."

"Yes, and I'm much obliged," Salmon replied, with a somewhat puzzled look.

"That gives you a pretty good early warning system," I continued, emphasizing the obvious.

"Yes." Now Salmon looked doubly puzzled. "We welcome the cooperation."

"Cooperation is a two-way street," I said. "I'd hate to have to limit attendance in the future."

Salmon nodded and I changed the subject. Within the week, I began receiving early copies of his papers.

THE INTERAGENCY GAME proved a little trickier. At the beginning, every time I convened the formal group that I chaired, fifteen agencies gathered in the room. There were too many chiefs around the table for serious bargaining, and the large number of spear carriers in the chairs along the wall meant that anything sensitive would appear in the next morning's papers. I called Jim for advice, and he invited me to lunch in the White House mess.

This wasn't your standard cafeteria. Low ceilings, a burgundy rug, and uniformed waiters gave the mess an aura of intimacy that fit its exclusiveness. We sat at a little table in the corner. "We should do this more often," Jim said. "I've been too busy with the damn social security bill."

"I've missed our talks," I said, glancing at the menu.

"Likewise." Jim beckoned to one of the uniformed waiters. "But I meant that it will do you good to be seen more often in the mess."

I looked around the small room. Two tables away, a Treasury under-secretary lunched with a special assistant to the president. Behind him, the deputy director of the Office of Management and Budget ignored her plump guest while she talked into her cell phone.

I explained to Jim the problems caused by the rigidity in the president's decision on the Middle East policy paper, and the way Locara stopped the interagency meetings from discussing the softening necessary for successful implementation.

"We've got to permit some exports," I said, "or we won't have any bargaining chips. Our critics in the region call the embargo part of our plot against Islam, and the Japanese companies are eating our lunch. But Kovic is too chicken to send the president my paper recommending a new decision. I need to get a chance to talk to Kent and explain it to him."

"That's not how it's done," Jim said, cutting into an inch of rare sirloin. "You don't need to teach a snake to suck eggs."

"I'm not following you," I said.

Jim put down his fork and explained.

"The president needs to look tough for domestic politics; you need some flexibility to implement his policy overseas. He knows that. Don't try to make him reverse anything publicly. Just create some running room at the margins."

"How?" I asked. "Every time I try at the interagency meetings, Locara interrupts and sings 'Hail to the Chief.' Then the others join the chorus."

"Wrong place." Jim spoke with his mouth full. "As we say in Montana, don't try to milk a steer. You can't get much done at those big meetings. You hold big meetings only to ratify things and so nobody can complain that they've been shut out of the process. You've got to eat more lunches."

I looked down at my chef's salad.

Jim followed my gaze. "Not that," he laughed. "You've got to meet the key players privately, so everything's wired before you get into the big room. Shut Locara out of those small meetings. And Alexa. She's too close to him. Find another entry into the Pentagon. Keep your changes marginal. Then Locara won't be able to stop you."

I pushed my plate away. A waiter came to clear it.

"How about dessert?" Jim said.

I shook my head. "No thanks. I'm full."

JIM'S STRATEGY WORKED LIKE A CHARM at first. I held fewer large meetings and settled minor issues directly with my counterparts in other agencies at small sessions where Locara was not present. More things on terrorism, proliferation, and the Middle East began to go my way.

But Joe Locara was too experienced in Washington to miss my tactics. Soon I began receiving memos signed by Jane Garcia but clearly written by Locara giving me explicit directions about how to handle many of the smaller issues. I knew, however, that the White House could not keep up with all the bureaucratic details, and I convened small groups to reinterpret the directives and sandpaper their sharp edges. I created more facts on the ground than Locara could effectively control.

Locara retaliated by setting up an ambush. He turned to his old friends on Capitol Hill. Soon I received a letter from Senator Peary inviting me to testify before his Foreign Relations subcommittee. The "invitation" was a command. Peary might be a member of our party, but he mistrusted the State Department, not to mention moderate Democrats, almost more than Republicans. I had already testified a dozen times in six months, twice before Peary's committee. I knew that when a senator says "jump," I shouldn't ask "why" but "how high?"

I walked into the amphitheater of the Senate Foreign Relations hearing room with my notebooks under my arm and support staff trailing behind me. I took a seat alone at the center of a long table, behind a small notepad, a pitcher, and a glass of water. The ice in the water sparkled from the bright TV lights. A black microphone on the table slanted at me like a hostile missile about to be launched. The lights made me squint as I looked up at the polished chestnut horseshoe where the senators sat behind their nameplates. I reached out to take a sip of water, but my hand trembled and the ice jingled in the glass. I quickly put the glass down.

I looked up at the four huge world maps on the wall. Above them loomed a large shield with the American eagle. Behind the senators, long blue drapes covered a window, and in front of the drapes, two dozen staffers perched, passing notes and leaning forward to respond to requests from their bosses. A staffer brushed the drapes, and they opened slightly to reveal a flash of daylight. Behind me were tables lined with scribbling reporters and rows of chairs for the public. The room was packed. Hundreds of eyes drilled my back.

As I sat waiting for the senators, Ian Doublett, Senator Peary's legislative assistant and a close ally of Joe Locara, sauntered over to the witness table. A pudgy man with stringy black hair and wire-rimmed glasses, he wore a rumpled blue suit, and there was a good four inches of paunch between his tie and his belt. I remembered Locara boasting how he and Doublett used to leak sensitive information to the press a week before a critical vote so that senators were boxed into voting for the pet causes of the staffers. And how Doublett would often start rumors about executive nominees who were coming before the committee for confirmation. He called it "tying a can to their tails to see how they run."

"I hope you're ready to defend the administration, Cutler." Doublett smirked.

"Of course."

"You know, no openings for the other party . . ." He let the sentence dangle as he leaned over the witness table. "As we told you, the chairman doesn't want to waste time on prepared testimony. We'll submit your statement in the *Record* and go straight to questions."

I nodded, hoping he would go away.

"We hear rumors about divisions in the administration. Of course, I don't believe . . ." Doublett was master of the unfinished innuendo.

The door behind the podium opened, and for once I was glad to see Senator Peary enter. Doublett turned quickly and scurried back to whisper something in the senator's ear and then took a seat behind him.

Chairman Peary sat behind a massive podium, rocking back and forth in his big black chair, one finger stroking his mustache. He had jowls like a basset hound that quivered when he spoke. He picked up a pencil, methodically turning it end over end, then tapped it silently against his other hand. Suddenly he leaned forward and, after a perfunctory greeting, fired the first salvo.

"Why are you permitting France to export chemicals to a fertilizer plant in Pakistan when you know the plant might someday be converted to chemical weapons production?" Scowling, he leaned over the podium, allowing the cameras to get the best angle on his famous profile.

I began to answer. "Senator, as you know, the same chemicals can be precursors for fertilizer as well as weapons. We're committed to rural development in Pakistan, and . . . "

Peary silenced me by waving his pencil. He paused for dramatic effect, turned toward the cameras, then back to me. He shook his head and fired again.

"Why are we continuing to coddle Pakistan when this new Islamist government is spreading poison to the Middle East?" he continued.

"We need good relations to be able to influence them to . . ." I began.

He cut me off again.

"Why are you allowing Japan to provide credits for their exports to Pakistan, when it is acting contrary to our policy on Islamic terrorism?"

"There is no strong evidence that Pakistan is supporting terrorists, Senator. Japan has its own policy, and there is nothing illegal about providing credits to Pakistan. We've indicated our preferences to Tokyo, but frankly there's not much we can do about it." Sweat began to form on my forehead.

Peary switched his attack to another direction. "Why is the State Department preventing us from stationing more troops in Israel, our one true ally in the region?"

"Mr. Chairman, I'm . . . "

Peary held up his hand, looked out over the packed room and then down at me, before firing his big gun. "Is it true, as some press reports say, that you're deliberately undercutting the president's policy by failing to cooperate with the White House staff?"

I flushed. The muscles in the back of my legs tensed. I longed to reply by asking Peary where he got his misinformation, but I swallowed the words. Responding to that cheap shot would be walking into Peary's trap. I knew there was no percentage in a fight. If I kept the tone polite and the answers long and technical, the TV footage would be too dull to run. If I fought back for even ten seconds, they would have a story. For once, I did not want to make the evening news.

I turned out right about the television coverage. It was easy to bore them, but the print people were more difficult to evade. Neither the picture nor the story in the *Washington Times* the next morning was very flattering, and it was only the first in a spate of hostile articles. All seemed to stem from leaks about past and pending decisions that smelled suspiciously of Joe Locara. One of his buddies was a key security reporter at the *Times* and little better than a flack for disaffected leakers in the administration. I responded by calling a few of the better reporters into my office and giving background accounts of the conflicts in the Middle East and the role of Pakistan. I explained what I was attempting to accomplish.

Locara escalated again. At least I assumed it was Locara. I could never pin it down. But whoever was out to get me was now playing hardball, and the next pitch was aimed at my head. I was sitting in my office when Julie buzzed to say that John Marcus was on the phone.

"I'm picking up rumors around town that you're planning to sell out Israel," Marcus said.

"That's ridiculous, where'd you get such crap?"

"I have two sources that say you blocked the effort to station troops in Israel and that you want to tighten controls on exports to Israel. Care to make any comment? On or off the record?"

"Who's spreading this horseshit?" I exploded.

"I never disclose sources," Marcus said, "but I know for a fact that the head of a major Jewish organization has asked the White House political people whether you're anti-Semitic. And it's on the HotNews Web site."

"Jesus," I was beginning to feel sick. "This is outrageous. You know that's a lot of crap."

"Care to make any comment?"

"You heard my comment," I nearly shouted.

"Hey," Marcus said, "Don't shoot. I'm a messenger."

As soon as Marcus got off the phone, I called Jim and told him what happened.

"This is serious," Jim said. "Gotta nip this sucker in the bud. If this spreads around town, you'll never shake it."

"What can I do?" My voice was rising.

"Two things," Jim said. "First, I'm gonna have a private talk with your friend Mr. Locara and tell him that if he doesn't knock it off, I'll cut his balls off. Then we'll have lunch."

"Lunch?"

"Yeah," Jim said. "I'll arrange a lunch at the Cosmos Club with a couple of our major Jewish donors and a couple of key columnists. You put on your best manners and show 'em what a good guy you are. That oughta help."

Jim was right. The hostile journalism began to give way to friendly stories. I knew I had won when I bumped into Rab White outside the secretary's office and he remarked admiringly, "Good ink you've been getting, Peter. The secretary always likes that."

THE GAME HAD ITS PRICE, of course. For the first time in over a decade, Jim and I found ourselves too busy for the spring pilgrimage to Cathedral Lake. We promised Abe we would not let him down next year, but next year seemed aeons away. And I realized that I hadn't written to Ali in months.

Sometimes when I put my feet up on my desk and tipped back to read a cable, I would look out the window and catch sight of guys playing softball or volleyball on the grass in front of the Lincoln Memorial. I hadn't relaxed in ages. Or I'd be talking on the phone to a congressman, and the sight of a plane taking off from Reagan National Airport out over the Potomac made me ache for Maine. My eyes would travel to the Winslow Homer picture of the fisherman.

Occasionally, if the weather was nice, I'd walk the few blocks from the White House to the State Department after a meeting. But more often I needed the official car, both for its air-conditioning and for a quick postmeeting strategy session with my staff before I hurried to my next appointment.

I was putting on weight from all the political lunches and dinners and the lavish spreads of foie gras at embassy receptions. Occasionally I found time for predawn runs in Rock Creek Park, but too many mornings I had to spend studying briefing books and option papers.

One night, I attended a reception at the British embassy. It was built like a palace, with a curving staircase, high ceilings, huge chandeliers, and large oil paintings. The British always served elegant food. I grazed at a table of hors d'oeuvres in lieu of dinner. My back was turned to the room as I shoveled up stuffed artichokes, asparagus rolled in ham, and smoked salmon on crackers. I had not noticed Dwight Carter approach, and when I turned around, I was startled by his presence. I had not seen him since our dispute at the Council on Foreign Relations, and I braced myself for another round of unpleasantries. Instead, Carter was cordial.

"How are you, Pete? You seem to be settling in pretty well."

"Can't complain," I said warily.

"You look good."

"I eat well," I said, holding up a crab cake.

"This amount of time in Washington makes anyone live like a native," Carter said with a smile.

I smiled in return.

"I hear you're still commuting."

I nodded, my mouth full of crab.

"Must be hard, not having your wife here."

"We're managing," I mumbled.

"Maybe I can help," Carter said. "I hear your wife's a very good editor. General Data controls several communications magazines. I'm sure we could find a place for her at one of our magazines. We're always looking for new talent. In fact, I think we could arrange a salary in the range of six figures if that's what it would take to get her down here. Would you like me to pursue it?"

I couldn't believe what I heard. "You mean a hundred thousand dollars?" I coughed down the last bite of food.

"Exactly," Carter said.

"Are there any special conditions?"

"Absolutely no strings attached."

Here was the answer to my prayers. Not only would Kate and I be together, but we could also build a financial nest egg. But why was Carter suddenly so interested in helping me? Certainly not out of charity or sympathy. I was the person who signed off on the export licenses that General Data needed. Bribery is illegal, but no law forbade hiring a spouse who was highly qualified for a job. It was a very clever approach that might even pass public scrutiny. But it was too transparent for me. I imagined trying to judge future license applications impartially and realized that I would never be able to do my job without second thoughts. I thought for a second of calling Abe to ask advice, but realized I already knew the answer.

"That's very kind of you to offer," I said, "but I'm afraid it wouldn't look right."

"Nonsense," Carter said, still smiling. "We're interested in attracting good talent. She would not be paid any more than we pay our other top editors. It would be good for us, good for her."

"That's probably right," I said, " and I know there is not a real problem, but I'm afraid it won't meet the Caesar's wife test."

He arched his eyebrows.

"You know," I said. "It has to look clean as well as be clean."

"Don't be silly," Carter replied. "It's perfectly legal and it's very common in this town."

"Thanks, but I don't think it would work," I said reluctantly.

"Well, think it over," Carter said as he moved away from the table. "The offer stands."

I knew I couldn't mention the offer to Kate. It would only confirm her mistrust of Washington. Things were tense enough between us. Besides, when I got back to Princeton on weekends, all I wanted was to collapse on the sofa. And all the kids seemed to do was bicker and fight.

Kate and I argued openly one Saturday evening while we dined at the Kleins' home. I was trying to explain how Washington worked, so I recounted a number of bureaucratic strategies.

"Some of it's almost comical," Rachel said.

"Yes, I want to laugh sometimes," I admitted. "But underneath, it's deadly serious. If we fail to control nuclear weapons and they fall into the hands of terrorists, there will be nothing to laugh about."

"Maybe men shouldn't be trusted with power," Rachel said with a smile. "All that testosterone makes them too competitive."

"Let me tell you about some of the women," I replied.

"It's not a question of gender, it's a question of maturity," Kate said sharply. "Why can't adults settle their differences openly without all that nonsense?"

"I know it sounds petty," I replied, "but if you don't do those things, you're out of the game."

"Maybe there's a message in that," Kate said.

"You're just like my father," I snapped. "You two always know the easy moral answer. But let me assure you, in Washington, the meek don't inherit the earth. If you turn the other cheek, some jerk will slap it."

Kate frowned at my tone. "Maybe your father was right," she said. "Why play games where you have to reduce yourself to that level? Maybe it's time for you to come back to Princeton."

"Or maybe it's time for you to come to Washington and learn what you're preaching about," I shot back.

Abe looked embarrassed. "We all want Peter back," he said to Kate, "but the work he's doing down there is very important." Then, turning toward me, "Of course, Kate's right. You should only indulge in such tricks to the minimal extent you need to get things done."

I started to reply, but Rachel quickly interrupted by asking if anyone would like another cup of coffee.

KATE FINALLY PERSUADED ME to take a few days during the children's vacation to visit my parents in Florida. I succumbed partly to stop her nagging, partly because of the dreary March weather, and partly because I had not visited them at Christmas. Moreover, Kovic was in Europe with the president for a week, and the State Department was relatively quiet. I could always talk to the office from Florida.

Lone Palm Village was an attractive retirement community near Tampa. The houses all looked alike, but they bordered a golf course and a large swimming pool. The community had its own infirmary and clubhouse. Everything was bright, but coming from the energy of Washington, I found it sterile and depressing.

The first morning, while my parents rested and Kate took the kids to a mall to buy bathing suits, I sat by the pool to sunbathe and catch up on unclassified reading. Somebody was taking her leave at the house near where I was sitting.

"Come see us if you're ever up north," a cheerful young voice said.

"Honey," a crackling voice replied, "I'll never get out of this place alive."

A car door slammed, an engine started, and I turned my attention to the Energy Department's analysis of world oil markets. The curves in the graphs showed American production declining and dependence on Persian Gulf oil rapidly increasing. All the numbers went in the wrong direction. I shook my head. Depressing.

On the other side of the pool, an elderly couple walked slowly down the path. He would jut one foot forward, then the other in angular progress, his right arm lagging behind. She shuffled slowly behind, her hand wrapped around the thumb of his right hand as though she were on a leash. Mutual tethering, I thought as I watched them eke along.

At lunch I watched my father slowly make his way through a slab of meatloaf. Kate and I had long since finished. The kids had left to play in the pool. Father's shoulders sloped forward, his chest sunken in, and the top of his round belly was just visible above the dining room table. Always small, he now seemed the size of a child.

Father cut his food carefully with his knife. The hand that held the fork shook as he raised it to his lips. His teeth were more yellow than white, and he chewed slowly and deliberately. When he spoke, remnants of partly chewed food were stuck along his gums.

At the other end of the table, Mother slumped in her chair. Her bosom, never ample, had vanished into a gentle slope from chin to stomach. The flesh on her thin arms hung loosely from the bones, and her skin was marked with large brown patches. She talked even less than usual, and what she did say was confused. She had forgotten the children's names and sometimes could not remember Kate. She leaned forward for her teacup with great effort. Even the simplest movements made her wince.

Behind Mother, on the sideboard, was a silver-framed picture of Jimmy and Monica, tanned, smiling, and ready to burst out of the photo. On the wall were the large oil portraits of my Cutler grandparents, plump, ruddy, captured in the prime of health. Between the portraits was an antique mirror that used to be in the living room in Blainesville.

I caught a glimpse of myself in its distorting glass. The hair at my temples was beginning to recede. I looked down at my hands. I imagined the beginning of faint brown spots and shivered internally. My eyes moved sideways to catch the sunlight reflecting on the tiled terrace and green lawns. I could hear the children splashing and giggling in the pool. I had a desperate urge to get up from the table and rush out to join them in the sun. Instead, I waited for my father to finish his careful chewing.

"We're so proud of you," Father said, finally putting down his fork. "Tell me again, what are you doing?"

I shuddered at the idea of repeating for a third time the duties of an undersecretary of state. Where once I had fought to protect myself from my father's questions, now I wished they were more demanding. It was painful to see him so incapacitated.

"I deal with all national security affairs," I said, "and that has meant a heavy involvement with the Middle East and Islamic terrorism for the past year."

"We're so proud of you," Father repeated, staring vacantly toward the sunshine. He nudged his bifocals onto his forehead and kneaded his eyelids with his knuckles.

Mother tried to get up to bring in the dessert, but she could not rise from her chair. Kate quickly insisted on going out to the kitchen. I sat silently, alone between my parents.

AFTER LUNCH, I went for a walk on the beach while Kate took the children to their tennis lessons. The sky had partly clouded over, and occasional breaks in the clouds sent shafts of sun to paint bright ivy patches on the dark water. I walked at the water's edge, watching the white crests of the waves break against the beach. Swirls of water laced

with foam broke over my ankles, crept up the sandy slope, then retreated, leaving behind a pattern of breaking bubbles and sand crabs
scurrying from their holes. I dug my toes into the sand as I walked, trying to deepen the pattern of my footprints, but when I looked back,
they had been swept away. Usually a walk on the beach revived me, but
today was different.

When I returned to their apartment, I found that Tony had called
from Washington. I dialed back eagerly. "There's an urgent cable from
the secretary in Paris," Tony reported.

"What's up?"

"The French are pressing hard on sales to Iran," Tony said. "They
claim that computer sales will help secure the flow of oil, but their real
gripe is that our laws are preventing exports by the French subsidiary of
General Data."

"So?"

"They're threatening to take legal action against the company unless
we make an exception. In addition, they've hinted that France will refuse any further cooperation on tightening controls on the exports of
missile technology unless we cooperate on computer exports."

"Just what I predicted," I said, shrugging my shoulders in self-
satisfaction.

"But here's the kicker," Tony said. "The president and the secretary
want an opinion on what the reaction will be at home if they give the
French what they want."

My mind raced ahead. It meant convening the interagency committee and taking soundings on the Hill. If I did not return, Locara would
chair the interagency meeting and begin the consultations without me.

"Are you coming back?" Tony asked.

"I just got here yesterday," I said. But I also felt my pulse quicken for
the first time in twenty-four hours. "I need a few minutes to think
about it."

But the answer was already running through my veins. I felt a satisfying rush of adrenaline as I began to think about strategy. This was a
defining moment for the policy changes I had been fighting for. This
was a chance for the president to experience firsthand the tightness of
the box that Locara had put him in. If I could work things out in

Washington while I had this window of opportunity, I would have a solid basis for a more flexible policy in the future. Then I could begin the round of international negotiations on multilateral export controls. This was the action-forcing event that I needed.

"Have a car meet me at the Delta terminal at 7:30," I told Tony, "and call a special session of the interagency committee for 8:00 P.M."

Kate was resting in the guest bedroom when I broke the news.

"No need for you and the kids to spoil your vacation," I said as I jammed shirts and underwear into a suitcase.

Kate sat on the bed, her arms hugging her knees. "This isn't just a vacation, Peter. This may be the last time you see your parents."

"I know. It couldn't have come at a worse time," I said, refusing to look at her and continuing to shove clothes into the suitcase.

"You're being a fool." Her voice rose. "So what if someone else chairs your precious meeting. These are your parents, for God's sake."

I stopped packing, walked over to the bed, and put my arm around her shoulder. "It's not that simple," I said. "This can be a turning point for the policy, exactly what I've been waiting for. I may never get another opportunity this good."

Kate shrugged, swung her legs to the floor on the other side of the bed, and buried her head in her hands. I knew by the slight heaving of her back that she was crying. For a moment, I was tempted to lie down on the bed and pull her to me. But the thought of George Vole, that unctuous weasel, and that slimy yuppie Locara using this opportunity to get control of my issue was too much. I returned to stuffing the suitcase.

Behind me Kate choked out. "You can't do this."

"I have to," I said.

"GOOD THING YOU CAME BACK," Tony said, handing me a file of papers. "Vole's soundings on the Hill haven't gone well. Peary is threatening new hearings if exceptions are made for the French."

"Maybe I can head that off by talking to Senator Rodriguez," I said as I shuffled through the papers Tony handed me.

"Locara has already called an interagency meeting," Tony said. "But now that you're back, he'll have to let you chair it."

It was a long night. I had to play bully at the interagency meeting, using the president's cable and the French threats as clubs. I called a dozen senators and congressmen, each time repeating the importance of French cooperation for any hope of negotiating a multilateral export control agreement. By morning, I was able to cable the president's party in Paris that there would be no serious repercussions in Washington if Kent met the French requests. One of the pleasant surprises of the whole episode was that Alexa Byrnes sided with me rather than Locara at the key meeting.

I EXPRESSED MY GRATITUDE to Alexa a few weeks later while we were sitting in the American Airlines Ambassadors Club at Kennedy waiting for a flight to London. I was heading the American delegation to a special meeting of countries that were the major suppliers of credits, weapons, and technology to the Persian Gulf. This would be the diplomatic centerpiece of my policy. We were seeking an agreement on a stiff code of conduct for suppliers to "regions of tension." Alexa was the Defense Department member of the delegation, and after two days at the Foreign Office, we were to attend a private conference on the Middle East sponsored by the Ditchley Foundation at its conference center near Oxford.

The lounge was crowded. We managed to find a vacant pair of chairs, pushed away the debris of empty glasses on the table, and put down our briefcases.

"I owe you one for last week," I said. "What'll you have to drink?"

Alexa laughed. "You can't buy Defense that easily, but I'd love a spritzer."

I gave the order to the waiter and turned back to Alexa. She wore an elegant, no-nonsense black business suit. Her blond hair was pulled back by a dark velvet band, and she wore small gold earrings. Her face was a little fuller than twenty years ago, but her figure was as slim as ever. Still the runner. I wondered how she found time. Strange to think how close we once had been in graduate school. I had been working with her for over a year now, and we had barely talked. It was all business. During the year, I had gone out of my way to avoid her whenever possible because she was Locara's bureaucratic ally as well as his girl-friend. I guess that's why I felt more political than personal gratification in the help she had extended last week.

"No bribes," I said. "But I'm grateful."

The waiter came with the drinks, and we raised our glasses in silent toast.

"I admired the way you handled that meeting," Alexa said. "You've grown over the past year."

"On-the-job training," I laughed.

Alexa smiled. "They never taught us this type of politics at Woodrow Wilson, did they?"

"I'll drink to that," I said, taking a sip of chardonnay. I looked at Alexa smiling and realized that I hadn't let myself think of her as a friend and former classmate rather than a bureaucratic rival.

When we boarded the plane, we were seated in different rows of the first-class cabin. I intended to skip the meal and catch a few hours sleep. After we were airborne and the seat belt sign was off, I went to the toilet. When I saw that the seat next to Alexa was vacant, I asked if she minded if I sat down for another drink before I retired. We started to talk about the London meetings but soon slipped into reminiscences about Princeton. Alexa asked about Abe.

"I knew he'd be an academic and that Jim would wind up in Washington," she said with a smile, "but I was never sure about you."

"Neither was I."

"Do you ever hear from Ali Aziz?"

I took a sip of bourbon. "We used to write each other a lot, and we always send cards on our birthdays. He's still working as an engineer in Pakistan's nuclear program. He writes less frequently now, and what he says is very guarded. His mail is probably censured."

"He was an odd fellow," Alexa said. "I could never figure him out. At one point I was sure he was going to stay in America."

I nodded. "Ali was always caught between his two worlds of Islam and science. I suspect he is having a hard time with this new government."

"It's a pity he went back." Alexa paused and held her wine glass to be refilled by the flight attendant. "He was odd but interesting."

"After all these years, I still consider him one of my best friends."

"And what about Kate?" Alexa asked, "Are you still together? I never see her with you around Washington."

"Oh yes," I said, a little too quickly. "She's still working at the Princeton University Press."

Neither of us brought up the subject of Joe Locara.

When the flight attendant came down the aisle with the table linens, I changed my mind and stayed for dinner.

It seemed only minutes after I finally returned to my seat that the intercom announced our imminent arrival at Heathrow. I hadn't gotten any sleep, but I did not regret my chat with Alexa. I needed the sleep more than the extra calories, but if I had renewed an old friendship and consolidated a new bureaucratic alliance, that was a nice night's work.

THE AMERICAN EMBASSY dominates Grosvenor Square in London. The building tries to meld with its surroundings, but the huge American eagle over the modern facade is anachronous, and the metal detectors in the lobby were unfortunate reminders of troubled times. When I arrived, part of the lobby was still being reconstructed to enhance security following a new terrorist threat two months before.

As soon as the Washington delegation had gathered in the ambassador's conference room, I opened the meeting. "I assume you've all studied the briefing books." I paused and looked around the table. "Do any of you wish to make any observations before we meet with the other delegations?"

"I have no quarrel with our instructions," said the Treasury representative, "but it's important that we not interpret the restrictions on credits to finance arms exports too narrowly. A number of our major banks are deeply involved." The point was so predictable that I let it pass without comment.

"Sir," said the two-star representing the joint chiefs, "I've been instructed to make sure that any language on the provision of advanced military equipment does not interfere with our potential to base supplies in Israel."

Again I merely nodded. Like most of the comments that followed, I had heard them all before. I was tempted to tell my colleagues to merely call out a number. Everyone would know which of the standard departmental positions the number referred to, and we would all save time and breath. But I also knew that this charade was important to build the consensus within the delegation that I would need when it came time to sell the results of my negotiations to the other departments back in Washington. I was grateful that Alexa said nothing. Maybe dinner on the plane was paying off.

I was optimistic after the consultations with the British. Perhaps it was because the American government officials had to mind our manners in front of foreigners, or perhaps the Foreign Office building created some sense of historical decorum.

"The Victorians sure built for empire, didn't they?" I said to my British counterpart as he ushered us under high ceilings, up a huge staircase, and past grand paintings on the walls.

Our two delegations quickly agreed that the British hosts would open the meeting at Riverwalk House the next day but would call on the Americans first so that I could set the tone of the discussion. We politely rehearsed our differences on export credits and agreed to leave the subject for the multilateral sessions on the next day.

If the Foreign Office building spoke of Britain's grand imperial past, Riverwalk House was the gritty present—a modern block construction along the Thames. After greeting the other delegation heads, I settled behind the placard designating the United States and half listened to the empty grace notes of the opening remarks while surveying the long table. Three delegates at the table and three along the wall for each country made the meeting too large, but every country seemed to find it impossible to exclude major bureaucratic players from the conference chamber.

I looked closely at the French delegate, knowing he would be trouble, hoping to elicit a smile. The Frenchman avoided my eyes, but I extracted a half nod from my German counterpart. I felt pride as my glance returned to my placard and little American flag on the green baize in front of me. But butterflies flitted about in my stomach. This was a crucial meeting. If I could negotiate a multilateral agreement among the suppliers of high technology, we could avoid a crisis in the Gulf. It would give us leverage on Pakistan. If my efforts failed, the hawks would prevail. Lives were at stake.

When it came my turn to speak, I appealed to the delegates' sense of history. I reminded them of the two Gulf wars and the devastation wrought by Al Qaeda. "Think of the damage that would be done to the world economy if there were a loss of Persian Gulf oil now that imports are rising." One or two people nodded. "Consider the horrors if a war escalates to nuclear or chemical weapons. Imagine the devastation of our cities that would occur if terrorists got access to nuclear weapons." Several people now seemed attentive. "In conclusion," I said, "if these multilateral efforts fail, there could be a crisis within a year. Our children will never forgive us if petty national differences prevent our grasping this historical moment."

I was sweating and trembling slightly, but I also knew that I had put my message across as well as I could. Not bad for an old Princeton lecturer, I thought, as I pressed the red button that shut off my microphone and settled back into my chair. Alexa passed me a note: "Nice job." I smiled at her.

The French delegate quickly punctured my satisfaction. He started with flattery, agreeing with my noble sentiments, but then went on the offensive.

"The government of France," he explained, "believes that the only way to ensure the flow of oil is through a rich web of trade relations. Arbitrary exclusion of dual-use technology will simply anger our friends in the Islamic world and might even provoke another oil embargo and further terrorism."

He stopped, pausing for effect, surveying the room. "Unfortunately," he commented acidly, "it sometimes appears as if some countries are not above seeking commercial advantage in their application of export controls. This, of course, annoys their friends and makes cooperation very difficult."

France was followed immediately by a pompous German delegate full of praise for European solidarity. I passed a note to Alexa, who was seated next to me. "Of course," I wrote, "particularly if solidarity allows German commercial interests to hide behind the ample skirts of

French rhetoric." Alexa smiled. Then the Japanese began to speak. I adjusted my earphones for the translation. Japan pledged cooperation but indicated difficulties with so many sections of our draft text that I began to appreciate the openness of the French objections.

The British delegate smiled politely as he took the floor, complimented me for presenting such an ambitious draft, and then went quickly to its weakest point. By designating the zone of tension as the Persian Gulf, it had excluded Israel. "Frankly, we in Europe do not regard this American proposal as adequately evenhanded. Unless we face the question of Israel more openly, we will never gain the confidence of the Muslim states in the region."

That bastard. Why didn't he warn me about this yesterday? Of course I knew of the objection. But I had hoped that the failure to raise the issue in the bilateral consultation yesterday meant the Brits would be more helpful. Instead, they were currying favor with the French.

Alexa passed me a note: "Perfidious Albion!"

I raised my hand and pressed the red button on my microphone. My pulse was throbbing.

"Of course, there is always a certain arbitrariness about where we draw boundaries, but why not start with controls on exports to the Persian Gulf and Southwest Asia, where the problem is most acute? We can come back to the question of the larger region at some later stage."

Looking around the table and seeing the blank response, I tried appealing to their political sense. "Let's be realistic," I said. "Efforts to define the zone for restraint in broad terms caused the failure last time we tried to negotiate a multilateral export control regime for the region. If we try to do more than is politically feasible, we'll fail again. Let's put first things first. In fact, several countries in the Gulf are rapidly approaching a nuclear capability, and Pakistan is already there. We need to act now before it is too late."

We wrangled for two days, clause by clause, an objection here, a reservation there, and occasionally a concession that moved the process along. I huddled with key heads of delegations, giving ground, holding firm, as we gradually removed brackets from around the contested language in the draft. I had to negotiate as much with my American compatriots sitting behind me as with the foreigners across the table. Every time I tried to soften the American position so that I could reach some agreement with the other countries, some bureaucrat threatened to raise the issue back home.

I decided to take some risks and call their bluff. Since I would approve the reporting cable that told Washington what happened, I knew I had time to light some backfires. My critics would attack the compromise, but I could make sure the cable created some damage control before I got back. Several times I overruled members of my delegation, deciding that the political risk at home was worth the prospect of getting an international agreement. Alexa continued to be cooperative. Only once did she side with the two-star from the joint staff, and that on a minor point.

Finally, on Friday morning, we had an agreed text for the delegations to take back to their national capitals. It was far from perfect. The French and British still held a reservation about the geographical scope, and the Treasury representative was seething about my compromise that weakened the language on export credits. "We'll fight this all the way to the top," Treasury threatened.

But it was a start. I was as exhausted as after a long run, but with the same glow of accomplishment. My opening rhetoric may have been flowery, but deep down I believed every word I said. I now had a framework for a multilateral approach, and the prospects of an imminent crisis had been lowered. I was doing something that would be worthy of at least a footnote in the history books.

THE EMBASSY CAR SPED UP the M-40 through the Oxfordshire countryside. I had heard good things about Ditchley, one of the great English country houses that Churchill used during the Second World War. It was now an elegant retreat for international conferences.

I was unprepared, however, for the beauty of the Georgian architecture. The three-story building of sand-colored stone was symmetrically connected by colonnades to two perfectly proportioned smaller buildings, each topped by a cupola. The main building was crowned with massive finials and two statues of heraldic angels. The car swung through iron gates past lawns as smooth as putting greens, and the tires crunched on the gravel of a circular drive. A massive oak door opened and a butler in a morning coat descended the stone steps to welcome us and usher us to our rooms. It was my first experience of a great country house. I raised my eyebrows at Alexa as we followed the butler up a broad carpeted staircase. "I feel as though I'm stepping back into history," I whispered.

She nodded and smiled.

The conference met in the library, a long room with two large fireplaces and twelve tiers of books on each wall. Close scrutiny revealed that above the fifth row the books were designed to be judged by their elaborate spines. It was an eighteenth-century English equivalent of the false front buildings in a western American town. Above the two marble mantles were gigantic eighteenth-century portraits of a worldly looking cleric and a portly squire in wig, velvet waistcoat, and knee breeches. They peered with satisfaction through the long French windows at the manicured park where pheasants and deer had been stocked for shooting pleasure.

After the session there was time before dinner, and Alexa announced that she was going for a run in the park behind the house. The idea appealed to me. I was curious to see the park and desperate to get some much needed exercise.

"Still on the run," I joked.

"Rarely miss a day," she smiled. "And for those days, I have an Exercycle in my apartment."

"Mind if I join you?"

"Of course not," she said. "It'll be like old times."

We ran on a dirt lane, past large oaks and chestnuts. The English countryside was a form of natural beauty so cultivated by man, so different from my beloved Maine wilderness, that I was amazed at how deeply I responded to it. I was elated by the bright green pastures and carefully clipped hedges. Fresh air filled my lungs. I smiled as we passed an enormous bull standing impatiently behind a wooden fence, separated from the cows chewing the grass nearby.

As I began to fall behind, Alexa turned her head and smiled. Out of shape though I was, the challenge gave me second wind, and I quickly caught up with her.

AT THE BLACK TIE DINNER, Alexa was seated on the right of Lord Watford, the conference chairman at one table, while I chatted with a Member of Parliament at another. After dinner, the groups rejoined for brandy in the drawing room, which was dripping with almost gaudy plaster cherubs. On the wall, larger than life, was a bas-relief of Diana the huntress, a robe loosely draped across one shoulder, exposing one breast, one hand holding a bow and the other the leash of a hound squatting patiently at her feet. Alexa's low-cut silk dress hung as lightly on her as did Diana's.

We sat facing each other at opposite ends of a red plush couch, sipping brandy. Any tension between us had vanished. I was feeling high on a mixture of political accomplishment, alcohol, Alexa's presence, and the opulent setting. As it grew late, we began to talk about Princeton. Other guests departed for bed, and we eventually had the room to ourselves. I rose to refill our glasses. As Alexa leaned forward to take the brandy snifter, the folds of silk fell forward, revealing a lace bra. I felt a surge of desire but glanced away quickly. I settled back onto the couch and Alexa looked down at the glass I had handed her.

"I like the way you've changed, Peter." She swirled the brandy and appeared intent on the streaks it made on the side of the glass. Then she looked up.

I raised my eyebrows, not knowing what to say.

"I should never have let you get away," Alexa said, smiling and looking back at the glass.

I smiled and shook my head. "It's a little late to think of that." Regretting the triteness of my comment, I added, "What about Joe?"

"I know you don't like him," she laughed. "But underneath his tough exterior, he's actually a good guy."

"You could have fooled me," I snorted.

She laughed again. "In any case, I decided to end it."

"How come?"

She ignored my question and looked at me with the full force of her blue eyes. I silently sucked in breath. I thought I had gotten over her long ago. How could this feeling still be there?

"We were so young at Princeton," Alexa continued, still fixing her gaze on me. "We've both changed a lot since then."

In the various times we had been together during the past year, I had chosen not to notice certain things about Alexa, like the down on her cheeks and the way she tucked her hair behind her perfect little ears. Suddenly they became irresistible again. I felt my will being torn into fragments. A small voice within me kept warning this was ridiculous, but another was pushing me toward her. The cacophony of inner voices was muddling my thought. I struggled to say something that reflected the first voice.

"Timing is everything." It sounded so inane after I said it that I dug in deeper trying to explain. "I mean, romance is no different than politics in that respect, is it?"

Alexa smiled and rose from the couch. "Well, if we're going to trade cliches, why not 'never too late' or 'strike while the iron's hot'?"

I forced myself to picture Kate.

"Well, at least I didn't say 'I told you so,'" I laughed. "It's nice to be friends again. We'll work more closely when we get back."

The red-carpeted staircase was broad enough for the two of us to ascend side by side. Remembering a lesson from Kate, I talked about the contrasting styles of the seventeenth- and eighteenth-century portraits we passed, savoring a sense of victory both in the vindication of the past and in resisting temptation in the present.

Alexa opened the door of her room and turned toward me. I put out my hand to say goodnight. Instead of shaking it, Alexa held it in both of hers and pulled me toward her.

"For heaven's sake, Peter, a little good night kiss won't hurt." She laughed. "I won't bite you."

I stepped forward. A small kiss would do no harm. But Alexa pressed her body against me, opened her mouth, and darted her tongue against my lips. Her hand reached into my hair, pulling me forward insistently, and my fingers ran over the smooth silk of her dress. I tried to think of Kate, but she was three thousand miles away. Why not? Just this once. Everyone is entitled to a moment like this.

Alexa drew me into the room and pushed the door shut. She loosened the sash that held the silk dress wrapped around her, and began to unbutton my shirt. For a moment, I hesitated. But too late. By then Alexa was standing naked before me. My pulse was rising. I simply could not turn away.

Alexa led me to the bed in the middle of the enormous room and pulled me down beside her. I kissed her breasts and ran my hand between her thighs. She gripped my shoulders tightly. Unlike the first time I made love to Alexa, when the ecstasy had been eroded by a sense of anxiety and uncertainty, I was sucked into this moment as quickly and completely as if I had placed my feet in quicksand. Memories from years ago blended with intense physical excitement in a driving, pounding torrent of passion.

Afterward I rolled onto my back, Alexa's head nestled on my shoulder and looked up at the canopy over my head. It was then that I thought of Kate. I was both empty and filled, satisfied and guilty at the same time. What was I doing here? After so many years of resisting temptation, how had I fallen into this situation? Alexa murmured and nudged her cheek against my chest.

I looked down at Alexa's body—the breasts a little fuller, the hips wider, the stomach not quite so taut as before, but there was none of the maternal bulge that was beginning to show on Kate. The unfairness of the comparison unloosed a strong surge of guilt. I looked down at my slight paunch and the love handles above my hips. Why would Alexa possibly want me? But as she turned to run her fingers over my chest, the sense of guilt vanished as quickly as it had appeared.

THE NEXT DAY, the conference broke into subcommittees. Alexa and I were assigned to different rooms, and I was glad since I desperately needed time alone to think. I heard little of what was said in my subcommittee. My mind was filled, alternately, with Alexa and Kate. A twinge of excitement pulsed through me every time I visualized Alexa's naked body stretched out next to me. Guilt and trepidation every time I thought of what I would say when I returned home to Kate. What would I do tonight? Dozens of times I resolved that I would go to my room alone, and dozens of times the image of Alexa melted those resolutions. The two halves of my mind had nothing to do with each other. When Lord Watford turned to me and asked my opinion, I drew a complete blank. I had no idea what was being discussed.

"Sorry," I apologized. "A sudden touch of jet lag."

"Quite all right, old chap." Watford replied. "We all understand."

I had to pull myself together. I was a happily married man with two wonderful children, as well as a senior official with an important responsibility. Last night was a momentary lapse, a single exception. I would explain to Alexa that we had made a mistake.

That afternoon, we went running again, but I could not find the right moment to tell her. After dinner, we joined different circles in different rooms. But when the others had gone to bed, I found myself inexorably drawn to Alexa's room. There she was waiting to enfold me, to destroy my resolution without a word. Just one more time, I rationalized. Tomorrow, at the end of the conference, we would go separate ways, she to Cairo for further consultations and I to Washington. I would return to reality and remember this weekend as a secret fantasy and a brief moment of recaptured youth. I would tell her when we got back to Washington.

CHAPTER 7

I SWIRLED THE ICE IN MY GLASS, listened to the clicking cubes, and looked out the window of the plane. In the east, the light was fading quickly and early stars appeared in the vast space. A flight attendant holding a white linen cloth interrupted my reverie.

"Mr. Cutler, may I bring you another refreshment?" she asked with the tone of forced cheeriness that seems to come with the uniform.

"Yes, thanks." I looked at the draft of the Gulf suppliers agreement lying on my tray and realized that I had not been concentrating on my most important accomplishment since joining the government. Instead, Alexa, naked, lingered in my mind. I tried to shut out her image but I couldn't. I gathered the papers and put them in my briefcase.

As I picked at the airplane food, I reminded myself how foolish it would be to let a weekend's weakness destroy a lifetime plan. I loved Kate and had been faithful to her for nearly two decades. Over the years several women students had let me know they found me attractive. Once the divorced wife of a colleague invited me to dinner when Kate was away. But I had always kept my distance.

Jim had never understood my loyalty to Kate. During a fishing trip several years earlier, Abe, Jim, and I had sat on the porch drinking beer and looking out over Cathedral Lake. Abe and I were lamenting the behavior of one of our faculty colleagues who constantly cheated on his wife. Jim found the discussion amusing.

"What's the hang-up?" he asked. "Isn't it a question of whether she'll find out or not?"

"That's typical Childress reasoning," Abe said disgustedly. "The point is not whether she knows, it's that you know."

Jim snorted. "That's not how the game's played in Washington. As they say, women are made to love the way money is made to spend."

"You don't really believe that," Abe said.

"Not entirely," Jim admitted, "but it's one reason I've held back from marriage. I don't think I could love just one woman. Hell, sometimes I've loved two at the same time."

"You may be able to love two women at once," Abe said, "but you can only be loyal to one at a time. It's a question of commitment."

"Abe's right," I said. "What's kept me honest isn't just a question of getting caught."

"What is it then?"

"I dunno," I fumbled. "It's kind of a personal integrity thing. You know, keeping a promise to someone I love."

Jim snorted. "Hell, you're just afraid she'd find out."

"No, I'm not," I protested. "Even if Kate didn't know, I'd know. And that would be hell enough."

Jim opened another beer and tipped his chair back against the cabin wall. "That's great," he said, "but it's unnatural for males to mate only once."

"Half do," I said. "Look at the divorce statistics."

"Try again," Jim laughed. "Marriage doesn't stop multiple mating. Washington alone would raise hell with your averages."

"The trouble with you, Childress," Abe replied, "is you've got all the subtlety of a dog around a bitch in heat. You don't know the difference between sociobiology and human ethics."

Jim chuckled, enjoying the stir he had provoked, and decided to add fuel to the fire. "The more a man mates, the more likely he'll be represented in the gene pool of the next generation. It's just a question of biology and statistics. Women don't have that power so they invented monogamous ethics to trap men into taking care of the few kids the woman can have. The trouble with you guys is that you've fallen into the female trap, and now you're trying to convince yourselves you like it."

"So much for the sacrament of marriage," I said, smiling and poking Abe lightly. "Childress has just liberated us."

Abe took a sip of beer and shook his head. "That's so crude, it's not worth a rise."

Jim leaned forward and looked very serious. "Darwin had a word for what's going to happen to people like you two."

"What's that?" I asked.

"Extinction," Jim said, followed by his long, low chuckle.

WHAT HAD HAPPENED TO MY COMMITMENT? How could I repair it? I made a decision. In little over an hour, the plane would touch down in Newark. Rather than catch my connection to Washington, I would rent a car, drive to Princeton, and surprise Kate. I could take an early train tomorrow morning and be a little late at the State Department.

Kate was asleep when I slipped into bed alongside her, and she responded with groggy surprise to my kisses.

Afterward she stroked my cheek. "What got into you?" she asked in a bemused tone.

"Nothing, it's just that I've been thinking about you."

THE NEXT MORNING, settling into a seat on the Metroliner, I pried the plastic lid off my coffee and took a long sip. The warm vapor rushed through my nostrils. Outside the train window, dawn burst over treetops. As the clacking of the wheels accelerated, I spread out the *New York Times* on my lap. The good feeling lasted until somewhere around Trenton, when I casually turned the page and was startled to see my picture next to a headline: "Administration Fails in London Talks."

My blood pressure rose with each paragraph. Senator Peary had released a letter to the secretary of state asking why officials violated the intent of the president and Congress by agreeing to a watered-down version of a Gulf suppliers agreement. Unnamed sources in the White House were suggesting that Peter Cutler, the American chief delegate to the London talks, had gone beyond his instructions by initialing a weak agreement. On deep background, White House officials were suggesting that the entire agreement might have to be renegotiated. I felt sick, then angry. Locara was trying to sabotage my accomplishment before the ink was dry by leaking to the press and stirring up trouble on the Hill.

When I reached the office, Julie greeted me by saying, "The secretary wants to see you immediately."

Kovic was seated by a table in the small hideaway room behind his big formal office. He did not rise or offer me a chair. He picked up a file of daily press clippings, folded open to the *Times* story.

"What the hell's this?" he asked, tapping the table with the file.

"Didn't my reporting cable come in on Friday?" I asked.

"This is the first thing I've seen," Kovic said, dropping the clippings file on the table. "What do you plan to do about it?"

"I'm sure it's an NSC staff leak. If I work quickly, I can get the agencies in line, convene the committee to approve the draft agreement on Wednesday, and release the story in time for the evening news. That should take the wind out of Peary's sails."

"I'll stall for three days," Kovic said. "But I've got to testify before Foreign Relations on Thursday. If you can't clean it up by then, I'll have to distance myself from the draft agreement."

"Okay," I said, thinking how Kovic's strong appearance belied his lack of spine.

Cleanup was more difficult than I expected. I had really screwed up. I never approved the reporting cable before leaving London on Friday. Nor had I telephoned instructions from Ditchley. As a result, the embassy held my cable over the weekend, which gave Locara three days to turn his version of the story into gospel. While I fooled around with Alexa, he had gone around Washington painting a picture of the agreement that would be hard to erase.

How could I have been such an idiot? How could I have forgotten to call the embassy? A horrible question occurred to me: Did Alexa have anything to do with this? After all, she and Locara were political allies as well as lovers. Maybe she was supposed to distract me while Locara did his damage.

By Tuesday night, I had Treasury, Commerce, and Energy in line, although I had to spend a lot of political capital to get them on board. I particularly regretted the promise to Commerce that the State Department would agree to an export license for the Dacla Chemical plant in Bangladesh. It was a marginal case, but with Kovic's deadline, I had no choice. The South Asia bureau was intransigent; hints to Walt Salmon about being excluded from staff meetings were not sufficient this time. They smelled blood. I could get even with them later if I won, but that didn't help now. Everything would depend on how Defense voted. I had to have to an alliance with Defense.

I called Alexa's office. Her deputy said she would return late Tuesday night and attend the Wednesday morning meeting, but he had no instructions. It was too late to call Cairo. The deputy bootlegged me a copy of the internal options paper Alexa's staff had prepared for her, but it did not tell me anything I did not already know. I slept fitfully that night.

THE COMMITTEE MET in the old Treaty Room in the Executive Office Building. As I entered the room, I spotted Alexa. She was talking intensely to Joe Locara.

There was no time to caucus. I gave Alexa a faint smile as I called the meeting to order, but either she did not see it or pretended not to notice. I began to feel anxious. Commerce and Treasury spoke first and supported the State Department position. Energy strongly opposed and announced that it wanted the draft agreement to be renegotiated. Beneath the table, I nervously twisted the wedding ring on my fourth finger, an old habit. Everything would depend on the Pentagon. Alexa waited until the other agencies had staked out their predicted positions before she asked for the floor. I held my breath.

"The Department of Defense supports the State position," Alexa said, "with one exception. We would like to see new language worked out regarding the interpretation of dual-use technology for chemical plants." I could live with that easily.

Alexa paused and then went on, "I was in London, and frankly I think what we have on the table is the best agreement that could be negotiated under the circumstances."

I let out my breath slowly, half afraid my relief might be audible. Alexa's sop to the Energy Department on chemicals was clever. It would keep them tied up negotiating details of language rather than mobilizing to fight a full-scale rearguard action against the treaty.

I looked over at Locara. He was scowling. I glanced at Alexa, but she was handing her papers to her military aide and getting ready to rush off to another meeting. I would have to thank her later.

I called Alexa at home after dinner, but she was out. I left a one-word message on her answering machine: "Thanks." Half an hour later, while I was lying on the couch studying a new report from Intelligence and Research, she called back.

"Today's been hell. I'm just getting home."

"The problem with travel is coming back," I joked. "I haven't gotten halfway through the pile on my desk."

"Have you eaten?"

"Yes. I'm just catching up on some unclassified reports."

"Come over and chat for half an hour while I have a bite. I'll show you some language on the chemical idea."

I looked at my watch: 10:00 P.M. Alexa had an apartment in a modern building in Arlington, convenient to the Pentagon. I could be there in ten minutes.

"Okay," I said.

SHE WAS SEATED ON A WHITE LEATHER COUCH, wearing a terry cloth bathrobe, her hair falling loosely to her shoulders. Dave Brubeck played softly from small black speakers on stark white shelves. The furniture was modern Danish, and a white shag rug covered part of the polished floor boards. A half-eaten omelet and salad were pushed to the far side of an oval glass coffee table; papers with the Defense Department seal were spread out in front of her.

"Here," she said, patting the couch. "Look at these while I open a bottle of wine."

She returned with two long-stemmed glasses and sat next to me. I was aware of her perfume. I slid slightly away on the couch and forced my eyes back to the papers.

"This is very clever," I said, after reading the papers carefully. "We let Energy hassle Commerce over their language defining relevant technologies, then you slip in this Defense draft as a compromise."

"That's only half of it," she said, smiling. "You pretend reluctance but finally agree that State will back it so long as it's a unilateral American statement that doesn't require renegotiating the international draft."

"What a devious woman," I said with genuine admiration. "I owe you one."

"Why don't you start with a little kiss?"

She leaned toward me. I knew I should tell her of my decision, but that would be impossibly churlish right then. I reached out, felt the warm pressure of her kiss. My resolution dissolved as her mouth opened. When she loosened the sash and shrugged off the robe, she was already naked. I realized I had lost again.

Afterward we lay side by side, exhausted, drained. Alexa ran her fingers through my hair.

"I want you to do something for me."

"Your humble servant, Madam."

"Come with me this weekend. I've rented a little cottage in the Shenandoah."

I was silent. I had told Kate I would go to Princeton.

"It would mean a lot to me, Peter. I really need to get away."

I looked hard into her eyes. I had made an extra stop at Princeton last Sunday. A quiet, secluded weekend with Alexa would be the perfect opportunity to end things in a civilized way. Given our schedules in Washington, any attempt to cut this off here would be too abrupt. I wanted a soft landing.

The next day I called Kate from the office. I told her that I had an urgent meeting with Pentagon officials related to the new Gulf agreement and that Kovic was pressing me on the subject. I felt guilty. It was not exactly a lie, but it was certainly not the truth.

"This agreement can bring peace in the Gulf," I said. "It's the most important decision I've ever been part of."

"But Peter," Kate pleaded. "Saturday is the championship game for Jimmy's Little League team. You promised him you'd be there."

"Oh shit," I said. "I totally forgot. But it's too late now. I'll have to make it up to him later."

"You'll have to explain it to him. I can't."

"The next weekend is my fishing trip with Jim and Abe," I said. "I'll come back to Princeton on Sunday night and take a later train on Monday morning so that I can have breakfast with the kids."

Silence on the other end of the line.

No sooner had I put down the phone than Tony came in carrying black binders marked "Top Secret: Code Word HANDY."

"Take a look at this," Tony said, dropping the binders on my desk. "Still inconclusive, but something may be heating up on the nuclear deal between Pakistan and Iran."

"Damn," I said. "That would be a disaster. I'm going to the Shenandoah this weekend to do a little strategic planning. I don't want to be disturbed, but if there's a crisis, call me. You have my cell phone number but here's a number for the house in case it's out of reach."

Alexa had found a secluded place in the Shenandoah nestled among green waves of Virginia hills. We drove past horses and cattle grazing behind chalky fences, and orchards filled with apple trees in blossom. We talked politics in the car, but when we reached the little farmhouse at the end of a dirt road, she suggested a long walk.

"No politics while we're walking," she said. "We're just going to soak up spring."

I was happy to oblige. "What a relief," I said. "I was afraid you were going to make me run."

"Later," she laughed.

We walked quietly for a few minutes. Alexa broke the silence.

"My father died last month. My mother told me when I got back from Cairo."

I stopped and picked up her hand. "I'm so sorry."

"I didn't know what to think," she said, leaving her hand in mine. "I guess I should forgive him now, whatever that means."

"You've come to terms with him?" I stopped and turned her toward me.

Alexa looked at me and nodded. "I can't let adolescent resentments govern my life forever."

She turned and started walking again. "I've decided to forgive both my parents."

We walked silently for several minutes.

"Funny the way it makes you think, when a parent dies." Alexa looked over at me.

I nodded.

"I hardly knew my father," Alexa continued, "but his death has changed my life."

"They still hold us, even when they're gone."

"For me, it's more like liberation," Alexa said. "I don't have to prove anything anymore, you know, that he was wrong to leave us."

We walked in silence again.

"Remember back at Princeton, when I turned down your proposal?" Alexa reached up and touched an apple branch that stretched out over the path.

"How could I forget?"

"I said I wanted power. But now that I have it, it's not enough." Alexa stopped and shook the branch so that blossoms fell onto the path.

"No," I laughed, "but it sure beats being powerless."

"Granted," Alexa smiled. "But you can't live on power alone."

"Some people in Washington seem to," I said. "Maybe it's like what Fitzgerald said about the rich. The truly powerful are different from you and me."

Alexa shook her head. "It's like junk food," she said. "Your ego always wants more."

I laughed. "When I was a kid, we never had junk food in the house. Now I seem to live on it."

Alexa smiled and we walked on for several minutes.

She broke the silence. "Thanks for coming, Peter. I really needed to tell someone about my father, and you were the person I wanted to tell."

She raised my hand to her lips and kissed it.

WHEN WE RETURNED TO THE FARMHOUSE Alexa started toward the kitchen but turned in the middle of the living room and smiled. "Which comes first?" she asked. "Lunch or love?"

"Guess," I laughed, taking her hand and leading her toward the bedroom.

Later we stretched a blanket on the lawn by the backdoor, brought out sandwiches and beer, and lay back to soak up the sun. Alexa wore a bikini; I was in shorts. I looked at her body. How could I give it up? I considered telling her now but decided my speech could wait until tomorrow on the drive back to the city. I closed my eyes and began to doze when I heard the phone ringing in the house.

I rolled on my side and grunted, "Who the hell . . . ?"

"I'll get it," she said. I closed my eyes again, but Alexa was back in a minute.

"It's for you. It's Kate."

I sat up quickly, knocking over a half-finished can of beer. Then I laughed. "Bad joke." But I looked up and saw she was not smiling. She was shaking her head side to side.

"Oh shit," I said, running into the house.

"Peter, where are you?" Kate asked. "I couldn't get you on your cell phone."

I hesitated. "At a retreat. A conference in the Shenandoah Valley." I shuddered at the lie.

"What's she doing there?"

"Who, Alexa?" I tried to sound casual. "She's part of the interagency committee."

"I got the number from Tony," Kate said. "The ring sounded like the end of the earth."

"It's pretty rural. We didn't want to be disturbed except for emergencies."

"That's what Tony said. But I thought you should know that Jimmy hit the winning home run this afternoon. He was sad that you didn't see it. I thought it might help if you called him."

"Put him on," I said.

"He's not here now," she said. "The coach took them all out for ice cream."

"Tell him I'll call as soon as this afternoon's meeting is over. I promise, but I have to go now."

I put the phone down, sat on a chair, and cradled my head in my hands. How could I act like this? I was not a duplicitous person. This was not the way I wanted to live. How had I come to lying to my wife and letting down my son? I had broken my promise to see Jimmy's game and now I had missed his moment of triumph. I would wait an hour and call him. But what should I do about Kate?

I went outside and sat on the blanket next to Alexa. I looked across the valley, got up, and paced back and forth. "I'm so torn," I said, "I feel like two people."

Alexa stood up, put her hand on my arm, and lightly kissed my cheek. "Let's not worry about this now."

I turned, looked into her eyes, and realized that I was the problem. I did not want to give up Alexa. I did not want to give up Kate either. Or to hurt her. I knew it was possible to be in love with two women. After all, I had done it. I just hadn't realized it was possible at the same time.

"Do you think she suspects . . . ?" Alexa let the question trail off.

"I don't know," I said, "But I think I have to get back to town."

We returned to the house, the spell broken, to pack for the long drive back to Washington.

UNTIL I WAS THERE, I didn't realize how much I had missed the spring trip to Cathedral Lake. As I stood on a rock ledge casting into a pool on the Penobscot, the sound of rushing water filled my ears and I inhaled the scent of ferns. Bright sun glinted off granite, and jade green shadows patterned the woods beyond. Occasionally I caught a fish and released it. Almost a distraction.

Every now and then, Washington flooded my mind and threatened to drown my pleasure. Could I get the Gulf suppliers agreement to work? How should I punish DOE? What was I going to do about Alexa? What should I tell Kate? But then I walked down the trail to the next pool, and the speckles of sun through the leaves changed my focus. I stopped to marvel at a birch that had stretched its roots around a huge boulder to draw sustenance from the mossy earth below. I sat for a moment on the giant hulk of a fallen hemlock and stared at little hemlock seedlings starting life in its rotting bark. A white-throated sparrow trilled its five descending notes from soprano to alto. I took a deep breath.

Kate and I used to come alone to Cathedral Lake when we were first married. Kate had little interest in fishing, but she loved the quiet untouched nature. As newlyweds, we sometimes paddled naked in our old canoe, alone in each other, letting it drift quietly across the lake. After such trips, we returned to the cabin and spent the rest of the afternoon making love and lolling in bed.

Later, when we brought the children, the pace was no longer so languid. They toddled down the dock in their life jackets, little orange bubbles bobbing in the lake among the yellow water lilies; learning to swim, catching their first fish, finally strong enough to paddle the canoe. I spent hours with Monica and Jimmy, teaching them how to handle a fly rod, how to tie on a fly, coaxing them as they played a fish, reminding them to wet their hands before releasing it.

Jimmy's first catch was a six-inch trout that he hooked by dangling the fly off the end of the dock. When it struck, he lifted the wriggling fish in the air.

"You don't pull them out of the water like that," Monica announced scornfully.

Jimmy was oblivious to the advice. He let the trout drop to the dock, pounced on it like a raccoon, and stood up squeezing the fish in both hands.

"I think we should let it go," I said. "It's pretty small."

When I saw Jimmy's face, I relented. "Okay. Take it up to the cabin to show Mom."

Jimmy shot up the hill, shouting for Kate, still gripping the trout as tightly as he could.

Monica looked at me in disgust. "Daaad," she strung out the word. "You should've made him put it back."

"No," I said, shaking my head, "but why don't you show me how to catch a big one?"

In the evenings, we sat around a campfire, listening to flames crackle, watching sparks fly to the dark sky. I told ghost stories. The kids huddled against Kate, knees pulled up against their little chests. After one of my better inventions, Jimmy pronounced it "so scary it made my feet sweat."

Now the kids had lost interest in the lake, and I couldn't remember the last time Kate and I had come up to the cabin alone. At least the guys kept up the tradition. And how I had missed it. At lunch, I tried to describe my newfound serenity. Abe could not grasp the contrast because he had no feeling for the chaos of life in Washington. Jim knew all about the crazed pace of politics, but he could not believe that I did not really care that he had caught twice as many fish.

"Hell, Cutler," Jim rubbed it in. "Even Abe caught more than you did."

"Yeah," Abe joined the banter. "This is a first. You must be losing it."

I truly could say I did not care, but I knew they would think they were sniffing sour grapes. So I stopped trying to explain, went out on the porch, and sat watching the reflections of Mount Katahdin in the mirror of the lake.

By evening, I was almost back to normal. After dinner, we sat on the porch, tipped our chairs against the cabin wall, and passed a bottle of bourbon. Rising trout dimpled the smooth surface of the Lake.

"Sorry I haven't consulted much," Abe said. "But I guess I just don't have a feel for what you guys are doing."

"Don't sweat it," Jim handed over the bottle. "Consultants are tits on a bull anyway."

"Yeah," I said, feeling the bourbon blaze a trail down my throat. "Washington's like a movie in fast-forward. You can read the script, but you can't get the feel unless you're in the middle of the action."

"You still enjoying it?" Abe asked.

"Love it." I took another swallow.

"Really?" Abe looked puzzled.

"Well, not in the beginning," I confessed. "At first I played bureaucratic politics in self-defense. But now sometimes it's for the fun of the game."

I handed the bottle to Jim, hoping he appreciated the bravado.

"You gotta watch that crap," Jim replied. "Falling in love with power games has ruined some pretty good men."

I was surprised by the seriousness in Jim's voice.

"There are three types in Washington," Jim continued, "people who want to do something, people who want to be something, and people who want to do in other people. The first kind are serious, the second type are blowfish, and the third kind are shits."

"Jim, I'm amazed," Abe interrupted. "You sound just like a Princeton professor lecturing about the evil of power without moral purpose. You're a political philosopher after all."

"Purely accidental," Jim smiled at Abe. "If a philosopher is right about the real world, it's purely accidental." Jim took a swig from the bottle and looked at me closely. "The most powerful people in Washington are the ones who can help others get things done, not the ones who play games for their own sake."

"I know that." I was slightly irritated. "You preached that sermon the first week I was in Washington. I just like to have a little fun sometimes."

"Does that explain your latest game?" Jim reached out and offered me the bottle.

"What do you mean?" I asked with an edge. I brought my chair down on the porch floor.

"A White House staffer tried to find a couple of undersecretaries last weekend to alert them to some new intelligence about Pakistan. It appears they both left the same emergency telephone number in rural Virginia. The story got around by Tuesday." Jim's chuckle had an extra low note.

"You look a little red, Cutler," Jim continued, obviously enjoying my embarrassment. "But you should've seen Locara's face when he heard."

In spite of myself, the image of Joe Locara learning that news brought a smile to my lips.

Abe had been watching this exchange with confusion. Now he brought his chair full four to the floor. "You spent the weekend with Alexa?" he asked. "I can't believe it."

I grimaced. "Boy, there sure are no secrets in this government."

Abe looked pained. I offered him the bottle, but he waved it away. His chair scraped on the floorboards as he swung around to face me. "My God, Peter. Kate had me substitute for you at Jimmy's Little League game last weekend."

I looked away.

"I never asked you to go to the goddamn game."

"Kate said you were working," Abe replied, "but that's not the point, is it?"

"Shit, Abe," I turned to face him, defiant.

He shook his head.

I turned away to look out over the lake again.

Abe reached over and put his hand on my arm. "Sorry," he said. "I didn't mean it to sound like that."

"It's a goddamn mess."

"Whatcha gonna do?" Jim was still tilting back.

"Got any good ideas?"

"I think you should tell Kate," Abe replied.

"She'll never understand."

"You might as well tell her before she hears it from others," Jim drawled, passing me the bottle. "If it's running around town, sooner or later it'll reach Princeton."

"Let me sleep on it," I rose from my chair and turned toward the cabin door. "Goddamn mess."

WE FLEW FROM Portland to Newark. Jim continued on to Washington, while Abe and I shared a rental car to Princeton. At first, we talked about Jim.

"Think he'll ever get married?"

"He jokes about being too busy," I replied.

"Funny," Abe said, "but for all his bravado, I don't think he's really at ease around women. I think they frighten him."

"I hadn't thought of that, but maybe you're right."

"I think he's afraid he'll turn out to be like his father," Abe replied.

"It's too bad. Jim would've made a great father."

"Do you think he knows what he's missing?" Abe asked.

"We'll never know," I said. "Unlike you and me, Jim keeps some doors closed, even to his closest friends."

"Maybe he doesn't like what he sees when he looks too deep, and he doesn't want others to see it either."

I shrugged, "Or maybe he just wants to keep his life unencumbered."

"A good life is never unencumbered," Abe replied, "and we shouldn't want it to be."

We rode in silence for a few minutes.

"What'd you decide?"

"I don't know," I replied, glad that I was driving so that I could avoid looking at Abe.

"Before you left, you told me my job was to help keep you honest."

"This wasn't what I had in mind." I kept eyes ahead, facing the glare of oncoming headlights.

"I don't mean Kate," Abe said. "That's only part of it. Washington has changed you."

"You'd better believe it," I pulled into the fast lane. "You swim with the current or you get washed away."

"Just thought I should tell you," Abe said, relapsing into a silence that lasted for the rest of the trip.

When I pulled into the driveway, it was nearly ten o'clock. I was half glad, half sorry to see the lights on. The kitchen was empty, with the remnants of the Sunday paper spread across the table. I put the fish in the freezer, went to the kid's rooms to chat for a few minutes, and came back downstairs. Kate was now at the kitchen table. I sat down on the other side.

"There's something I have to tell you," I said. Kate looked up, and I saw that her eyes were red. I reached across the table and picked up both her hands. "I'm having an affair, and I don't know what to do about it."

Kate did not say a word. She did not even look surprised. She did not scream or become hysterical as I had feared. She just looked at me. Gradually tears welled up. She pulled her hands back and placed them in her lap out of reach.

"I'm sorry. I never wanted to hurt you."

"You didn't have to tell me." She let the tears flow down her cheeks without trying to wipe them away. "I know. Someone called. He said it was Alexa Byrnes."

"It's very recent."

Kate picked up a dish towel from the back of a chair and dabbed at her cheeks.

"I'm sorry."

She pressed the towel to her face and shook her head.

"I don't want to leave you."

"It's not up to you," she said.

"Let's not do anything hasty."

Kate looked at me, tears blurring her eyes. "The call came Friday after breakfast. It was a man's voice. All it said was, 'Do you know about your husband and Alexa Byrnes?' I didn't go to work. I just stayed in my room and cried all day. That night, I told the children I was sick. I never thought you'd lie to me, Peter." Her speech was punctuated by faint, choking sobs.

"I'm so sorry, Katie." I got up from my chair to put my arms around her, but she put out her hands to fend me off.

"No." She spat the word. "It's bad enough that it's her, but how could you lie to me like that?" Her face was strained.

Arms outstretched, I moved toward her again.

"No," she screamed, "No, no, no, no." She swept the remains of the newspaper off the table, creating a blizzard of paper between us.

Shaken, I stepped back.

"What's going on down there?" Monica called from the top of the stairs.

"Nothing." I walked quickly across the kitchen. "I just said something that hurt Mommy's feelings. Go back to bed."

When I turned to Kate, she seemed more in control.

"I've been thinking about this since Wednesday," she said. "I want to separate for a while." She rose from her chair and walked to the sink. She turned on the faucet and splashed water onto her face. She held a towel to her face for a long moment and took a deep breath.

"We can still put things back together," I moved toward her and held out my arms again.

She shook her head and backed away. "Or I can have an affair, or we can go our separate ways. I've had since Wednesday to consider all the options, as you would say." Now her eyes were dry.

"I've said I'm sorry. I promise I'll end it. What else do you want me to do?"

"I don't know," she moved toward the stairs. She turned on the bottom step, trying to hold herself rigid. "You can start by sleeping downstairs."

KATE DID NOT GET UP to say good-bye when I slipped out at 6:00 A.M. to catch the early train. I did not know whether she heard me leave or not. The train was not crowded, and I drifted into a half sleep, replaying the previous night's argument in my head. I had not slept well on the living room couch. As I dozed, I heard the clacking of the wheels and passengers wrestling baggage in the aisle. I dreamed of Kate, of Alexa, of the State Department, of the house in Princeton. But the last dream recaptured the intensity of Saturday's apotheosis in the Maine woods. I woke up in Philadelphia with a clear decision. I would call Kate as soon as I reached the office and ask to come home next weekend. I would put things together again. The decision sustained me all the way to Washington and from Union Station to the Department.

When I reached my office, Tony was waiting with a handful of black folders. I started to wave him out of the office so I could call Kate, but in his excitement he did not notice.

"Here it is," Tony handed me the folders with a look of triumph. "Look at these new reports from HANDY. We've finally got proof that Pakistan is about to transfer nuclear weapons to Iran. I've got a car waiting. There's a meeting at the CIA right now."

"Oh my god," I said. "This is a disaster."

CHAPTER 8

THE STATE DEPARTMENT CAR RACED up the George Washington Parkway toward CIA headquarters in Langley. Out of the corner of my eye, I noticed a blur of trees. I had classified documents spread out over the backseat. One was an agent's report that Pakistan and Iran had negotiated an alliance promising to consult if either were "attacked by hostile neighbors." Nothing startling. Earlier reports from Jerusalem and New Delhi had already alerted us to that. Such pacts were a dime a dozen in the Middle East.

I let out a soft whistle, however, when I read HANDY's report of a secret protocol that provided for the sharing of "technology relevant to production of all modern weapons and the transfer of ten prototypes." This was backed up by an intercept of a conversation between the Iranian Foreign Ministry and its embassy in Islamabad, which told the Iranian ambassador he was authorized to increase the offer for "examples of modern technological assistance" to $5 billion over a three-year period, and to assure the Pakistanis that expected increases in oil prices will mean that Iran will have no difficulty in making the scheduled payments. Read together, these two pieces of intelligence were stunning. Did Ali know about this? Was his lab involved?

I looked up from the papers in my lap and glanced out the window. Through the shadows of the trees, I caught a brief glimpse of sunlight glinting off rapids in the Potomac. The image glittered in the distance for a moment, then vanished as the car rounded a curve. I had to remember to call Kate. But how could I think about my personal crisis at a time like this? Here was a national crisis. I had to concentrate. Pakistan. How good was the intel? I picked up the remaining report I had yet to read. I tried to skim it but was interrupted by the need to produce my State Department identification when the driver stopped at the outer gates of the Agency. The car sped through the parklike CIA campus and pulled up in front of a modern white building with long rows of windows. I jammed the partially read report into my briefcase and locked it shut. My fingers were putty.

I mounted the steps under an arched portico, entered a large marble lobby, and crossed a black and white chessboard floor inlaid with a huge insignia of the Central Intelligence Agency. On the marble wall to my right were four long rows of gold stars honoring members who had died for their country.

After more checking of credentials, a guard ushered me to a windowless room on the second floor. A large map of Pakistan was pinned to an easel. A group of people huddled over a table in the center of the room, intently studying large photographs. I recognized Alexa, Joe Locara, Wilbur Solomon from DOE, and Luther Cabot, the white-haired deputy director of the CIA. I did not recognize the Agency photo interpreters and analysts who were pointing to details in the photos. As I entered, the group looked up as though startled in some illicit act, briefly acknowledged my presence, and quickly bent over the photos.

"This is where they assemble and store the weapons," Cabot pointed at the photos, to bring me up to speed. "General Ziad doesn't trust any of the subordinate commanders. After the coup, he centralized the weapons storage in this heavily guarded depot. That protects him against any new coup plotters seizing the nukes, but it also means they have all their eggs in one basket. The Paks call it the Jamal Waheed Nuclear Research Laboratory."

I snapped to attention. This was Ali's lab.

Cabot continued. "They say it's a civilian lab, but we know it's also being used for weapons. Look at these double perimeter fences, with guard towers every hundred yards. Note the double gates at the rail spur as well as at the road entrance. These little circles are antiaircraft missile sites. These little dots are the ventilation adits. The main entrance has double steel blast doors." His fingers circled the perimeter of the top photo. "The weapons part of the plant and the storage vault are underground. They really dug deep after they saw what our cruise missiles did to the Iraqis in 2003."

"Could we take it out with an air strike?" Locara asked.

"Not unless you want to use nukes," Cabot replied. "That sucker sits under twenty feet of prestressed concrete. Only other way to take it out is to insert a clandestine team of special forces."

"What are those buildings on the surface?" I asked.

"Nothing important," Cabot replied. "Just some civilian research and support services." He nodded to one of the photo interpreters. "Let's look at this one on the machine."

The computer-enhanced image was enlarged on the screen as the analyst pressed keys that zoomed in. The details stood out more sharply.

"This is a different angle. Note the shadows. They show that the gray spots in that other picture are earth berms to prevent low-level cruise missile attacks. They use berms and balloons on wires to protect the ventilation adits and to force missiles to fly high so the antiaircraft missiles can get at 'em."

I stared at the satellite picture. Could Ali be down there somewhere among the gray spots in the photo? "What's this?" I asked, pointing to a dramatic white streak from among the jumble of black and gray shapes.

"That's just a landing strip. Things that stand out clearly aren't necessarily the most interesting," one of the photo interpreters replied with the condescension of a specialist.

"So HANDY has sent us the missing piece of the puzzle?" I asked.

"His latest report makes it all fall in place. The overheads fit with the intercepts and the humint," Cabot responded in the jargon of the intelligence community.

"Any dissenting interpretations?" I asked, stepping back from the photos and taking a seat. The huddle dissolved as the others followed my lead.

"Defense Intelligence is on board," Alexa said. "They've been leaning in this direction for the past six months." She pulled out a folder with the Defense Intelligence Agency seal on its cover and put it on the table to establish a bureaucratic place marker.

"The official national intelligence estimate had Iran three years away from the bomb," Wilbur Solomon said, as if to remind us of his presence.

"Obviously we'll have to revise that," Cabot said defensively. "No one expected Sunni Pakistan to be willing to sell to a Shiite country. We know that some of their renegade scientists helped the Iranians with centrifuge technology years ago, but selling a complete weapon would be unprecedented."

Cabot had an annoying habit of holding his glasses and pointing with them. Occasionally he placed them back on his nose, then removed them for emphasis. "We now think that after the Iraq war, Iran decided it would be safer to buy as well as build. In any event, they have been shopping while building. And when the Islamists took over in Pakistan, they saw an opportunity. They figured if they could persuade the Paks to sell 'em, they could quickly mate the warheads with their mobile Scuds and confront us with a fait accompli. Then we wouldn't dare to invade."

"Couldn't we destroy the weapons after they reach Iran?" Solomon asked.

"We never did find many of the Scuds in Iraq back in '91," Cabot replied with a shrug. "Mobile missiles are damn difficult targets. You can hide 'em in any culvert."

"That's a risk for Israel," Alexa said. "Scuds can't reach us, but they could hit our allies and our troops in the region."

"And there is a good chance they will transfer one or two to their terrorist cells," Cabot continued. "They figure if the terrorists can smuggle one into our harbors on a cargo ship, or into a city aboard Air Cargo, they can deter us from invading."

"Hell, all they have to do is tell us they have done it and send a little sample in the mail," Solomon added.

"So once the bombs reach Iran, the game is over," Locara said.

"We might get some . . ." Cabot let his thought trail off into a mumble.

"So much for Pak promises," I said, thinking of the number of times Pakistani officials had assured us they would not help other countries obtain nuclear weapons.

"They lied to us all through the '80s when they were developing their bomb," Cabot said. "But the Reagan administration didn't press too hard because we needed their help getting supplies to the Afghan mujahideen during the Cold War. General Zia al-Haq was a problem. We were getting pretty good cooperation from General Musharraf, but things have been more difficult since General Ziad took over." He rose from the table, walked over to the map on the wall and studied some detail, then returned to the table.

"How would they transfer them?" I asked.

"They could transport them by road, ship, or air."

"Could we intercept the shipments?" Alexa asked.

"Not unless we had perfect intelligence on the coordinates," Cabot replied. "The bombs aren't that big. They could be hidden in any of the thousands of shipments that go in and out of the country every day. We can't stop 'em all."

"What are the Paks' motives?" Jim asked.

"The economy's broke and the radical military government's using Islamic solidarity to gain some legitimacy. Selling to Iran is a twofer. They get hard cash and an Islamic blessing thrown in." Cabot took his glasses off and waved them in his hand. "And some of our people think it's also a way to put pressure on India."

"And Iran?" I asked.

Cabot sprawled back in his chair. "They fear that if they try to develop the bomb themselves, we or the Israelis may destroy the plant before they can finish. The closer they get, the greater the risk of preemption. They know we have pretty good imagery of their nuclear facilities. They figure it would be like getting caught with their pants down. Buying a fait accompli from outside is their insurance against preemption. And getting some of it into the hands of terrorists gives them an extra insurance policy. The only thing that's held them back has been finding a seller."

"Would they really pass them to the terrorists?" Jim asked. "I thought they were keeping their distance from Al Qaeda."

"They don't like Al Qaeda for religious reasons," Cabot replied. "But they have their own Shiite terrorist cells that they feel they can control."

"What about destroying the bombs after they're transferred to Iran but before they go mobile?

Cabot shook his head. "We couldn't be sure of their location. And we can't be sure we have tabs on all the terrorist cells. Tehran rolled up most of our humint assets six months ago."

"What's that mean?"

"We had some people pretty well placed in Iran," Cabot replied, "but one got careless. The Iranian secret police caught him and tortured him. He compromised the whole damn network."

"What happened to them?"

"You don't want to know," Cabot said. "It wasn't very pretty. Killed their families too."

"Guess we'll have to get 'em before they leave Pakistan," Locara said. "If we can. What do we know about their location?"

"HANDY is an excellent humint source, but we also have others in Pakistan," Cabot said. "I should warn you that it's closely held information."

"Are we sure this is the only location?" I asked.

"Ninety percent confidence," Cabot replied. "But you can never be sure in this business."

"Can't the Israelis take care of the Pak plant?" Alexa asked. "They bombed the Iraqi reactor in '81."

"If it's too well hardened for us, it's too hard for them too." Cabot replied. "We've got to put some boots on the ground."

"But that doesn't rule out Israeli covert action," Alexa said.

"The last thing we want is to spread the Arab-Israeli conflict to South Asia," I snapped. "We can't risk reinforcing the fundamentalist propaganda about a clash between Islam and Crusaders and Zionists."

Alexa looked annoyed at my tone. "That's not self-evident," she said icily.

"These are policy questions, not intelligence issues." Joe Locara interrupted, the hint of a smile twisting the edges of his mouth. "Save them for this afternoon's meeting at the White House."

THE MEETING with the president was scheduled for three o'clock, but Jane Garcia wanted the principals for a prebrief at two in the Roosevelt Room. I arrived early. Garcia sat at the end of a long table beneath portraits of Teddy Roosevelt in a khaki uniform on a horse and Franklin Roosevelt in a gray suit holding a pen. She looked tired as she sat with her elbows on the table and kneaded her temples with her fingertips. She glanced up at the sound of my approach.

"You've caught me on a bad day," she said.

"Guess we've got a mess."

"Last thing the president needs right now, what with fighting the Congress over taxes and the economy turning sour."

The director and deputy director of CIA joined us. Secretary of Defense Castle arrived with Alexa and an admiral from the joint chiefs. Wilbur Solomon came at the same time as Kovic and Joe Locara. Jane Garcia read from an NSC paper that Locara had prepared. She wanted to be clear about the options we would place before the president. Option 1 was a diplomatic effort to dissuade Pakistan from implementing the secret protocol of the new treaty. Option 2 was an American covert action to destroy Pakistan's nuclear facilities before any transfer could take place. Option 3 was a preemptive military strike by American and Israeli forces at the exact time of the transfer before the weapons could be mated to the missiles in Iran. Option 4 was to encourage Israel to act alone.

Kovic leaned forward and looked around the table. "I'm sure we all agree," he said, "that we should always try diplomacy first."

"Not if it wastes time and loses the element of surprise," Castle interjected. "If they know we're on to 'em, they can move the weapons secretly and disperse them all over the country, or give them to the terrorists. Remember the trouble we had finding weapons in Iraq? The only sure way is to kill these critters before they leave their nest in Pakistan."

The admiral spoke with the authority of his ribbons and braid. "It's our considered military judgment," he declared, "that there will be no way of taking out 100 percent of those weapons once they've left their depot in Pakistan."

Kovic seemed taken aback, so I entered the fray. "That's a real risk," I said, "but it has to be set against the certain costs of a hostile reaction to American citizens and interests in the Islamic world if we launch what appears to be an unprovoked air strike into Iran or Pakistan."

Castle was shaking his head, so I changed tack. "Besides, suppose we miss the timing or the weather's bad. Suppose there is more than one depot. We wind up with the worst of both worlds. We miss the weapons but we pay the political . . . "

"I've heard all that crap about political costs before," Castle interrupted, pushing away the papers on the table in front of him. "State always has a hundred reasons for sittin' on our ass."

"Well, you can double those costs if we get the Israelis involved." I paused for effect. "It won't wash to appeal to nonproliferation. We're already accused of hypocrisy for not doing more to stop Israel's nuclear program. That's why there's all this talk of an Islamic bomb. The only low-cost option is the diplomatic one. We should try to convince the Pakistanis to change their minds."

"And just how do you propose to do that?" Castle asked, his Texas accent dripping with sarcasm. "Say please?"

"We can threaten to cut off aid," Kovic interjected.

"We can't compete," said Locara. "Our aid is trivial. Iran is offering much more." He leaned smugly back in his chair.

"But if we get the Japanese, the Europeans, and the World Bank to cut off aid and loans too, we begin to get near the ball park," I replied.

Alexa jumped in. "You'll never persuade Pakistan unless you get India to be less threatening, and I doubt they'll do anything helpful." I looked at her closely, trying to figure out if she was cultivating favor with Castle or was angry at me.

"Maybe we can persuade the Russians to use what influence they have left in India," Kovic suggested.

Cabot intervened briefly, waving his glasses. "It's not the Agency's job to make policy recommendations," he said, "but I should point out that if anyone is interested in option 2, it'll take several weeks to perfect our existing covert action plan." After his little speech, he replaced his glasses and looked smug as a child with a lollipop.

At the end of going over the same arguments, Jane Garcia called a halt. "Well, I think we've aired the options. We'd better move across the hall now."

We moved to the Cabinet Room and waited ten minutes for the president to arrive. Kent was always late. It had become a trademark of his presidency. Some people chatted quietly, others looked over their papers. I sat next to Locara, but we studiously ignored each other. I let my eyes rove around the long white room with its arched windows and gathered green draperies. An American flag stood near the fireplace, and two urns bracketed a clock on the white mantle. I leaned back in the big brown leather armchair and admired the smooth finish of the long oval table. I tried to catch Alexa's eye, but she was absorbed in some document.

The president finally arrived. I was surprised to see Jack Reese and Jim Childress come in with him. Jim looked over and smiled faintly. We stood until the president took the big chair in the middle of the table between the secretary of defense and the secretary of state. I looked closely at Kent. I hadn't seen him up close for some time. His face was etched with far more wrinkles than I remembered, and there was more gray around the temples. He looked like a man under pressure with a low rating in the public opinion polls.

Jane Garcia summarized the pros and cons of the four options in a concise, fair-minded way, but that did not stop the rest of us from rehearsing the same arguments for Kent that we had presented in the Roosevelt Room.

Finally the president intervened. "Once we let countries start selling the bomb, we're on the road to disaster, but from what I hear, options 3 and 4 are too costly. Let's try a combination of 1 and 2."

Kent paused and looked around the room. Silence. "We'll give Tom Kovic and his boys a month to see if they can make any progress on the diplomatic track. After all, the covert action plan is not ready anyway. During that time, the CIA will put the final touches on its plan in case diplomacy fails."

He looked around the room again. "Anybody see any problem with that?" I held my breath, expecting Castle to object, but the blanket of presidential authority seemed to have quieted even the voluble Texan.

After a pause, Jim spoke. "Mr. President, we'll have to notify the intelligence committees on the Hill."

"Of course," Kent said. "Anything else?"

"We'll want to keep this under close control," Reese said. "If something goes wrong, it could damage your presidency."

"The polls show us down below 40 percent approval rating on foreign policy," Jim said. "We can't afford to blow it on the proliferation issue, what with the midterm elections in November."

Kent nodded.

"But we can't risk a bungled job either," Reese said. "Remember the damage Ollie North did to Ronald Reagan."

"No loose cannons," Kent said with a grimace. "Let's have Jim sit in on all the planning and keep me directly informed."

"Another thing, Mr. President," Reese said. "We should try to keep this out of the papers as long as we can."

"Then we can't have Air Force Two landing in Islamabad," Jim said. "Once those silver birds fly, reporters are gonna flock after them."

"We can send Cutler to Asia on commercial flights with minimal staff," Kovic volunteered. "And I'm already scheduled for the NATO summit in Brussels. We can talk to the Europeans then. And Secretary Castle is going to be in Beijing for the military-to-military talks."

Reese looked at his watch and whispered something in the president's ear. Kent nodded and pushed back his chair. "All right," he said, "That's how we'll proceed. Let me ask you all to exercise the greatest discretion in discussing this matter beyond this group."

Kent vanished with Reese and Jim through the door to the Oval Office. I was gathering up my papers when I became aware of Alexa standing behind me.

"Would you like to come over for dinner?" She spoke softly so that she would not be overheard.

"We need to talk," I said, "but let's go out." I did not trust myself to go to Alexa's apartment. "I'll make a reservation at Mario's for 8:30."

I LIKED MARIO'S because it had not been discovered. It was a new restaurant in an old house in Alexandria. I could always get a table and rarely ran into anyone I knew.

I was already sitting at a table when Alexa came in. I had downed a gin and tonic to fortify my resolve, but when she walked across the room, I almost lost it. She was wearing a linen skirt with a white silk shell that showed off her slim, tanned arms, and she looked gorgeous.

We talked about the White House meeting while we ate the antipasto. We agreed that Kent chose the correct options, though Alexa was more pessimistic than I that diplomacy would work. After the waiter filled our wine glasses, I proposed a toast to our political reunion.

"I hope that's not all," Alexa said, smiling and clicking her glass against mine. "Or are you trying to tell me something?"

"Kate knows," I said. "She's threatening to leave me."

"I can suggest a solution for that problem," Alexa said. She smiled and started to raise her glass for another toast.

"No," I blurted. "I've decided I want her back."

Alexa rocked the chianti back and forth in her glass. "What are you telling me, Peter?" she asked slowly.

"Well," I said, avoiding her eyes, "I want to remain good friends."

Alexa continued to rock the wine in her glass. She was quiet for some time. She finally looked up, closer to tears than I had ever seen, but she held them back. "Is this some kind of a game, Peter?"

"No, not at all."

"If Kate's leaving, why can't we continue?"

"I have to go back to my family," I said, staring down at the table. I focused on the red light reflected off the wine glass onto the tablecloth.

"That doesn't make sense," she said, looking at me intently. "What about us? Were you just acting?"

"No, of course not."

"Last weekend." Alexa said the words softly, pausing. "I haven't been that happy in years." Her eyes were moist. "Weren't you too?"

"Yes," I admitted.

"Then why spoil a good thing?" Alexa asked. "Kate bores you. Admit it."

I shook my head.

"It's hard to explain." I was silent for a moment, then spoke quickly.

"Last weekend I went up to Maine. I hadn't been there for some time. I was overwhelmed by this tremendous sense of peace. I was in the middle of the woods and Washington seemed so small and far away. Suddenly it no longer seemed important."

"What's that got to do with us?" Alexa asked.

"It showed me that simple things and basic commitments have to come first," I looked into her eyes. "You've always entranced me. You still do. You're wonderful. But I made a commitment to my wife and family. That's the kind of person I really am. I lost sight of that during the past year."

"People change," Alexa said. She fingered one of her gold hoop earrings. "We're not at Princeton anymore. I'm no longer scared of the M word. We're the same kind of people, Peter. We both want the same things in life. Power and love."

"Maybe," I sighed and shook my head slowly. "But our life cycles seem to be out of phase."

"That's profound." A tone of sarcasm entered Alexa's voice. "Is that the best you can do?"

"Sorry," I said. "What I meant is that in the end, it has to do with the commitments we make. I made mine early, and now I have to live with them."

My efforts to explain had the opposite effect of what I intended. Had I been less absorbed in trying to understand my own torn feelings, I might have noticed Alexa's face hardening as I stumbled along in my explanation. Her eyes were no longer soft and sad. They glittered with anger. She drew back in her chair, wounded but ready to strike back.

"I've been around, Peter, but yours is the sleaziest trick I've seen." Alexa pushed her chair back from the table. "You were just using me for your goddamn power games."

"No. You don't understand."

"Oh yes I do. You damn hypocrite." Her eyes glared. "You were just using me."

"No," I protested. "That's really not it. I meant what I said."

Alexa stood up and pushed her napkin into her plate.

"You'll regret this," she hissed as she turned away.

I was too stunned to follow her. I sat paralyzed as she walked to the door. Eventually a waiter came and asked, "Is anything wrong with the veal, sir?"

"No," I said, looking down at Alexa's unfinished meal with a sense of déjà vu. "Everything is fine."

Later I called Alexa's apartment but got the answering machine. "I'm sorry. It's not what you think," I told the machine. "I haven't changed my mind, but let's talk about it." She didn't call back. Nor did I have a chance to see her at meetings before I was caught up in a whirlwind of travel.

I did reach Kate. She was very cool on the phone. I told her we had to work things out, but I couldn't come home that weekend because something very important had come up.

"No, I can't discuss it over the phone. It's highly classified."

Kate's laugh sounded hollow. "Don't you have anything more original? You've already used that line."

"You've got to believe me. It's true this time."

"You can't just call and say you're sorry and expect me to trust you again.'" Her tone turned angry.

"I'll make it up to you, Katie. I promise. I just can't come home this weekend."

"It doesn't matter, Peter," she said icily. "I've decided to spend a month in Europe. Robert Carney has been very understanding, and I can write there."

"Where'll you stay?"

"I'll visit my sister in France, and I'll leave the kids there and travel. No itinerary. I need distance to be able to decide what I want to do about our marriage."

"Give me a chance," I pleaded. "Wait till I'm back from this trip. I can explain then how important it is."

"I'll call you when I get back in mid-September," she said.

"Maybe I could meet you in Europe."

"No," Kate said. "Don't even call."

The phone clicked dead. She had hung up.

I HALF DREADED my long trip: Los Alamos and Honolulu for briefings, then Tokyo to get Japanese help on sanctions, on to Islamabad and New Delhi to meet the protagonists, and then home via Moscow in search of Russian help. I could not afford to fail.

The first stop was Los Alamos for a briefing on the technical issues that might come up during my discussions in Pakistan and India. I was met at the airport by the assistant director of the Los Alamos National Laboratory. We drove past dramatic pink and brown canyons, stark battlements of eroding rock, with stubby New Mexico pines softening their lower slopes. I noticed a few low gray buildings on the nearby mesas. They seemed out of place.

"Is that where they made the first bomb?" I asked.

"No," the official said, "the ones on the left are physics and energy experiments. That other one does environmental work. We'll show you the bomb places later."

We spent the morning sitting around a table in a windowless vault called the Blue Room. A lighted sign on the wall read Top Secret, Restricted Data, followed by a series of compartmented code words indicating the classification level of the meeting. A young technician flashed a PowerPoint presentation on a screen to illustrate how the construction of nuclear weapons based on highly enriched uranium differed from those based on reprocessed plutonium, and how an atomic fission bomb differed from a hydrogen fusion bomb.

"Atomic bombs release energy by splitting atoms; hydrogen bombs release energy by fusing atoms together. That's a lot more powerful," the technician said. "Basically, fusion is the sort of energy that powers the sun."

"What do we know about Pakistan?" I asked.

"We don't think Pakistan has hydrogen bombs yet," the technician said, "but they may be able to get up to thirty or forty kilotons from their fission weapons. That's about two or three Hiroshimas."

"How big are these things?"

"Any size and shape you want," the technician replied. "Some of the bombs in the early '50s were so big that an eight-engine plane could carry only one. Today some are small enough to fit in an artillery shell." He paused for a moment before adding, "Or a suitcase. That makes it easy for terrorists."

"How many do the Paks have?"

"We estimate several dozen, maybe a few more."

"Is that all?" I asked. "They've been working on this since the Reagan years."

"It's not easy to make the fissile material," the technician replied, switching off the computer. "And they used several on those tests back in '98. Follow me, and we'll show you some bombs and how they're made."

I followed him into a top secret display area with models of nearly all the nuclear weapons that the United States had made since 1945. Some were to scale, others life size.

"This is a model of Big Boy that flattened Hiroshima and that's Fat Man that we dropped on Nagasaki," my guide said with the matter-of-fact tone of a curator in an art museum. "That little fellow there," he pointed to a three-foot-long conical cylinder, "packs ten times the wallop of the two originals put together. And we can easily fit three of those in the nose cone of one missile."

As I followed the guide down the aisles, I remembered a phrase from a Catholic bishops report that I read in graduate school: "We are the first generation since Genesis with the capability of destroying God's creation." In this technocratic setting, the words cut into my mind with a new hard edge. When we finally emerged into a room with windows, I took a deep breath. I felt light, almost giddy after the shadows of the underground museum.

"Where do we go from here?" I asked.

"Over to Q building to show you plutonium handling and then to the assembly plant."

At Q building, I donned a white smock, gloves, and paper booties over my shoes. We entered a room where a guard inspected my picture badge and radiation dosimeter. A machine scanned my handprint and confirmed my identity before allowing a door to open. We passed through an airlock chamber into a long laboratory. Technicians in white coats manipulated materials inside glass boxes by putting their hands in the built-in rubber gloves. I was joined by the manager of Q building, an older man with gray hair and an impish smile. I did not catch his name.

"Here," the man said, soon after introduction, "put out your hand."

He placed a lump of silver metal shaped like a grapefruit half in my outstretched palm. It was slightly warm and weighed a few pounds. "That's enough plutonium for half a bomb," the manager said with a wink. "Don't worry," he added, responding to my look of alarm. "It's nickel coated and we've used it for display since 1952."

I stared at the silvery, innocent-looking object in my palm. Two of these could wipe out a city. In a flash, this little lump could vaporize all the political power in Washington. It was completely unreal.

"I guess I'll never have so much power in my hands again," I said.

"You have no power until we give you the other half," said the doctor, flashing his smile again.

"But if I had two halves and clapped them together, I could destroy Los Alamos?" I asked, handing back his silver hemisphere.

"No," he said, "Your muscular force clapping the halves together might release enough radiation to kill a few of us in this building, but you need the power of conventional explosives to get enough neutrons flowing to sustain a chain reaction. We'll show you that next."

In the assembly building, I was shown how large hemispheres of conventional high explosives are fitted around a plutonium core. The simulated explosive material was pink and looked like balls of bubble gum.

"So now we've got a bomb?" I asked, looking at metal spheres surrounded by pink plastic.

"Not yet," my guide explained "You have to connect these electrical lenses around the surface of this pink basketball and time the explosions so that the device implodes symmetrically and forces the plutonium into a critical mass that produces a fission explosion. If the timing is off, you just blow the device apart."

"You won't get a nuclear explosion?"

"Nope." The scientist shook his head. "You'll just spread the plutonium around. Most of the people in the plant will eventually die of radiation sickness. That's pretty awful, but it doesn't have the power of a nuclear explosion."

"Is that what would happen if someone were to blow up a laboratory building like this?"

"Yeah," he laughed. "We'd be goners for sure. That's why security is so tight."

As I deplaned in Honolulu, I was greeted by Mike Sanchez, a bright young foreign service officer who had flown in from Washington to accompany me to Tokyo, Islamabad, and New Delhi. He and a young lieutenant in a spotless white navy uniform led me to a van for the short drive to Camp Smith. The van driver was an Asian American woman with long black hair and beautiful skin the color of Kate's. By now, Kate must be flying in the opposite direction.

Camp Smith was on a hill with a spectacular view over the Pacific. A marine guard saluted sharply as the van pulled up under the portico. Another guard saluted as the navy officer escorted us down a hall lined with offices bearing strange acronyms. We stopped at CINCPAC, the commander in chief of the Pacific Forces. Admiral Jones led us from his office to the briefing theater. He introduced me to the other commanders from all four services and invited me and Sanchez to a large horseshoe table where cookies and iced tea had been placed before two of the chairs. I tipped back in my chair as the lights dimmed, and curtains swept back automatically from a large screen. Above it were three digital clocks labeled Honolulu, Washington, and Zulu. A briefer stood at a lectern near the screen, reading the viewgraphs that explained how Japan and China would respond to the proliferation of Pakistani nuclear weapons.

As he droned on, I rocked in my chair and struggled to keep my eyes open. My head jerked. Embarrassed, I pinched my legs under the table to shock myself awake. The pain worked only for a while, and I found myself drowsing again. Finally I asked a question as a desperate means to stay awake. The discussion was desultory. I could not wait to get back to the airport.

I slept as much as I could on the plane but felt drained when we reached Narita Airport. Fletcher Barnwell, our ambassador, briefed me on the ride into Tokyo. Barnwell had delivered the president's letter to the prime minister two days ago, so the bureaucracy would have studied the American request that Japan help us put pressure on Pakistan. As far as the embassy could tell, the Japanese were divided on how to respond. The vice minister of foreign affairs would host a dinner for me that evening in one of the finest traditional restaurants. I should not try to raise the Pakistan issue at that time. They knew I would be tired, and dinner would end early.

As the car crawled along in heavy traffic, past an endless parade of boxlike buildings with neon icing, I found my attention to the ambassador's words fading in and out with the flashing advertisements. Thirteen time zones had taken their toll. How could I persuade the Japanese to help us? When I finally checked into the quiet comfort of the Hotel Okura, just up the hill from the brown tower of the American embassy, I looked longingly at the bed with pajamas and slippers carefully laid beside it. But I knew that if I lay down, I would not be able to get up again.

The restaurant was exquisite—an old thatched house with bamboo and rice paper walls, set in a perfect Japanese garden. When Vice Minister Sato learned that I was interested in Zen gardens, he insisted on a short tour. We followed a winding stone path past trimmed and twisted pines, carefully placed rocks, and a carp-filled pool. A candle glowed a soft orange in the stone lantern behind the pool.

I told Sato that I had learned about Japanese gardens from my wife. Mentioning her name brought a momentary spasm of pain. Kate always said that Cathedral Lake was like a large Japanese garden.

We left our shoes at the door of the restaurant and sat on tatami. Each course was a work of art, accompanied by blossoms and carefully arranged on a pottery or lacquer dish. Again, the beauty in the detail made me think of Kate. Fortunately Sato kept the conversation light and polite enough for me to survive both my mind's distraction and my body's jet lag.

The next morning, Ambassador Barnwell and I sat on blocky chairs across from Foreign Minister Takashi and Vice Minister Sato, with the inevitable cups of green tea on a low table between us. I explained the American position and offered to share photographic evidence. The Japanese officials seemed only mildly interested in the satellite photos of the Pakistani plant that Sanchez removed from a locked briefcase and spread out on the table.

"You must realize, Cutler-san," Sato said, "that what you are asking is very difficult for us. Because of our dependence on imported oil,

Japan needs the goodwill of the countries in the region. We have used our foreign aid to build that goodwill. Now you ask us to destroy our investment."

"If we let nuclear weapons spread in the region, your oil will be in even greater jeopardy."

Takashi looked at his hands. "Maybe yes, maybe no. Even a nuclear Iran will want to sell oil."

"If there's no war," I said. "And if terrorists get hold of the weapons, Tokyo is just as vulnerable as Washington."

"Of course we wish to help President Kent," Takashi continued. "But I wonder if he understands the problems we face. As you know, Japan depends heavily on its ability to export high-tech products. When your Congress threatened to retaliate for our sale of supercomputers in the region, it caused a great deal of difficulty for us."

"I'm sure the president understands your problem," I said.

"We are very glad to hear that," Sato replied.

The conversation rambled a bit after that, but I came away with the impression that the Japanese would back us on the threat to withdraw aid and loans from Pakistan. In the car to the embassy, Barnwell confirmed my impression.

"But," the ambassador added, "when you said 'the president understands,' they read that as saying yes to their point about computer exports. I hope you can deliver that back home, or we'll have another of those classic misunderstandings."

"Yes," I said optimistically. "I think I can pull it off."

CHAPTER 9

I SOARED WITH THE PLANE as we took off for Hong Kong. I was
determined to bring off a diplomatic coup. Success meant more
than an ego trip; it meant our national security. If Pakistan sold the
bombs to Iran, there was a high probability that Iran would step up its
threats to Saudi Arabia and Israel. And if they passed weapons to Islamic terrorists, we could be in real danger at home. September 11,
2001, had been a hideous wake-up call. But suppose it had been nuclear? We would have lost the lower half of Manhattan. I shuddered
and shook my head, trying to free my mind of the images.

Enormous clouds loomed over the Pacific. I thought of Los Alamos
and the pictures of nuclear explosions, the searing flash, the puffing ex-
pansion as the cloud sucked life out of the earth below, transforming it
into a deathly vapor. The mushroom clouds slowly unfolding were
strangely beautiful, and the enormity of an explosion that brought the
power of the sun to earth instilled awe. How could the explosion be
both horrible and beautiful at the same time? Could I make sure that

horror never happened? Could I prevent such weapons from falling into the hands of some renegade commander or religious fanatic?

When Sanchez and I arrived in Hong Kong for a layover, the American consul, Tiffany Rogers, was waiting at the airport with the latest cables. She looked serious as we entered the VIP lounge, and when she opened her briefcase and handed me a file of cables, she warned, "I'm afraid there's some unpleasant news. It's in the cable on top."

I opened the file: "Please advise UnderSec Cutler that father hospitalized with aneurysm. Operation scheduled tomorrow. Tampa Methodist Hospital. Cutler authorized to suspend mission at his discretion."

I sat back in my chair and reread the cable before handing it to Sanchez. Aneurysm sounded serious. If I flew back now, I might get there before my father went into the operation. But how could I abandon my mission at this point? I could call my mother, but that would be futile. The last time I tried, she did not remember who I was.

I told Rogers I wanted to call the hospital in Florida. After some difficulty, we finally got through to Tampa Methodist, but all they could tell me was that my father was in intensive care and that the operation was scheduled for tomorrow. They could not advise me on whether to come home. I put down the phone and stared at the window, but I did not see the planes taxiing on the runway. I saw my father, thin and frail, smiling feebly from a white hospital bed. Then I saw the gray plume of a mushroom cloud slowly spreading across the sky. I heard Secretary of Defense Castle telling the president that diplomacy had failed and it was time to attack.

I shook my head and looked at my watch. I had to hope my father would forgive me.

"Okay," I said to Sanchez, "let's go."

Islamabad is an artificial capital that was created in the 1960s. It sits at the foot of the green northern hills far from Pakistan's teaming population centers of Karachi and Lahore. As the plane circled to land, I could see signs of the planners' early intentions, though squatters quarters and vendors stalls had added a more normal chaos in some areas. The government section consisted of blocky white buildings laid out in a grid. There were none of the spectacular glass towers of Hong Kong. A residential area was dominated by a graceless modern mosque with four minarets at its corners. They reminded me of ballistic missiles ready for launch. I wondered if I would see Ali. His laboratory was in a remote area of the southwest, but he often came to Islamabad. I had cabled the embassy to see if a meeting could be arranged.

The previous American embassy had been destroyed by an angry mob reacting to false rumors about American desecration of the holy shrine in Mecca. This embassy was built like a fortress. I met with Ambassador John Rogowski in his spacious office. Rogowski arranged a call to the hospital in Tampa.

"The operation has been successfully completed," the hospital official reported.

"Is he going to recover?"

"He's in the ICU," the official replied.

"What's that mean?" I asked, exasperated with the unfamiliar jargon.

"It means his condition is very serious."

"How serious?"

"The report says stable."

"Should I come home immediately?"

"That's up to you."

"What do you advise?"

"I'm afraid I cannot advise you," the official replied. "I'm authorized only to report that the patient is in the ICU, in serious but stable condition."

"Thanks a lot," I shook my head, hoping that he would hear the sarcasm in my voice.

I put down the phone and sat quietly for a moment. I imagined my father lying under a sheet, hooked to tubes, unable to communicate. But if he woke up, he would know that I had come. It would mean a lot to him. This might be my last chance to tell him how much I loved him. But suppose I arrived too late and he did not wake up? I was on the brink of a diplomatic breakthrough. Success might save millions of lives. Surely Father would want me to stay and finish the job.

I drew a deep breath and returned to the situation in Pakistan. After a few minutes, however, Rogowski put a finger to his lips and nodded toward the door, suggesting that we go to the secure room. We moved to a windowless room in the center of the building. Inside was a large Plexiglas bubble set on insulators. Within the plastic bubble were tables, chairs, maps, and phones. The ventilators made a humming noise that helped dampen other sounds. We entered the bubble.

Rogowski's aide used a pointer to show me the location of the nuclear weapons facilities on the map of Pakistan. When the ambassador briefed me on what to expect tomorrow, I had to listen carefully over the low hum of the ventilators.

"General Ziad is very committed to the treaty with Iran. He was cautious at first, but now he is betting on a very dangerous gambit. The economy has gone downhill since the coup, and the Islamic military government is not popular with some of the population. Ziad sees this deal as two for the price of one. He proves his devotion to Islamic solidarity, and he gets a nice cash bonus to boost the economy."

"What about the foreign minister?" I asked.

"Mahood's as smooth as a London lawyer, which is what he was," said the CIA station chief. "He defended some of the terrorists at the Old Bailey, which earned him credits with this new bunch. But he has little power of his own. The military uses him to handle foreigners because he's a good negotiator, but the Islamists don't trust him. Sometimes they listen to him, but General Ziad has the last word."

"I think I get the picture." I rose from my chair and stretched. "By the way, did you get my cable about arranging a visit with a nuclear engineer named Ali Aziz? Would it be okay for me to see him?"

The station chief arched his eyebrows. "We wanted to talk to you about that," he said. "But it's very sensitive. Ali Aziz told you he runs a nuclear research lab in the southwest, but in fact that lab is a cover. In reality, he's also the manager of their nuclear weapons assembly and storage plant."

"I know that," I said with a shrug. "They told us at the CIA, but do you think . . . "

"That's only half of it."

I sat down again and focused on the station chief. "What . . . "

"There's more," he interrupted me, and handed me a piece of paper labeled Top Secret Code Word HANDY, "but first I'll have to ask you to read and sign this nondisclosure form."

After I fumbled with my pen and signed the paper, he continued. "Ali Aziz has been helping us. He is one of our key sources."

"My God, you mean Ali is HANDY?"

The chief of station nodded. "That's very closely held information."

"You mean he's the source of those reports I've been reading back in Washington?" I was still incredulous.

"Some of them. The best ones."

I sat for a moment trying to absorb it. My eyes traveled to the plastic ribs of the bubble we were in.

"What made him help us?" I finally asked.

"Not money," the CIA man said. "He almost stopped when one of our men offered to pay him. But Aziz hates this government and all it stands for. He was involved in a group of intellectuals who were promoting the idea that Islam is compatible with liberal democracy. During the coup, the new government killed several of his friends. I guess they left him alone because they needed his skills. Actually, it was Aziz who took the initiative. He approached us soon after the coup."

I shook my head. "When we were students together, we used to talk about Islamic democracy."

"He takes the democracy part very seriously. He's still very religious, but he doesn't believe in spreading Islam through terror."

"What about the bomb?"

"He believes Pakistan must have the bomb for defense against India, but he objects to selling it to Iran. He's the one who tipped us off. Probably thought the U.S. could put diplomatic pressure on the government before it was a done deal."

"So I guess this means I can't see him?"

"On the contrary, we want you to see him. The embassy passed along your message. He's in Islamabad this week and expecting you to call. He'll give you something for us."

I hesitated. "I don't want to put him at any risk."

"They know about your friendship. They censor his mail. They expect you to see him. Might even wonder if you don't. But be careful what you say. They watch him closely. His room is bugged. Best place to meet is in a restaurant. Noisier the better."

"Can I call him?"

"Yes, but remember, the line will be tapped. He will suggest lunch at Ahmed's. We know the place well. You'll be watched, but you can talk quietly. At the end of lunch, he'll hand you a large tourist book with pictures of Pakistan. Unwrap it and make a show of flipping through the pages. The diskette with his message is hidden inside the cardboard of the back cover. They can't find it without destroying the book. You're safe because of your diplomatic status."

AHMED'S WAS CROWDED, NOISY, AND HAZY with cigarette smoke. The headwaiter in a flowing brown robe and white turban escorted me past walls draped with oriental rugs. The odor of smoke mixed with the sweet smell of kebabs barbecuing on a large grill at the far end of the room. My eyes adjusted slowly to the dim light, and I did not recognize Ali until he rose from behind a small table by the wall. He had put on some weight, and streaks of gray flecked his hair. His face was less angular, the high cheekbones less pronounced. But the bright black eyes and brilliant smile had not changed. He had not yet grown one of the new politically correct beards.

"You look the same."

"Likewise, my dear friend," he smiled. "And the lovely Kate?"

"She's fine." I could not bear to talk about my current marital situation, but Ali noticed my hesitation and raised his eyebrows.

"We're going through a rough spot, separated for a while. But I'm sure it will just be temporary."

"I'm so sorry to hear that."

I quickly changed the subject. "And Fatima? I'm sorry not to see her."

"She's well and sends you her regards. We have wonderful news. After all these years of waiting for Allah to send us the blessing of children, she is finally pregnant. It's Allah's miracle." He smiled broadly.

"Helped by a few new little pills."

"Wonderful," I exclaimed, reaching across the table to shake his hand. "When are you expecting?"

"October," he replied. "It's my ray of hope."

"I was a late arrival for my parents too," I said.

"I hope it is a boy just like you." He grinned. "And how are your young ones?"

"They're just fine," I said. "Monica is about to enter high school, and Jimmy thinks about nothing but baseball."

"How about Abe and Jim?" Ali asked. "Do you still see them?"

"I see Jim all the time because of our jobs." I did not say, more than ever because of your country. "And I see Abe at times when I get back to Princeton. They're both doing great and send their best."

"Such different men," Ali smiled, "but I remember them both fondly. Please convey my warm regards."

There was a moment of awkward silence after we had exhausted the obvious.

"Sorry I can't offer you anything stronger than fruit juice for an aperitif," Ali said as the waiter appeared. We ordered lamb kebab with a yogurt sauce and flat chapati bread.

Ali waited for him to leave and then continued. "This place served alcohol to foreigners before the coup, but now everything has changed."

"For you too?" I spoke softly.

Ali leaned forward over the table and lowered his voice. "It's not the same country I came back to."

"Have you thought of leaving? I could try to help with the visa."

He half smiled. "My dear Peter. They have taken away my passport. They will never let me travel again. I know too much, and they don't trust me. See those two chaps with the khaki shirts at the table across the room? Those are my bodyguards. Supposedly they protect me because of my position, but it also means someone is always watching me. I spent several days under detention after the coup. The only reason I'm not in jail is they think I've changed."

"Have you?"

"Not in the least, but I keep my views to myself now. You might say I've gone underground."

"Remember our long arguments at Princeton?"

"Of course."

"Do you still think Pakistan needs the bomb?"

"More than ever." Ali nodded vigorously. "India still threatens us. But there are other things I don't approve of. I deal with those in my own way."

"Isn't there any way I can help you get out?"

"No, but I can help you. I'll give you a little souvenir to take back to the embassy at the end of lunch. You'll love the pictures. They say a picture is worth a thousand words. In this case, it is quite true." Ali laughed, but it was a bitter laugh, and his eyes did not sparkle as he smiled.

"Isn't there anything I can do for you?" My voice rose. How could I help him? Get him out of here?

Ali leaned back and shook his head. "I'll manage. Now let's talk of other things."

A PROTOCOL OFFICER ushered me into Foreign Minister Mahood's office. There I confronted a slight owl-like man wearing large horn-rim glasses over a prominent nose. His unprepossessing appearance was deceptive; once he opened his mouth, words flowed smoothly. Mahood was extremely cordial. He introduced his deputies, asked me to be seated, and bid a white-coated servant to bring tea. He then launched into a flowery discourse on the importance the new government attached to maintaining good relations between our two countries.

Responding at my host's level of rhetoric, I described the American interest in Pakistan's economic development. "We hope, however, that nothing will arise in our relationship that would jeopardize my government's ability to encourage your growth."

Mahood smiled and nodded.

"I must tell you, Mr. Minister, of the great importance the United States attaches to stopping the deadly spread of nuclear weapons. We would regard any actions that contributed to such a spread as an unfriendly act."

Mahood's smile vanished.

I continued, "We would have to take appropriate responses."

I spoke in diplomatic generalities, careful not to disclose exactly what American intelligence knew about Pakistan's intentions for fear of revealing the source of the information. Nonetheless, I sensed that I could not win at that elevated level, for Mahood replied not in sentences but in paragraphs, each elegantly crafted, clearly rehearsed, enveloping my points and always stinging with a poisoned barb.

"My dear Mr. Cutler," he replied, drawing out the word "dear." "We share your views entirely." He lingered on the last word as well. "That is why we have been so concerned about development of the Israeli nuclear arsenal. I am so glad that we see eye to eye. It would be far better to have nuclear disarmament in the Middle East. After all, we have always regarded efforts by our Islamic brothers to obtain nuclear weapons as only a second best. Mankind must go beyond the old balance of power and learn to live as brothers." He spread his hands to punctuate his remarks.

"Let me be specific," I said, trying to deflate the rhetoric and bring the conversation down to firmer ground. "We would regard the spread of nuclear weapons to Iran or any other country in the region as a threat to our national interest as well as to world peace, and we are prepared to take serious steps to prevent it. I hope I have made myself clear." I looked directly at Mahood.

"Exactly," Mahood said, returning my stare. "It has long been the policy of my country to oppose the introduction of nuclear weapons into any region. It's a great pity that the Zionist intruders have chosen to introduce them into the Middle East. My country stands prepared to cooperate in any international endeavor to rid that region of the nuclear scourge."

I ignored this rhetorical restatement of Pakistan's official policy, as I knew Mahood could later claim that the transfer to Iran was made necessary by Israel's intransigence. "I'll be blunt," I said. "If your country were to renege on its pledge not to transfer nuclear weapons, we could not continue to allow financial resources or private investment to flow to your country. Moreover, after recent discussions, I have every reason to believe that would be the position of other major donors and banks. And that would only be a first step."

Mahood stopped fencing and looked serious. "Speaking hypothetically, of course, if a country like Pakistan were to suffer such sanctions, it would merely encourage the aggressive intentions of some of its neighbors," he said. "I can't imagine such a policy succeeding without assurances of security of borders in a region."

"I think we see eye to eye on that," I responded. "I intend to stop in New Delhi after I leave Islamabad. President Kent has already written to the Indian prime minister expressing the depths of our concern about the situation."

Mahood nodded. "Let me raise another question." He signaled the servant to fill the teacups again. "Your Congress goes on and on about human rights in our country with absolutely no understanding of the anarchy and corruption that prevailed under the previous government. It will be very difficult for our governments to reach any understanding under such circumstances."

"There's not much I can do about that. Congress reflects public opinion in a democracy, and human rights are deeply held values. The American people will not tolerate torture in any form or at any level."

"Of course," the foreign minister replied. "And we have our own commitment to Islamic values and Islamic democracy. Each country has its own way. That is all we want your Congress to understand."

"Let's not overload the circuits," I said. "I'll be blunt again. If we fail to reach an understanding on the nuclear issue, I foresee a crisis in the relations between our countries. I hope my message is clear."

"Oh absolutely, my dear Mr. Cutler," Mahood said, peering at me through his glasses. "You are just as clear as the finest crystal."

Mahood thanked me for my visit and presented me with a silver cigarette case embossed with a crescent as a memento of the visit. It was very similar to the one Ali had given me years ago. I thanked him politely. Now I had two of these things, I thought as I left the foreign ministry, one priceless and one worthless.

In the car riding back from the Foreign Ministry, Ambassador Rogowski assured me that there was no question about whether Mahood understood the message. The only question was what General Ziad would do about it. And for the answer, we could only wait.

As we left the highlands, our little two-engine airplane flew low over the Punjab plain where the Indus River had flooded the land. Some villages stood as little islands, their roofs floating like toy boats on a brown sea. The sun glinted off the water with a golden glow, and the shadow of our plane swept across the glistening surface like a little arrow.

How strange, I thought, that these people, speaking the same tongue but divided by religion, spent so much of their energy scheming against each other rather than joining to fight nature's primeval cruelty. But if India or Pakistan ever unleashed their nuclear genies, it would make the floods below seem benign. I would need all my persuasive powers in New Delhi.

Although it was Sunday and government offices were closed, Ambassador Baker met us at the airport. The streets into the city were swarming with people moving at varying speeds. Pedestrians, bicyclists, bullock carts, and cars all competed for the same thin ribbon of pavement. I sat in the backseat clutching the door handle as the driver bore down on the accelerator, horn blaring, swerving at the last minute to avoid an oncoming obstacle. I was unprepared to see people cooking, washing, and defecating by the side of the road. As the air-conditioned limousine swept past poverty, I wondered how a country could have the power to produce nuclear weapons while its people lived and died by roadside ditches.

"This will be a tough nut to crack," Baker warned. "Delhi is already fed up with Islamabad over Kashmir, and they're in no mood to cooperate."

"How much do they know about the transfer to Iran?"

"Their intelligence is pretty good," he replied. "I suspect they know most of the story."

"What I need is some gesture to sweeten the pill if Pakistan pulls back."

"Not out of the question," Baker replied, "But not easy."

Baker had invited me to stay in Roosevelt House, the ambassador's residence. It was a delightfully open building set in a large garden. As soon as I arrived, I called Florida and received an uninformative update: "condition unchanged." I called the house in Princeton on the chance that Kate might have returned early from Europe. No answer.

We lunched in the shade of a small pavilion in the garden. Sue Baker asked about Kate, whom she had met in Washington. I pretended everything was fine.

"She's very busy," I said. "She's been promoted to senior editor at the Princeton Press. It's a very important position. She's in charge of art and literature. Otherwise she might have moved to Washington."

THE NEXT MORNING, we drove around the great arch of the India Gate past red stone walls decorated with finials and cupolas, the architecture of imperial power. The British built the government section of New Delhi in a monumental style with wide boulevards. My car drew up before the palatial Foreign Office, and I was ushered in to Rajit Singh, the foreign minister, who received me cordially. His handsome brown face was framed by straight white hair and pierced by dark eyes. As he spoke, the muscles in his cheeks vibrated all the way back to his ears. The phrases rolled out in long waves of large words whose rhythms were at odds with his clipped accent. After listening for a few minutes, I dispensed with diplomatic pleasantries and got straight to the point.

"I know Ambassador Baker has told you of the depth of our concern about the possible nuclear transfers between Pakistan and Iran. We're prepared to make serious efforts to prevent such transfers, but we can't do it alone. We'll need your help." I sat forward in my chair.

"More specifically," I continued, "we feel that Pakistan will require security guarantees as part of the price for canceling the secret protocol that is the heart of their new treaty with Iran. We would hope that your government might reinstitute the negotiations on mutual inspection of nuclear facilities and a pledge of no first strike."

Singh looked at me sharply. "We are very concerned as well. Our sources confirm what Ambassador Baker has reported to me. But you don't understand those people as we do. Just look how they are behaving over Kashmir. They say they have stopped support for terrorism there, but that is a lie. They don't want security; they want a larger Islamic state. We have extended the hand of peace a hundred times, only to have them spit on it." He looked at his aides, who nodded solemn assent.

"Perhaps you're right," I said, "but this situation is too serious to treat as normal." I frowned. "It needs urgent attention."

Singh nodded and I plunged ahead.

"It merits another try. If we can tell the Pakistanis that you'll make a new effort, that'll be of great assistance to our diplomacy."

Singh sighed. "I wish I had your American optimism, but I know these people. We come from the same background. They have never got over their need to try to prove they are equal to India in order to justify their foolish secession. But how can they be? We are ten times their size."

"Let's look ahead rather than back," I said. "If our efforts fail, you'll be worse off. Why not risk another try at negotiating a no first strike pledge and a mutual inspection regime?"

Singh smiled a tired smile and looked around at his aides again. "If you want something to say to them, I will discuss the matter in cabinet and see if we can help you. But even if we make an offer, you should have no illusions that anything will come of it so long as they are stirring up trouble in Kashmir."

"All we need now is some help," I replied. "We can work the details later."

"All right," Singh said. "If your president wants some little gesture, we will help him."

MOSCOW WAS MY FINAL STOP before returning to Washington. I couldn't wait to get home. I needed to take care of the situation with Kate. I was dying for American food. Although I tried to drink only bottled water, I had still managed to catch a bug. I felt awful. Pills had stanched the diarrhea, but I could eat very little. But the stop in Moscow was important. If I could persuade the Russians to use their remaining influence in Central Asia, and if Castle and Kovic were successful with China and Europe, we would close the diplomatic circle.

An embassy car whisked me from Sheremetyevo Airport to Spaso House, the ambassador's residence, a nineteenth-century mustard yellow mansion with a massive rotunda. As I waited for the militiaman at the iron gates to check my documents, I noted with pride the American eagle spread out on the gatepost. Once settled in my room, I tried to call Florida but did not get through. I would try again after my visit with the foreign minister.

Foreign Minister Kisalov seemed distracted when we entered his large office, a long room of blond birch with parquet floors and three chandeliers. We sat at a pale oak table. A waiter brought small cups of coffee and tall crystal glasses of tea. After a few formalities, I briefed Kisalov on the visits to Tokyo, Islamabad, and New Delhi and explained how helpful it would be if Moscow would instruct its ambassadors to reinforce the American message. I hoped he would bring pressure to bear in Central Asian areas where Russia still had considerable influence.

Kisalov used an interpreter, though I knew he spoke English quite well when he wanted to. Kisalov nodded intently with slightly squinted eyes as the interpreter spoke. When he replied, his right hand drew circles in front of him as if to help spin out his answer. He said he shared the American concern. After all, nonproliferation had always been a high priority for Russians. But he urged me not to overestimate their influence in Teheran or other capitals in the Central Asian region. These were not regimes that listened to reason. Moreover, he explained, his government was deeply embroiled in domestic problems. He personally was preoccupied with working out the troubled relations between Moscow and the Central Asian republics. He would do what he could, but the Americans should not expect too much.

All in all, it was a mixed meeting. On the way back to the embassy, Walker and I discussed how to summarize it fairly in a reporting cable without discouraging the political process back in Washington. Walker's assistant greeted us with a grim look on her face. She handed me a cable that had just arrived.

"I'm afraid it's bad news," she said.

The cable was brief. "Regret to inform Reverend Cutler died last night. Funeral services arranged for Friday. Department has booked first flight Thursday to Miami via London. My personal sympathies. Kovic."

I could not move. As I stared at the capital letters on the page, they gradually blurred. I dropped the paper.

Walker took my elbow. "I'm so sorry, Peter. Is there any way we can we help?"

I shook my head. They left the room and closed the door. I put my head in my hands.

The embassy placed a call to the director of Lone Palm Village to confirm the arrangements. They also tried to find Kate by calling her sister's house in France, but couldn't reach her. She was traveling and had left no numbers.

A car took me back to Spaso House. I lay on the bed for an hour. When Walker returned, he asked if I wanted any dinner. I thanked him but said that I wanted to go for a walk.

I wandered Moscow in a trance. I was vaguely aware of store fronts and passersby, but my mind was in Blainesville, talking to my father, apologizing for being so difficult, for not being with him at the end. I wandered into a stream of traffic, and a militiaman came over and scolded me in Russian. I looked blank. He shrugged and turned away.

I walked until my feet ached. Eventually I saw the lighted red brick towers of the Kremlin. I followed around the park of spruce trees until I found myself entering Red Square with Lenin's plain pink marble mausoleum on my right. Crossing the large paving stones of the square, I confronted the garish majesty of St. Basil's Cathedral with its wild profusion of striped onion domes in all sizes and colors.

Finally exhausted, I managed to find a cab to take me back to Spaso House. I went straight to my room and quickly fell asleep but woke up trembling in the middle of a dream. I had been in Florida trying to get back to Washington. Father pleaded with me to stay. He grabbed the sleeve of my suit jacket, but I tore it away and ran out the door, slamming it behind me. Blood dripped from a torn fragment of cloth, leaving a trail of little red dots on the sidewalk. "I'll come back and clean it up later," I said.

I kicked off the blanket and buried my head in the crumpled pillow. A sob caught in my throat. "I loved you so much. Why didn't I tell you in time?"

FATHER'S FUNERAL was held in the community room of Lone Palm Village. The bare room doubled as a chapel on Sundays, and a visiting chaplain conducted the service. Father had left detailed instructions for the funeral before he entered the hospital: a plain closed casket, white lilies, and his three favorite hymns. I sat on a metal folding chair in the front row along with Uncle Ben and two cousins from Boston. Behind us were some fifteen or twenty elderly people from the nursing home, all strangers to me.

Mother was wheeled in and placed next to me. I kissed her carefully. She looked frail and her leathered cheek was dry against my lips. She stared vacantly ahead. She did not speak, but at times made soft whimpering sounds. I reached over to pick up her hand. It was shriveled and weightless. Her gold band hung loosely on her finger. She gave no indication that she recognized me.

I stood when the piano started a hymn and sang the words from memory:

> Oh God our help in ages past,
> our hope for years to come.
> Our shelter from the stormy blast,
> and our eternal home.

I choked on the second verse. Sometimes in Blainesville I had stood in my father's church without singing. It had been an adolescent form of silent protest. My mind filled with the sound of the old organ in that little church.

I thought of how Father teased Mother. He said he hoped she would play the piano at his funeral. She always replied with a shocked "Oh, Horace, that's terrible." Father would laugh and wink at me.

After the service, two men lowered the casket into the grave. They were sweating. The oppressive Florida sun bleached us all into monochrome. Mother had already been wheeled back to the infirmary. The chaplain said a brief prayer. Someone handed me a shovel. I dug some dirt from the pile and threw it into the grave, watching the powdery soil sprinkle down on the plain wooden cover of the casket.

I spent the next day in Father's apartment, going over his possessions, packing up boxes. I found his favorite fly rod, a little seven-foot bamboo, beautifully finished and smooth to the touch but without much power. We had argued about it during our last fishing trip together. It was autumn. The leaves were down and a stiff breeze had roughened the cold waters of Cathedral Lake. Father was having trouble casting, and I blamed it on the rod.

"It's too small," I said as I paddled the canoe. We were moving parallel to the shore and casting toward trout lurking by sunken logs in the shallow water. Waves slapped against the prow, and the spray stung our faces. "You can't fight a wind like this with a rod that size."

"It doesn't matter," Father said. "I like this rod."

"Here," I replied, picking up my nine-foot Winston graphite from the bottom of the canoe. "You'll do better with this."

Father shook his head and continued to cast his little bamboo. "This is what suits me," he said.

With my hands off the paddle, the wind swung the canoe, and a wave splashed water over the side.

"Damn, you're stubborn," I said, putting down my rod, picking up the paddle, and digging furiously into the water to straighten the canoe into the wind.

Father looked at me and smiled. "Better get used to this rod, Peter. It's yours when I die."

I ARRIVED BACK in Washington deeply depressed. My nose and throat were congested, and I had a throbbing ache in my right ear. My desk was a disaster area. Despite Tony's best efforts to sort the material into piles with notes indicating priorities, everything was urgent. The strategic arms paper needed my immediate okay before tomorrow's meeting. The Koreans were reopening the question of shared costs in developing a new fighter plane. Intelligence reports suggested trouble in Brazil. A meeting would be held on Pakistan at the White House at two o'clock. Tony said there had been a number of meetings in my absence, and he pointed to a thick file. I tried to work my way through the most urgent pile, but I couldn't concentrate with the drumming in my ear.

I finally went down to the State Department clinic. The doctor looked in my ears, in my throat, sat back in his chair, picked up a prescription pad, and began to scribble something illegible.

"You've got a low-grade infection," he said. "Take these antibiotics and go home and go to bed."

"I can't go to bed," I protested. "I have a meeting at the White House this afternoon."

The doctor gave me a quizzical look. "Why do you people think you have to kill yourselves?" he asked, and signaled the nurse to send in the next patient.

I filled the prescription, bought some aspirin, and returned to the office to prepare for the meeting. By skipping lunch, I was able to get through most of the Iran and Pakistan file for the two o'clock meeting. Planning for covert action—Project High-Tech—had been progressing despite my absence. Several cables and intelligence reports from the embassy in Israel suggested that Jerusalem was impatient with the pace of the diplomatic track and was pressing hard for stronger actions.

My suspicions were confirmed when I joined the meeting in the Executive Office Building. Pakistan was the only item on the agenda. To my surprise, I found Jim in the chair. Alexa was there, along with Locara, and three people from CIA's Directorate of Operations. Jim rose when I entered, came over, and put an arm around my shoulder.

"Sorry about your father, Peter," he said. "Hope you got my cable and flowers. Let's chat at the end of this."

There were other murmurs of condolence around the table.

The D.O. official continued his briefing, tapping a wall map of Pakistan with his pointer.

"The insertion should be pretty straightforward. We fly the choppers in over this desert area. No known bases in the area, and we fly below radar level from a cruiser stationed here." He moved the pointer and tapped twice.

"The team leaves the choppers here, and has to make it by foot to this rendezvous by 23:00." Tap. Tap.

"There they meet with one of the guards we have paid off. He waits for the midnight change of shift and escorts them past the guard towers to the perimeter fence just outside the ventilation shaft. Here." He tapped another map of the local area.

"We penetrate the perimeter fence here, using fiber bridging to cross the mined area, and enter the plant with ropes down this ventilator shaft." Three taps. "Now I'll turn you over to Bob. He'll show you how we take out the plant."

"This bay is where the finished weapons are held," another man from the Directorate of Operations said. He displayed a floor plan of the plant on a large screen.

"This is the best place to get 'em all at once before they're transferred. From here, they're taken by elevator to the surface when armored convoys come for them," he said, circling an area of the blueprint.

"After we plant the explosives, we'll use this elevator to get to the surface. Then it's only thirty yards to the perimeter fence. Our team can cover that and cut the two strands of wire in something like ninety seconds. During that time, we'll divert the guards by an explosion on the opposite side." He tapped the other end of the blueprint.

"What happens to the people in the plant?" I asked.

Bob looked as if I were a guest arriving at the time a party is scheduled to end. "We've been over that," he said. "By ringing the fire alarm two minutes before the explosives are timed to detonate, we can be sure that the staff has time to evacuate via the personnel elevator near the entrance."

"But what if the plant manager or maintenance people try to find out the source of trouble after the alarms ring?" I asked.

"That's why we detonate in two minutes, so they won't have time to discover and disable the explosives."

"That's not what I meant," I continued. "Suppose they're still in the plant when the explosion occurs."

Locara looked at me in annoyance. "This isn't tea at the faculty club," he sneered. "We're talking about stopping a transfer of nuclear weapons that could lead to millions of deaths. Of course there are some risks."

My head throbbed but I persisted. "But what about HANDY? He helped us. Don't we have an obligation to get him out of there?"

Locara shook his head, and the man from Operations looked over at Jim with exaggerated exasperation.

Jim nodded. "That's a good point. Let's come back to it when we go through the mock-up down at the Farm." Then, looking at me, "On Friday we're gonna fly down there to walk through some models they've built in the last month. It'll be a final dry run."

Overwhelmed by my earache, I tuned in and out as the three experts led the working group through a series of drawings, charts, and photographs. I would bide my time and talk to Jim privately.

At the end of the meeting, Jim waited for the others to file out and then led me next door to his office, which overlooked the West Wing of the White House. I could not tell which part of the hum in my head came from my earache and which from the air conditioners. Jim told his secretary to hold the calls.

"How ya bearin' up, ole buddy?" Jim looked at me carefully. "I gotta tell ya, you look like a carcass the coyotes chewed."

"It's hard," I said, "but we all face it sooner or later."

"He was a good man."

"How far have we gone down this track?" I asked, changing the subject. "Haven't you seen my reporting cables? We have a good chance for a diplomatic solution."

"Nothing's decided for sure," Jim replied, tapping a pencil against the palm of his left hand, "but after we briefed the Hill and those Israeli intelligence reports came in, the president was put under a lot of pressure for more rapid action. He told me to get this option ready to go by next week. He's afraid that if we wait too long, something will leak, and the Paks will move the weapons before we can act."

"A week's not enough time," I said. "Kovic doesn't go to Europe until next week. We won't have all our diplomatic ducks lined up for the big squeeze."

"It's the Paks who set the timetable, Peter," Jim replied. "I'd prefer diplomacy too, but not if the horse is about to leave the barn."

"We don't know that for sure," I said. "Mossad always does worst-case analysis. That's understandable because Israel's under the gun. But we shouldn't automatically swallow their story."

"Well, we've got till next week before anything gets decided," Jim said.

"What about Ali?" I asked. "What if he's killed?"

"Let's work that problem down at the Farm," Jim said. "Maybe the operations boys can come up with a solution. Besides, there's something else I wanted to tell you." A sheepish grin crept across his face.

"You want to talk about women now?" I asked. I had seen that shit-eating grin many times.

"I've been seeing a bit of the blond bombshell," Jim said, laughing, "despite all the times I warned you about her."

"Alexa?" I asked incredulously.

"Hope you don't mind, ole buddy?" The question hung for a moment. "You told me you were goin' back to Kate."

"Yes," I finally said. "We're finished." My ear was pulsing. Could this really be happening? I didn't know what more to say.

"Good," Jim said. "I had a long dry spell, and what with this committee, I put in a lot of late hours with Alexa."

"Well, good luck," was all I could manage. Looking at my watch, I added, "I've got to go brief Kovic."

"Okay," Jim said, clapping an arm around my shoulder. "Get some sleep so you can enjoy our day in the country tomorrow."

THE ANTIBIOTICS WORKED, and I felt somewhat better the next day. The throbbing had subsided, though I was left with an annoying deafness on my right side that made me twist my head to hear better at meetings. The pressure hurt my ear drums as the Gulfstream took off from the general aviation area and traced its way down the Potomac toward the CIA's secret operations base that everyone called the "Farm." I watched the glistening river, etched with inlets and bays, gradually widen until we passed over a large peninsula, circled twice, and landed on an isolated strip of asphalt carved out of the forest.

An unmarked van pulled up to the plane. Guards issued us special red badges and drove us to a building that looked like it had been designated temporary a half century ago. At the entrance, another guard checked our badges against photo identification and asked us to read and sign a nondisclosure form before we were allowed to enter a briefing room.

Inside, we were greeted by the head of the Special Forces group responsible for the covert action.

"I'm Mike," he said. "We don't use last names in this business. I'll be your tour guide while you're here."

I studied him closely, wondering what type of person specialized in such dangerous operations. He certainly had the look. He appeared to be in his late twenties or early thirties. He had sandy hair, an open face, and a warm smile. He had the build of a football player and would fit right in on any Big Ten campus. He was surprisingly easygoing. Too American, I thought, but then remembered he would not have to blend with the crowds in Pakistan. He didn't need an entry visa.

"This operation won't be a piece of cake," Mike said. "As you know, our mission is to destroy the weapons before they leave the depot, and it's heavily guarded. Let's start with the map."

Pakistan flashed on the wall screen across from us. Mike used a laser pointer to guide us. "We start from a cruiser stationed here." The little red dot of the laser light wobbled over flat blue ocean near the tan coast of Pakistan. "Our ships are often in this area, so they won't raise any suspicions.

"We will be inserted by Seahawk helicopters flying just over the water at night, well below their radar. First bird has our team of seven commandos; second flies backup and rescue equipment. Coast is lightly patrolled here, and the area inland is mostly desert."

The red dot made its way inland. "We put down here, camouflage the choppers near these hills, and do the rest on foot. Can't fly closer because of villages near the depot. The birds have the new quiet engines, but we can't risk any sound detection."

"Communications?" Alexa asked.

"Each man has GSL on his wrist, and we can talk to each other, the cruiser, CENTCOM, or even Washington for that matter. But we won't. Don't want to risk intercepts. When we do communicate, it will be in encrypted microbursts."

"How far on foot?" Locara asked. "Any danger of running into stray villagers?"

"About twenty clicks," Mike replied, using the military jargon for kilometers. "We have very detailed maps of that terrain, including several hiding places. We'll send one man dressed native to scout before the rest of us move forward."

"Now if you'll move over here," Mike pulled a cloth off a display table and exposed a scale model of the Pakistani nuclear plant, reconstructed in perfect detail, showing guard towers and the double strand of fences.

"We approach the perimeter from this ravine at 23:00. The guards in this tower are on our payroll." His finger casually brushed the little tower.

"We use shears to cut through this fence, but first we route this cable around the hole we make so there's no short circuit that would trigger their alarm." His thick fingers gracefully stretched a little wire around the hole.

"Now comes the tricky part." He ran his thumb along the sandy space separating the outer and inner fences. "This sand is three meters wide. Not only does it show footprints, but it's laced with sensors and mines."

"Will you have time to use mine detectors?" Locara asked.

"Nope," Mike smiled. "We'll go right over 'em."

"How?" Jim and I asked at the same time.

"Graphite bridges." Mike looked triumphant. "They're portable lightweight components we will carry with us and assemble on site. They will keep us two feet above the surface of the mines. Then we cut the inner fence and make our way over to this ventilation opening. We pry off the screening and go down the shaft on rope ladders."

Several of us nodded in genuine appreciation.

"Now if you'll look over here," Mike pointed to another model, this one a cutaway of the interior of the plant.

"We come down here near a maintenance closet, just around the corner from where the weapons are stored. His fingers walked down the little cutaway corridor, then paused and rested on a yellow spot.

"This is where we place the explosives."

"What are the red arrows?" Jim asked.

"That's our escape route. We've got five minutes to get out before that sucker blows."

"Is that enough time?" I asked.

"That's what we'll show you next," Mike smiled. "If you'll follow me, I'll take you out to our set."

We left the briefing room and walked a few hundred yards through bright sun to a large, dark shed. When the door was closed and flood-lights switched on, we saw a life-size replica of a section of the Pakistan assembly plant and its perimeter fence. Mike pointed to bleachers where we could observe the whole set.

"We keep a roof over this part because we don't want anyone peeking." Mike waved an arm at the rafters. "Nowadays, anybody can buy one-meter resolution photos on the Internet, and I'll bet the Paks would pay plenty for these shots."

Mike introduced six athletic young men by their first names. "Now for the run-through. There's a stopwatch on the wall," he said. "Our target is five minutes to place the charges and get up the elevator, then ninety seconds to be out through the fence. I'm starting the clock."

I watched in amazement as the athletes scaled obstacles, placed satchels of explosives, inserted fuses, connected wires, and scurried to the mock perimeter where they quickly cut through two strands of razor wire with large shears and assembled another graphite bridge. Mike stopped the clock with twenty seconds to spare. I joined in the spontaneous applause from the stands. We filed back into the briefing room.

"Any questions?" Mike asked

"Can you really get enough power in those small satchels?" Locara asked.

"You'd be amazed what you can do with the new plastics," Mike responded. "And don't forget, we have to carry the stuff. The smaller the better."

"What about guards in the tower where you cut your way out?" Alexa asked.

Mike grinned. "Also on our payroll. We expect a little absenteeism that evening."

"What about the manager and maintenance staff?" I asked.

"They're over here on the other side of the guardroom. Can't see us." Mike tapped an area of the scale model with a metal pointer.

"Surveillance cameras?" Alexa asked.

"We've made a videotape of normal operations. One of the guards we've bought puts it on the monitor in the control room before we disable the camera. From where the manager sits, everything looks normal."

"Is there some way to warn him?" I asked.

"He gets the same warning as everyone else," Mike replied. "We will pull the fire alarm as soon as we're up the elevator and clear. In response to your concerns reported to me yesterday, we've added another minute and a half. That gives people three and a half minutes to get out before the big bang. That's more than enough if they don't dawdle."

"What Peter means," Jim interjected, "is there some way we could warn our informant separately?"

"Not without spoiling the operation," Mike replied. "The informant fed us information about the transfer because he opposed the government's plan to sell the bomb. But he's got a technocrat's passion for his plant. He has no idea we're planning to blow it up. He's not giving us access to the plant. We're getting it through the guards we've bought."

"But suppose he tries to find the problem rather than evacuate?" I asked.

Mike shrugged. "That would be a fatal mistake."

I DECIDED TO RAISE THE QUESTION of Ali privately on the plane going home. Jim and Alexa were sitting next to each other. I leaned over their seats.

"We've got to talk about this."

"About what?" Jim asked.

"About Ali."

"You heard the answer," Alexa said sharply. "He gets the same warning as everyone else."

"We can't do that to a friend," I said, looking directly at Jim.

"It's a real bitch," Jim said. "Let me see if I can get 'em to add another thirty seconds to the warning time."

When I got back to my house, I was still chewing on the same question. I couldn't get the picture of Ali out of my mind. I heard his generous laugh and his funny, formal English. I needed to talk to someone about my doubts, but whom? Kate was off somewhere in Europe, and all my efforts to reach her had failed. My father was dead, and Jim was caught up in the covert operation. Abe was the only person I could turn to. I knew I was taking a dangerous risk in discussing something so sensitive, but I was desperate to voice my anxieties. I had a permanent knot in my stomach. I needed help. I proned Abe.

"Yes, I'll be home tomorrow. What's up?"

"I'll tell you tomorrow."

"Is it about Kate?"

"Something I can't talk about on the phone."

"Sounds spooky," Abe laughed. "I'll come to your house after lunch."

I sat on the train to Princeton, idly watching the blur of buildings and trees slide by. How strange it would be to return to a house without Kate. What if she had changed the locks? I suppose I could always break in. Had she really decided our marriage was finished? But my key turned in the lock, and I pushed open the front door. Maybe there was hope.

I walked around the house, taking in the familiar objects, Kate's clothes in the closet, an empty glass in the sink. I couldn't stand being there alone. I picked up the phone, asked Abe to come earlier than planned and pick up a pizza. There was still beer in the refrigerator. I busied myself trying to tidy up the kitchen, stewing, waiting.

After we finished the pizza and Abe had offered condolences about my father, I asked if he was prepared to enter a dangerous area. He looked puzzled. "You still have clearances as a consultant," I said, "but you're not cleared for the subject I want you to help me with today."

"Maybe you shouldn't tell me then," Abe said with a slight smile. "After all, I don't need to know in either the technical or the personal sense of the term."

"I know, but I need your help. Just promise me it'll never go beyond the two of us."

"Of course," Abe replied.

I described the situation in Pakistan, my travels, and the covert action plan. I felt a twinge of guilt about this disclosure, but I rationalized my indiscretion with the certainty that Abe wouldn't repeat a word of it. I told Abe that I was torn. I could not really be sure that our diplomacy would work in time. If we destroyed the Pakistani bombs before they were transferred, we could possibly save millions of lives. Even if a few lives were lost, what are a few compared to the prospect of millions?

"But then I think of Ali," I said, picking up the half empty can of beer from the kitchen table. "What if something happens to him?"

Abe shook his head. "It's easier to plot the death of abstract people than real ones, but that doesn't make it right."

"But what about the lives we may save?" I asked. "How do we weigh them in the balance?"

"How sure are you about those you'll save compared to your knowledge of those you'll kill?" Abe asked, scratching his beard.

"We can never know for sure, but if it's just a question of comparing risks and consequences, then the plan probably makes sense," I replied.

"No," Abe looked at me intensely. "Because you're not in a position to play God. You can never know the expected utility. For example, what's the probability that Iranian nuclear weapons will bring stable deterrence to the region rather than war? And you don't know for sure that they will hand anything over to terrorists. Once you've destroyed the Pakistani plant, won't they build another? Is this really their only depot? And what's the probability that Ali will be killed? There are too many unknowns."

"But if there's no God, humans have to make the best estimates we can and live with the consequences," I said, playing devil's advocate.

"You can't know the consequences," Abe countered. "All you can know for sure is what acts are wrong. Killing a friend is one of them. And you don't need God to know that."

"That's old clean-hands Abe," I said, trying to relieve the tension. "But it won't work in the real world. Remember the joke about Kant. 'His hands were so clean that he had no grip on anything.'"

"He had a grip on his integrity," Abe said. "Some moral choices are awful. Remember Sophocles? You can be Creon or you can be Antigone. You can't be both. At some point, you have to choose."

"That's fine in a seminar on theory," I replied, "but this is politics. I can't put my integrity ahead of the lives of millions of people."

Abe continued to look serious. "Then let the Israelis do it."

I was surprised. "Isn't that hypocritical?"

"If I were faced with my imminent death, I might be tempted to make a desperate choice that would sacrifice my integrity," Abe said. "That's where my moral crisis would begin. But we're not faced with their choices. You don't have to kill a friend to create some unknown greater good in a distant region."

"It's too late," I sighed. "If I resign, they'll just go ahead anyway. And if I try to warn Ali, it will spoil the mission and Pakistan will send the weapons to Iran. There's no way out."

CHAPTER 10

I REPLAYED MY DISCUSSION with Abe a hundred times on the train back to Washington, thinking of refinements and rejoinders I might have added to bolster my argument. Abe had a point, but he was also naive. He had no feel for the way politics actually works. But I kept coming back to Ali. Among all the unknowns was one certainty: the evil of killing my friend. Could I prevent that without undermining the whole plan?

When I got home, I dialed Jim's apartment and asked if I could come over for a beer.

"Sorry, Peter, not tonight. I've got some pretty intense consultations going on with the Defense Department right now. How about tomorrow night?"

"I go to Brussels with the president and Kovic tomorrow afternoon. I'd like to discuss something privately before I go."

"Guess I gotta give equal private time to all the undersecretaries," Jim chuckled. "Let's meet in my office at 7:00. I'll have some breakfast brought in."

THE BLUE PLATES with the presidential seal were already set on Jim's conference table when I arrived a few minutes late. Jim was sitting at the table thumbing through the daily press clippings.

"Hey ole buddy, you been out fishin' the Potomac?" Jim said. "Our bacon 'n eggs are gettin' cold."

I could not resist a jibe in response. "Too much heavy lifting last night, Jimbo?" I smiled. "You look all tuckered out."

"Now, now," Jim said with a grin, wagging a finger. "We never play kiss and tell in this business."

When I finished my eggs, I pushed away my plate and got to the point.

"I've been thinking a lot about Project High-Tech," I said, "and I think we should slow it down."

Jim pushed his chair back from the table and raised his eyebrows. "It's a little late for that."

"You told me we had time."

"It's a moving train, Peter, and we don't own the timetable."

"But you could still turn it off?"

Jim shrugged. He took a sip of coffee.

"We have to change to a plan where Ali isn't harmed." I said. "We owe him that."

Jim looked pained, put down the coffee mug, and sat quietly for a moment. "We're not sure he'll get hurt." He paused for a moment, then continued. "I don't see how we can let the life of one person, even a friend, alter government policy."

Without letting on that I had spent the weekend in Princeton, I repeated Abe's arguments. Jim looked unconvinced.

"What kind of an argument is that?" he asked. "Sure, I'd like to avoid any risk to Ali, but that seems incredibly selfish. You can't make policy that way. The president has asked me to solve this problem."

"I agree, in part," I admitted. "But we aren't sure about the risk to the others. There are too many unknowns. The clear and present danger is to Ali. And we don't know if the plan will really work. It has too many moving parts."

"For Chrissakes, Peter. We can't ignore millions of people just because someone we like is endangered. You're sounding like a goddamn academic. This is the real world. Risks are unavoidable."

I scowled but kept silent.

"Sorry," Jim continued, responding to my look of annoyance. "That was a cheap shot. I've been under a lot of pressure. The last two weeks have been hellacious." Jim rubbed his large hand across his forehead and then raked his hair. "It's a bitch, but that comes with the territory. Sometimes all the choices are bad. Then you've gotta ask how you help the most people."

"No," I replied, "you admit you can't answer that question and that sending a friend to his death is wrong."

"I wish you'd quit saying that. We're not sending Ali to his death." Jim looked exasperated. "He'll hear the alarm. There's a good chance he'll get out."

"Not Ali," I said, heatedly. "He'll stay and try to fix the goddamn problem."

I knew I wasn't making any progress. I pushed aside my coffee mug and leaned forward. I softened my tone and switched to a new pitch. "We don't have to argue about this. We have alternatives. We can wait and see if our diplomatic option works. And we can use the time to develop a better plan that doesn't endanger Ali."

Jim shook his head. "Time isn't on our side. They could move those bombs any day now."

"Are you sure?"

"The Agency isn't certain, but DIA thinks so, and their reports have stirred up the hawks on the Hill. Peary's breathing down the president's neck. So are the Israelis."

"Then let the Israelis make their own move. Let them do the dirty work."

"Whoa, cowboy," Jim sat forward in his chair. "Aren't you the guy who argued a few weeks ago that we shouldn't let the Arab-Israeli conflict pollute the politics of South Asia? I thought I remembered a little speech about not feeding the fantasies of the bad guys who claim there is an alliance of Zionists and Crusaders."

I felt myself reddening. "From that point of view, American action is better, but it's not if we have to do something wrong."

"Bullshit, Peter." Jim began to look agitated. "That's the old clean hands crap. You know the answer to that as well as I do. In the real world, it's a self-indulgent luxury."

"Not if we have alternatives," I replied angrily.

"We don't," Jim shook his head and scowled. "It's too late. You can't paint vertical stripes on a moving train, Cutler."

He glanced at his watch and rose from his chair. "I've gotta be in the Oval Office for the morning briefing in five minutes." He walked over to his desk and gathered papers into a leather file with the White House seal.

"Promise me not to do anything until I get back from Europe?" I asked as we walked briskly down the halls of the old Executive Office Building.

Jim looked annoyed. "You know I can't promise that."

"Okay," I nodded "but promise me you'll think about it."

"Sure," he said with a chuckle. "That's not hard."

THE OFFICIAL PURPOSE of the Brussels trip was a long planned signing ceremony for the new biological weapons verification protocol. The president's role was all pomp, but it would play well on the six o'-clock news, and, given the polls, he needed it. Kovic and I would use the visit to NATO headquarters to press the Europeans on Pakistan. It was crucial to gain more time for diplomacy. But first we needed to get the president on our side.

Air Force One, a blue and white 747 emblazoned with the United States of America in big gold letters, sparkled in the bright afternoon sun. We staffers were asked to enter through the rear steps that descended from the belly of the plane. The front steps were reserved for photo ops: the president and Kovic. I watched from behind the huge engines as the two men waved to the cameras from the top of the stairs. I entered a staff compartment just behind the large conference room and spread my briefing books on the table. While others were settling back in their big beige chairs, scanning the TV monitors, I was preparing my pitch.

I was tempted to talk to Kovic right after wheels up, but I waited until dinner was finished and the stewards had cleared away the dishes. Kovic and I wandered to the back of the plane to jolly up the press for a few minutes. I had carefully crafted his remarks to keep the press pointed at the story of chemical and biological arms and the problems of verification that was on the formal agenda of the NATO summit. Thus far we had been amazingly successful in avoiding leaks about Pakistan. We returned up a long aisle to the forward cabin just behind the president's office. Kovic was in a jovial mood, probably in response to the press secretary, a man who assiduously practiced the Washington adage of "always flatter up."

"I've got some talking points you might want to use with the president," I said, putting a sheet of white paper on the table in front of him. Kovic picked it up, read it, and handed it back to me.

"What's this all about?"

"I think the High-Tech working group is moving too fast," I said. "At the rate they're going, any diplomatic success you score on this trip to Brussels will be overtaken by events. I think you might want to let the president know that you need another week to show how the diplomatic track is progressing."

"Are they really moving that fast?"

"Looks that way."

"Has he approved the action yet? Notified the Hill?" Kovic asked, arching his eyebrows as he sipped his coffee.

"Not beyond planning, but he's under strong pressure to give it the green light. That's why we need to talk to him now."

Kovic put down his cup. "Here, give that back to me."

I slid the paper across the table again. Kovic took a pencil from his shirt pocket and added a few words. "Okay," he said. He picked up one of the phones by his chair and asked to see the president.

The president had been resting in his stateroom in the front of the plane, but he agreed to meet us in his adjoining office. When we entered, he was already seated in his big chair in front of a credenza with phones, tape decks, and a large TV. He was wearing a blue satin flight suit with POTUS and an eagle embroidered on the pocket. He looked tired.

Kovic introduced the subject using the talking points I wrote and then invited me to make my case.

"There is a good chance that we can solve this with diplomacy, Mr.

President. High-Tech is high risk, and if it moves too fast, we will lose our best option."

"Senator Peary and his friends are pressing me to act quickly." Kent sighed. "They say it's now or never. They claim the Paks are about to move the bombs."

"But we'll pay a high price if we use force before we have exhausted the diplomatic option. Even the Brits might vote for a resolution of condemnation in the UN. And we will be setting up our enemies in the Islamic world. They'll use this as a stick to beat us and a way to gain more recruits. It's bound to generate more terrorism."

"That's not as bad as a nuclear Iran threatening Israel."

"I agree, but we may be able to avoid both. And in any case, we have to show the allies that we have exhausted all the alternatives before we use force."

"You really think you have a diplomatic alternative?"

"We've got pressure from the Japanese and Chinese, and some carrots from the Indians. All we need is the Europeans to close the noose."

"Think the Europeans will play ball?"

"There's a good chance." I nodded my head forcefully. "We'll know in a day or two."

"And that will bring the Paks to their senses?"

"It's our best shot."

"Wish I were as sure." The president sighed again. "If we blow this, Peary will make my life hell. Not to mention the midterm elections."

"Just a few more days," I pleaded.

"Okay, a few days," he said with a backhanded wave of his hand. "Now let me get some sleep." Kovic and I left quietly and shut the door.

As I settled back into my seat, the knot in my stomach was gone for the first time in days. I had gained a temporary reprieve. I needed some sleep to stave off a return of the bug, but my mind was racing over the points I would need to make to get a clear commitment from our allies. Time was tight. I dozed fitfully until a steward awakened me for breakfast and landing in Brussels.

Over the next two days, Kovic and I earned our pay. NATO headquarters hosted the summit, and we spent much of the first morning seated behind the president as he presented the formal agenda in the large council room. After the president departed, however, we huddled for hours with our counterparts in the bilateral meeting rooms, urging them to warn Pakistan of possible economic sanctions or worse if it were ever the source of a transfer of nuclear weapons or technology to another country. We had to impress on them that their messages to Islamabad must be sent quickly if they were to have any useful effect. We started with the Brits and used their promise of help to move the Germans, which in turn brought in the French. One by one, we worked our way through the long list of countries, pleading, cajoling, threatening. Only Turkey held out, for domestic political reasons, and we could live with that since we were seeking coordinated démarches rather than a unanimous council resolution.

When we finally got into the cars for the motorcade back to Kovic's plane, I was physically exhausted but exhilarated by our success. We had the Paks in a corner. My plan was working. We could stop the bombs without sacrificing Ali. I could not wait to get back to Washington to consolidate our gains and watch the diplomatic option play out. I tried to call Jim from the plane, but there was no answer.

THE PLANE LANDED at Andrews Air Force Base late Tuesday night. By the time the bags were loaded into the cars, it was after midnight. Despite the hour, I decided to call Jim from the car to give a firsthand report of the progress we had made. I rehearsed my pitch as the phone rang. But a sleepy female voice answered.

"Oh, Peter," Alexa said, sounding groggy. "I thought you might be Jim."

"Where is he?"

"Called to an unexpected meeting."

"What's up?"

"Oh, you know Washington," she replied, evasively. "People never leave you alone."

"I wanted to tell him about our success in Brussels," I said. "It's more important than ever that we put High-Tech on hold."

"I don't know about that," Alexa said.

"You have to help me persuade Jim."

"I don't have to do anything for you," she snapped.

"There's no sense risking lives if we can solve this with diplomacy," I said. "Think of Ali."

"Peter," Alexa responded sharply, "This isn't a secure line."

"Sorry," I said. "But please help."

"I'll tell Jim you called."

The phone went dead.

I COULDN'T SLEEP. I was still on European time, and the flight had brought back the congestion in my throat and ears. I was in my office by 6:00 A.M. When Tony arrived, I pressed him to get the files on the High-Tech working group meetings that had taken place in my absence.

"It's funny," Tony said, "but we haven't received anything from them this week. I called the White House, and the NSC staff guy said he had no records of any meetings that you should have attended."

I went into my inner office, picked up the green phone, and called Jim on the secure line.

"Hey, ole buddy," Jim greeted me. "How's the tourist?"

"We've got the Europeans on board."

"Yeah?" Jim replied. "That's good news."

"Didn't Alexa tell you I called?"

"Nope." I made a mental note.

"All we need is time to tighten the diplomatic noose."

"How long's that gonna take?"

"They promised to get their messages out this week."

"We're down to short strokes." Jim sounded stressed. "The Paks could move those suckers any day now. We just don't know. Once they're gone, those European messages aren't worth squat."

"Just give me a few more days."

Jim chuckled. "You State Department guys always want more time."

"Is something else going on?"

"You know I can't answer that."

"Are there meetings I should be going to?"

"Hard to say," Jim let out a strained laugh. "This town's full of meetings."

"Are there any High-Tech meetings?" I added a hard edge to my voice.

"The president was a little worried about some of the stories that mentioned Pakistan last week. He wants things tightened up so . . ." Jim let the sentence taper off.

"Just tell me if I've got time to . . . "

"For Christ's sake, Peter," Jim's voice was now brittle. "Don't push me." Then, softening again, "Come over for a beer Sunday night, and we'll have a long talk."

"Why not tonight?"

"Bad week. I'm backed up 'til the weekend," Jim said, ending the conversation.

I put down the phone and looked out the window at the sun setting fire to the marble memorials. Jim had never been so evasive with me. Obviously something was up. He had been struggling not to lie to me. I had to give him that at least. If Jim had lied, he might have thrown me off the track, but his evasions were almost as frank an admission as if he had blurted out the truth. If he was willing to have a long talk on the weekend but not before, then something was likely to happen in the next few days. Clearly I had been cut out of the action. I called Tony into the room.

"You still friendly with your counterpart over at Alexa Byrnes's shop?

"We trade a little information from time to time." Tony sounded apologetic.

"Call him and ask if she's going to the High-Tech meeting today. Tell him I want to give her something that's tightly held, but if she won't be there, I'll use a courier. And while you're at it, call your friends at NSC and ask if I'll see Joe Locara at the meeting."

Tony smiled and left for his cubicle in the outer office. He was back in a few minutes. "She'll be at the meeting out in Langley at 10:00, and so will Locara," he reported with a look of triumph.

"Well, that answers one question," I said, waving Tony out.

What should I do? I could call Jim again and tell him that I knew about the meeting. But how would that help? It wasn't going to get me back into the loop, and it would just put Jim in a tight spot. They didn't want me there because they did not want to hear my argument that the diplomatic option was working. They were afraid I would delay them. I could resign as a matter of principle, but what would that accomplish? I would have clean hands, but it would do nothing to help Ali or advance the diplomatic option. What about Kovic? I called his assistant.

"I need to see the secretary."

"The secretary will be tied up with testimony on Capitol Hill most of the day."

"It's urgent."

"The best I can offer is five minutes before the morning staff meeting. He has to be in the car right after that."

KOVIC DID NOT LOOK HAPPY to see me. "Well?" he asked skeptically. "What's so urgent?"

"High-Tech is going ahead," I said. "It's not only risky, it also means the end of everything you just accomplished at NATO. They're not giving us time for the diplomatic option to work. You've got to call the president."

"He knows my views," Kovic said with a tone of irritation.

"But they went ahead in our absence," I said. "I think it may happen in the next few days."

"If that's what he's decided, that's what we'll have to go with," Kovic replied.

"You won't at least call?"

"No," Kovic said, shaking his head. "He's the one that got elected. Hard choices are what presidents are paid for."

Before I could protest further, Kovic rose from his chair. "Now we've got to go across the hall for the staff meeting."

I took my seat third down from the head of the big table in the secretary's conference room, but I could not concentrate on the discussion of strategy for the upcoming congressional hearings on the foreign aid bill. How could I save Ali? How could I delay things so that our diplomacy had a chance to work? And if they went ahead with the covert action, was there a way to warn him to get out without spoiling the mission?

Any official message was bound to look suspicious. A private message might arouse less suspicion, but what kind of a code could I use that Ali would comprehend and others would not? I thought of the birthday cards that Ali sent each year. Ali knew my birthday was in March. If I e-mailed him an urgent invitation to a birthday party in August, he would know something was up. But it was awfully short notice, and there was no way Ali could drop his work and fly to the United States for a phony birthday party. Besides, they would not let him out. But at least he would know that something strange was happening. How could I make him understand that the message really meant that he should absent himself from the plant for a few days?

I needed a second strand to my strategy, another way to convey only to Ali what the strange private message was about. I also needed to find a way to buy time for the diplomatic option by slowing down Project High-Tech. But how could I slow it down when I had been cut out of the action and Kovic had become such a coward? And then it came to me.

I HAD AGREED to see John Marcus of the *Post* before I left for Europe. We were to talk on the record about the president's speech in Brussels and the verification procedures for biological arms agreements. Marcus sat in my office, and I tipped back in my chair and put my feet up on my desk. I kept the conversation on the details of verification and European attitudes until the very end of the interview when Marcus put his notepad in the pocket of his rumpled suit and got up to leave.

"So all in all, you got everything you wanted on this trip," Marcus said.

"Yes," I replied, taking my feet down off the desk and standing up to say good-bye. "On both issues."

Marcus snapped to attention. "What was the other issue?" he asked, raising his eyebrows. "I thought this trip was all about verification."

"Sorry," I said, "I misspoke. I really can't say anything about the other issue."

"Pakistan?" Marcus looked at me closely.

"I really can't discuss it."

"Is there something in those rumors?" Marcus asked. "Were you in Brussels asking for European help on Pakistan's nuclear weapons?"

"No comment."

"Come on, Cutler," he implored. "Don't be coy."

"If you want anything," I said, "it'll have to come from Brussels. Keep me out of it. No footprints."

As soon as Marcus left my office, I sent a quick e-mail to Ali. Very bland, but he would know something was up.

"Greetings. Hope all goes well with you. It would be great if you would take this week off and come to my birthday party. It would mean a great deal to me."

IT WAS STILL DARK when I stepped outside to pick up the paper. I had been awake since five, suffering from a headache and congestion. When I heard the delivery truck noise and the smack of the paper against the pavement, I put on my bathrobe and slippers and ran outside. I tried to read the front page by the street lamp, but the light was too dim. I hurried back to the kitchen and spread the paper out on the table. There it was, with a Brussels dateline: "US Presses Europeans for Pak Sanctions," the headline said. "Kovic Hints Further Steps" read the subhead.

I quickly devoured the story. "Secretary of State Thomas P. Kovic recently asked NATO allies to join in cutting off aid and loans to Pakistan if that country proceeded with a plan to assist the nuclear weapons programs of other Islamic countries such as Iran. According to informed sources in Brussels, the Europeans agreed to cooperate in slowing the spread of nuclear weapons in the Southwest Asian region. One official said that the Americans had implied that if the Europeans did not cooperate, the United States would take unilateral action. The use of force was not excluded."

Perfect. Cable News would have broadcast the story on its worldwide service by now, and it would be on several Web sites. That was just enough of a leak to help Ali interpret my private invitation to leave. He could put two and two together, combining his private message with the public leak. It was like double key encryption on the Internet.

The public message makes sense only if you have a private key. He would be the only one to understand. Plus the leak would probably make the CIA wary of going ahead with any covert action right now. That would slow things down and buy more time for diplomacy. What's more, the substance of the story reinforced the view that our diplomatic solution was working. The threat of force could hang in the background to strengthen the diplomacy, but there would not be precipitous action. And with a Brussels dateline, nothing could be traced to me. It had worked just as I planned.

I spent the morning on routine matters at the office. No inquiries from Kovic about the leak. No calls from the White House about anything.

I celebrated by leaving the office early in the afternoon to go home and take a nap. I still felt the remnants of my illness, and jet lag from the trip to Europe had left me tired. Now I could afford to invest a few hours in recovering my health. With the pressure off, I succumbed to exhaustion. I took the phone off the hook, stretched out on the bed, and fell into a deep sleep.

I WOKE UP JUST BEFORE 7:00, feeling slightly better. I made a gin and tonic, settled into a chair with my feet on the coffee table, and flicked on the television. I took a sip of my drink as I watched the NBC logo and opening music fade. A picture of General Ziad came on the screen.

"Good evening," said the anchor. "In our top story, an explosion in a Pakistan nuclear plant has cost the lives of six Americans. Fourteen Pakistanis, including the plant manager, were also killed in what promises to become a diplomatic catastrophe for the Kent administration."

My head snapped back as if I had been punched in the face.

"The government of Pakistan is claiming that a team of saboteurs damaged a peaceful nuclear facility. Pakistani officials say that six Americans were caught in the act and killed. Another American escaped. The details of the operation remain murky, but it appears that a CIA covert operation has been compromised. White House officials refuse all comment on the matter."

The picture switched from the anchor to a White House correspondent. She held a mike out to the press spokesman. "I'm afraid I can't comment. It's standard policy to neither confirm nor deny rumors about intelligence matters." The picture switched to Capitol Hill. A reporter thrust a microphone under the jowls of Senator Peary, who complained about the bungling nature of the Kent administration. He called for a full congressional inquiry.

I sat stunned.

The screen turned into a map of Pakistan. A little red star flashed in the southwest, where the explosion had taken place. A grim-faced President Kent ignored questions from reporters as he made his way to a waiting helicopter on the White House lawn. A reporter interviewed some Georgetown professor about Pakistan's nuclear program. Then commercials.

"Oh my god," I cried. "No, no, no, no, no!"

I clicked the television to mute. Silence rang in my ears. It could not be true. I shook my head and rubbed my fingers over my forehead. I buried my face in my hands. Ali was dead. And Mike and his team. Could I be responsible for twenty deaths? But I had not told Ali or John Marcus anything substantive about the plan. I had simply put Ali on alert and told Marcus to keep looking. Nothing could be traced to me. Each of my two messages was innocent by itself. Or maybe not.

A wave of nausea hit my body. My clever ploy had been too clever by half. I had done both too much and too little. My leak had not prevented the CIA from going ahead with High-Tech, but my message to Ali had somehow alerted the Pakistanis and turned the mission into a slaughter.

Images and sounds filled my mind. The muffled thumping of specially designed helicopter engines as Mike's team flies low over the desert of southwest Pakistan to their preplanned base camp. Men pull the camouflage net over the helicopters after preparing them for quick exit. They slip packs of tools and explosives over their dark fatigues, their faces painted black. They communicate through hand signals as they walk single file for three hours to the nuclear storage facility.

The CIA had shown us pictures of this mountainous desert: large rocky outcrops, sparse vegetation, few villages. It was all etched in my mind. A scout goes ahead of the others, making sure they do not stumble across any locals. He checks the luminous dial of the wrist receiver that reads his exact position from the global positioning satellite. He whispers at his wrist and a microburst of message bounces off a satellite back to Mike and his men huddled at the last hiding place. Okay to move forward to the next designated spot. They need to reach the vicinity of the plant by 11:00 P.M. to have time to rest and to rendezvous with one of the guards the CIA hired.

It was all supposed to go like clockwork. As the midnight shift changes, the paid-off guards look the other way as the silent file of Americans scurries past the watchtowers to the double fences. They quickly cut the wires of the outer fence and assemble their small graphite fiber bridge to cross the ten-foot strip of mines that separates the two fences. They cut the inner fence and make their way to the ventilation shaft that leads down to the subterranean storage area. They remove the metal cover and scramble down rope ladders into the shaft. They regroup in the maintenance room. Mike and two others move down the corridor to the nuclear storage area, while the rest draw their guns and provide cover. The Americans quickly place the little packets of plastic explosive and connect wires to the timers. Then they take the elevator to the secondary surface exit before shrieking alarms turn the whole area into bedlam.

But then the clockwork stopped. My imagination failed. Did the wrong guards find them, open the elevator door, and shoot them like pigs in a pen? Did they get to the exit and find it blocked? A firefight with hostile guards unwilling to unlock the portal? Did they get out to the perimeter fence, only to be gunned down from a watchtower as they desperately scrambled through it? How could something like this happen? They had gone over it so many times.

I fought the sickening undertow of guilt, struggling to regain my mental footing. It was not my fault. Mike's men would have been killed anyway. High-Tech was a hare-brained scheme with too many moving parts. I was right to question it, and they were wrong to go ahead. They should have allowed more time for diplomacy to work and also to work out a better contingency plan.

I knew I was lying to myself. If I had not leaked the warning to Ali, I would not be feeling guilty about the deaths. If I had done nothing to try to save Ali, I would have felt another form of guilt. I was simply trying to do the best I could in an impossible situation. I had to try to save my friend's life, and it was not clear that my message was what caused the plan to fail. But I still felt sick.

I saw Ali sitting at his desk in the manager's office. Startled by the emergency alarm, he rushes to the door, brushing past employees who are running to the emergency exit. Ali ignores the danger and makes his way to the storage area. Did he find the satchels of explosives? Was he frantically ripping out wires when the force of the explosion tore him apart? Did he encounter our men? Did they shoot him? My stomach lurched. I had to know more.

I turned on the television again to see if there was any further information, but now the pictures were riots outside the American embassies in Cairo and Amman. I went online and checked several Web sites, but they merely repeated what I already knew. How could I find out what happened? Jim. I dialed his office on the secure line that had been installed in my home. Betty put me through right away.

"What happened?" I asked, skipping the usual niceties.

"We had to go ahead with High-Tech. We were afraid they might move the bombs."

"Oh my god."

"Those goddamn stories in the press may have tipped 'em off, or maybe a guard betrayed us," Jim said, his voice sounding taut. "Maybe they knew something was up and put on extra guards. The guys we bought let our people in as planned, but the new guards in the towers shot them trying to get through the fence on the way out."

"Mike?"

"Dead. Cut to pieces by the machine guns."

"All of them?"

"One got out. Choppers flew him back to the cruiser."

"And Ali?"

"You were right. He stayed in the plant and tried to find the goddamn problem." Jim replied, choking. "Goddamn engineer. It's a fuckin' mess."

"And the bombs?"

"We blew them up. And now the place will be too hot for the Paks to use for years. But apparently they weren't all there. There seems to be another depot somewhere. Intel wasn't as good as we thought it was."

"I feel sick," I said.

"Christ," Jim said, "How do you think I feel? At least you were clean on the last stage."

Not really, I thought. I hesitated, nauseated, head spinning. I felt a sudden urge to blurt out the truth, but my instinct for self-preservation kicked in.

"I'm at home," I fumbled. "Call me if I can help."

I poured another drink. My hand shook and the gin bottle clinked against the glass. I saw Mike, beaming, proud of his team's acrobatic escape through the simulated perimeter fence at the Farm. It seemed so easy then. It was all so abstract, so impossible to grasp, so distant from the mere words I said to John Marcus in my office. Yet my words may have killed people as surely as if I had pulled a trigger.

Ali dead? What did that mean? I couldn't believe that I would never pick up the phone or send him an e-mail or see him again.

The phone rang, and I jumped off the couch to answer.

"You bastard, Cutler," Jim's voice was choking with fury.

"What're you talking about?" I asked. Fear crept up my throat.

"Don't give me that shit," Jim was shouting into the phone.

"I don't know what you're talking about," I said. My voice rang hollow.

"Liar," Jim spat the word into the phone. "Locara was just here. Says Marcus virtually admitted to him that you were the source of the leak. You deny it?"

I was wordless.

The phone was silent for a long moment. "Cutler," Jim's drawl had turned slow and hoarse, "I'd been saying that if I caught the bastard who did this, I'd cut his balls off."

CHAPTER 11

I DON'T KNOW HOW LONG I SLEPT. As soon as I woke up, I was hit by the memory of being fired. How could they do this to me? Rubber-kneed, I leaned against the wall as I staggered into the bathroom. I looked at myself in the bathroom mirror. My face was wan, my hair was tangled, and I needed a shave. I took my temperature. It said normal, but that seemed like a lie. My head was still pounding.

I went to the kitchen and took a Diet Coke and a piece of stale bread from the refrigerator. I forced myself to swallow. I had to pull myself together. Maybe go to the office. I picked up the kitchen phone, rang my old number, and asked for Tony.

"What're they saying?"

"It's not very nice around here, Peter."

"What do you mean?"

"There's an intelligence report that you won't like," Tony said. "A lot of people on the seventh floor have seen it."

"Any word from the White House?"

"No," Tony said, "but Locara was here yesterday looking around the office. Didn't say why."

I bit my tongue. "What about calls?"

"Lots from embassies. We've told them you're not available."

"And the press?"

"There's quite a list. Do you want to return any of them?"

"No."

"John Marcus dropped by day before yesterday to ask when you're coming in."

"Sounds like I should lay low for a while."

"What do you want me to do with the boxes?" Tony asked.

"Store 'em. I'll be in touch in a couple of weeks."

The doorbell rang. When I opened the door, I found a woman holding two sun-bleached copies of the *Post* that had been left on the doorstep.

"I'm Janice Cooper from Channel 7," she said. "I thought you might like to tell your side of the story." Behind her were two men, one with a television camera fixed on me. The other thrust a microphone in my face.

I stared at them for a minute, blinking into the sun and the camera. Should I talk to her? What would I say? I didn't have the energy.

"I have nothing to say to you."

I took the papers from her hands and closed the door. I thought for a second about the terrible impression that would make on the screen tonight, but I had stopped caring.

I went to the kitchen, dropped the rolled-up papers on the floor, and sipped my Diet Coke. Should I fight back? Get a lawyer? I could prove that I had opposed the operation and that I had been working on a better alternative. Why should Jim get off? A spark of anger ignited under my lethargy. I could offer to take a lie detector test.

I thought of the polygraph test I took at the CIA last year, remembering the humorless inquisitor who smeared a chilly layer of Vaseline on my skin before the little patches with electric wires were attached. I felt nervous despite the fact that I had lived a conventionally clean life up to that point. I had passed that test with ease, but how would I react now if I were asked about my wife, my father, my personal relationships in Washington, my little remarks to Marcus? Forget about the lie detector test.

My cell phone rang. John Marcus.

"I'd like to tell your side of the story."

For a moment I was tempted. But what about Reese's threat to involve the Justice Department? And what would it accomplish? I was finished, exhausted.

"There's nothing to tell. Sorry."

I put down the phone, realizing that I couldn't stand Washington a moment longer. The house in Princeton was empty. There I could escape the press. Be alone. Figure out how, in less than a year and a half, my life had fallen apart. I used to be a faithful husband, doting father, inspiring teacher, and good citizen. Now I was none. What happened to me?

I reached Princeton in late afternoon. As I pulled into the driveway, I noticed that the lawn was badly overgrown and Kate's garden was full of weeds. The air in the house smelled stale. Dishes were in the sink where I left them after my last brief visit with Abe. The hanging fern in the window had withered. I lugged my suitcase upstairs. My side of the big double bed was rumpled where I had hastily made it. Kate's side was perfectly smooth.

I slid back the closet doors, picked a hanger from my nearly empty half, and stared at the rows of dresses and shoes that filled Kate's side. I lifted the hem of a black silk dress and rubbed it between my fingers. My eyes welled up, and I had to wipe them on the back of my sleeve. In the bathroom, Kate's nightie was hanging on a hook on the back of the door. Her hair dryer was on the shelf. Why didn't she take it to Europe? Where was she right now?

I walked down the hall into Monica's room. Her quilted bedspread was covered with stuffed animals. There was the big blue panda I won for her at the Fourth of July carnival when she was six. It was almost as big as she was, but she wrapped her little arms around it and lugged it around for the rest of the day. I went over to her bureau, which was littered with lipsticks and earrings. She and Kate had argued fiercely about whether she could wear makeup to school.

I paused at the door to Jimmy's room. His new Little League trophy sat on his desk: a golden Roman column with a little player crouched on top, bat forever ready to strike. I had not been there to see him win it. I grimaced at the memory of the Shenandoah. Jimmy's weathered baseball glove lay next to the trophy. On the wall was a picture of the two of us in Maine, each holding a salmon, completely happy with the world, with each other.

Returning downstairs, I went to the liquor cabinet, took out a bottle of Beefeater and a glass, and slumped down into the living room couch. I lacked the energy to go out and attack the lawn, or even turn on the television. Instead, I focused on the streaks of light from the western window slowly working their way across the dusty air.

The sharp ring of the phone jolted me out of my stupor. I decided to answer on the faint chance it might be Kate.

"Cutler?" It was John Marcus. "Glad I got you. Tried your cell phone and everywhere else."

"I told you I'm not taking calls."

"This one might interest you," he continued. "My sources say the White House is planning to nominate Joe Locara for your old position. I'm doing a story for tomorrow's paper. Any comment?"

"Not that you could publish."

I hung up. Insult added to injury. And yet I was not all that angry. After all our battles, Locara had finally won. Oddly, I didn't really care.

I DID NOT LEAVE the house for several days, except for a brief trip to the store. Mow the lawn, weed the garden, clean the house? Why? It was all so pointless. I drank, watched a little television, ate the contents of the freezer, and let dishes pile up in the sink. I tried to read but couldn't concentrate. Mostly I lay on the couch, drifting between sleep and waking.

On the evening of the fourth day, I was shocked by the sound of the doorbell. At first I didn't get up, but the bell kept ringing. I went to the door and slowly opened it. Abe pushed in.

"So here you are," he almost shouted, grabbing me by the shoulder. "I called Virginia, called your office, called here last week. I just happened to see the lights on and your car in the driveway."

"I just got here," I lied.

He pushed past me and sat in a chair. I was annoyed. I just wanted to be alone.

"I've been worried about you," Abe said. "I called Jim at the White House, but he wasn't very helpful. I told him it didn't seem right that they were blaming you for all this."

I sat down on the couch and almost smiled. "Calling Jim is like calling heaven for the phone number of Judas."

"What's that supposed to mean?" Abe looked puzzled. I told him what had happened since our last talk in this room a few weeks ago. It seemed like a few years.

"So I betrayed Jim and he betrayed me," I concluded.

"It doesn't have to end there." Abe was looking disapprovingly at the half-empty bottle of gin on the coffee table. "Jim will cool off. Give him more time, and then we'll all go up to Maine together."

"That's optimistic," I said. "But I'm not so sure this can be repaired."

Abe continued. "What're you planning to do now?"

"I have no plans," I looked away, wanting him to leave. Abe was such a boy scout. What an academic. What did he really know about power, about the real world?

"You shouldn't feel so guilty about those deaths," he said firmly. "There were many other causes besides you."

"It's not just that," I sighed. "In the past year, I have forgotten what I really care about. I've ignored my wife, my father, my friends, myself. This isn't me. But I don't know how to go back."

Abe got up from his chair and sat next to me on the couch. He put his hand on my arm. "You'll find out by little steps," he said.

I shrugged and looked away.

"Come back and teach. Live here with Kate. Rachel got a card from her in Europe. She'll be back soon to put the kids in school. Next year, invite Jim to go fishing. It's the little acts of engagement that count."

"What the hell's that supposed to mean?"

"Think small," Abe said with a smile. "Don't try to paint on a grand canvas. Life's really in the details."

I was too tired to argue. His proximity and insistence made me uncomfortable. His optimism was oppressive. He was making my head ache. I needed silence. "Can I get you a drink?" I asked, standing and moving toward the kitchen.

"Come over for dinner," Abe said, following me toward the kitchen. "Rachel will be furious if she learns you're eating alone."

"I've already eaten," I lied. "Maybe tomorrow."

"Okay," Abe said, moving toward the door. "I'll be in New York tomorrow, but I'll come back early so we can have dinner."

"Don't worry about it," I said.

"No, I want to," he replied. "Let's say seven."

He wrapped his right arm over my shoulder and gave me a squeeze. "I'm glad you're here," he said, smiling. "Tomorrow night, we'll talk about getting you a course to teach this fall."

As soon as he left, I poured a drink and slumped back on the couch. Could I really go back to life in Princeton? Soon Kate and the kids would return from Europe. But would she take me back? Or even let me live in the house? On my brief trip to the store, I saw two former colleagues at a distance. I was sure that they whispered to each other as they turned to avoid me.

Princeton was impossible. Even the prospect of a dinner with Abe and Rachel filled me with dread. I couldn't stay. I no longer belonged. I had to get out of there.

IT WAS A LONG DRIVE to Maine, mile after mile of tedious interstate highway in the pouring rain. The windshield wipers slapped back and forth monotonously. I suddenly had a crazy urge to let the car swerve into the concrete divider. It'd be such an easy way to end everything. Maybe suicide made sense. I had screwed up everything in Washington and had nothing to go back to in Princeton. And I could not live at Cathedral Lake forever.

The rain pounded against the windshield. Could I really end my life? Would that atone for the deaths I caused? Show those people in Washington that I was the master of my fate? End things on my own terms?

If so, how? No short cuts. No swerving the car off the road. The right ending had to be in the middle of Cathedral Lake.

For miles I debated the merits of my shotgun versus drowning. At first it was just an intellectual exercise. The shotgun had the virtue of speed. Cut a hole in the bottom of the canoe with an ax and then pull the trigger as the water rushed in. Option 2: the gun has two barrels. Use one to blow a hole in the bottom of the canoe. That would make a smaller hole than the ax, and the canoe would fill more slowly. Plenty of time to turn the other barrel to my head. A third option was to tie a rock to my legs, paddle to the middle, and tip the canoe over. That would be less messy. But why should that matter? Either way, I would leave a note in the cabin. Put it inside a glass jar in the middle of the table so the mice would not get it. Someday, someone would find it.

Working through these scenarios got me through a hundred miles. It was like the games we used to play to distract the kids when we drove to Maine. We would go for hours looking for the letters of the alphabet on road signs or seeing how many state license plates we could identify. Kate was infinitely patient with the kids. She even wrote some poems for them in the car. I used to hate those drives, but now I choked up at the memory.

Then I ran through everyone's reactions. What would they think when they heard the news? Locara wouldn't care. I was finally past caring about him too. Alexa? Also past caring. Jim, as angry as he was, would be crushed. And so would Abe.

How would Kate react? She would be hurt at first, but at least she would be free of me. She would have no trouble finding a new man, a better man. The kids would be shocked. It would be hardest on them. Maybe I was being selfish. How could I do this to them? Should I drop this idea? On the other hand, I wasn't much good to them anymore.

GRAY CLOUDS DRIFTED LOW over the dark fir forest as I bumped the last mile along the dirt road. I stopped at the trail to Cathedral Lake and pulled well off the road. I left the keys in the ignition so that the car could be moved easily when someone found it. As I got out, cold rain stung my face. I pulled on a green poncho. This time I did not have to worry about a pack basket.

I made my way down the soggy trail to the lake. My boots made a familiar squishy, sucking sound in the swampy areas. I tripped on a tangle of roots and pitched forward. I put out my hands to break my fall, picked myself up, and wiped my dirty hands on some wet ferns by the side of the trail. There had been an unusually early frost. The maples had turned, but the rain had knocked many leaves to the ground, leaving naked gray branches. When I reached the cabin, the lake was shrouded in mist, and I could not see the rocks on the other side. I went into the cabin, unlocked the storage closet, and took out my grandfather's shotgun and a box of shells. I noticed Father's bamboo fly rod leaning in a corner. I took it out as well. There were canned peas and instant mashed potatoes on the shelf. Might as well catch a trout.

I took the fly rod out of its case and rubbed my forefinger over the smooth tan wood that was held together by neat wraps of thread and shellac. As I gently coupled the metal ferrules of its sections, I thought of the day my father gave it to me. I rubbed my eyes with the back of my fists and then picked up the rod and walked down to the dock.

As I eased the canoe onto the water, I could see only half of the misty lake. Shadowy spruces lined the right shore. Nearing the middle, a chill wind marked a new squall. Raindrops marched, row after row, into the surface of the water. For a moment, the drops were replaced by early snowflakes, equally driven, but making no mark when they vanished silently in the dark water.

I pulled the poncho tighter around me as I paddled. The mist began to lift. Now I could see the tall pines on the eastern shore. There was little movement in their big black trunks, but the upper branches undulated in the wind. Ahead a pair of loons, bodies low in the water, oval heads and long bills thrusting forward, moved like dancers—splitting, turning, rejoining, diving, and reappearing fifty yards away. Lost for a moment in the mist, the male called to his mate: ou-ou-ou-ee-ee-ee-oouu-oouu-oouu. I shivered.

I was jolted to attention when the rod tip jerked into the water and the rod was nearly pulled out of the canoe. For a moment, in spite of myself, I felt the old thrill of excitement. I seized the rod and let the fish strip line from the reel. It fought deep into the lake. When I brought the fish to the canoe, tired, lying on its side, I admired the purple speckles on its sides and the red belly of a male in spawning colors.

I slipped my left hand under the fish and lifted it from the water. I hesitated for a moment, wondering if I should kill it. Finally I took the fly from its hooked jaw and bent its head back with my right thumb. The ruptured gills gushed brightly. I lay the body on the ribs of the canoe and admired its beauty. It gave a last quiver.

When I reached the dock, the lake was clear of mist, and the cold breeze moved the low gray clouds rapidly across the sky. For a moment, a break in the west let in slanting rays of sunset. The sun scattered rows of gold on the waves of the lake until the order was suddenly shattered by a shift in the wind. How could I let this go? I was glad it was clearing. I would cook outside on the rocks in front of the cabin.

I placed birch bark under pine kindling in the outdoor fireplace, struck a match, and watched the yellow flames slowly grow. The fire warmed me, and the pungent birch smoke filled my nostrils. I listened to the trout sizzling in the black iron frying pan. Suddenly I was ravenous. I thought of Abe and his comment about life being in the details. Maybe I could rebuild my life from the bottom up. Forget Washington and what those people would think. To hell with them. I took a sip from a half-empty bottle of bourbon I found in the closet, but I drank carefully. I wanted a clear head this night.

After dinner, I sat on the porch for a while. It was cold, but I wanted to watch the lake. The sky cleared and the first stars appeared above the pink afterglow of the sunset. How could I leave something so beautiful? I drew a deep breath. The air smelled fresh. I inhaled deeply again. Maybe I was being ridiculous. Was this really atonement or just a final act of ego? Damn. I was losing my will. This was the time to move. It was now or never.

I went into the cabin to write my note. I thought of the various long explanations I had devised in the car. Now they seemed pompous and pointless. Instead, I took a sheet of paper and wrote four short lines: "I'm sorry, but I can't live this way. I love you all. I don't know how else to show you how sorry I am. Please forgive me."

I folded the paper, put it in an empty pickle jar, and placed the jar in the center of the table. I picked up my grandfather's shotgun and the box of shells and walked to the door. Normally I would place a lantern in the window, knowing that if I lingered late, it would stretch a rippling thread across the water to guide me back to the cabin. Not tonight.

I closed the cabin door carefully and clicked shut the padlock in the latch. I walked slowly down to the dock. I better not linger. Kneeling in the canoe, I put two shells in the shotgun and snapped it shut. I placed the gun in the bottom of the canoe and pushed off from the dock.

Slowly I paddled to the middle of the lake, rested my paddle across the gunwales, and lay back in the bottom of the canoe. The light was dim. Stars poked holes in the blue-black canopy above me. A half-moon rose over the spruce spires to the west. I picked up the shotgun and cradled it on my chest. The metal was cold.

I thought of the times I had drifted here before and how different life seemed then. I thought of my father and his favorite quote about being filled with awe by the moral law within man and the starry heavens above him. I wondered if I would see him soon. Probably not. I thought of Monica and Jimmy and Kate, and how I loved them. Would they forgive me? Could I really leave without saying good-bye? Perhaps I should stop, reconsider. Why was I doing this? Who was this gesture for? Was it really an apology to others? Was I really free of Washington, or was this a juvenile way to strike back at Jim, Alexa, and everyone else? Maybe this was all wrong. Maybe I should simply accept their rejection. Wouldn't Abe's small steps of engagement, of swallowed pride, be a harder form of atonement?

But then I remembered my former colleagues turning away from me at the store in Princeton. And Kate's anger in the kitchen. I had vowed in the car not to succumb to last-minute cowardice. I stroked my cheek with the cold muzzle of the gun, encouraging intimacy.

Why wasn't I at peace with my decision? Why was I so reluctant to give up the struggle? What was holding me back?

I tried a prayer. "Oh God . . . oh God . . . please help me in my time of need . . ." Nothing followed. My eye caught the distant silhouette of Mount Katahdin. "I look up to the hills from whence cometh my strength," I said out loud, but I could not think of the next line of the psalm. My eyes filled with tears. "Damn," I said, choking a sob. "Damn, damn, damn."

I sat up in the canoe and reached into my pocket to pull out a handkerchief to wipe my eyes. The shotgun fell from my chest to the bottom of the canoe. An enormous sense of relief overwhelmed me. I picked up the gun, opened it, and took out the shells. I held them over the edge of the canoe for a moment and relaxed my grip. They made a little splash and disappeared into the blackness. All that remained were a few bubbles on the surface of the lake. I took a deep breath, picked up the paddle, and dipped into the dark water. The stroke erased the bubbles from the shells and replaced them with new ones. I paddled slowly toward the shore where the dock and cabin should be. There was no bright lantern to guide me tonight. I was steering by memory and my faith in small things. The canoe glided smoothly and picked up speed. Each stroke, I said to myself, was a small act of engagement.

ACKNOWLEDGMENTS

ANY PEOPLE HAVE CONTRIBUTED to this book, both as inspirations and critics. To thank them all would require another book, but I want to single out the special help of Linda Conway, Pat Deutch, David Ignatius, William S. Cohen, Richard Sennett, and Stephen Dobyns. I also benefited greatly from the superb editorial advice of Kate Darnton and Lindsay Jones at PublicAffairs. I am grateful to them all, but especially to Molly Nye, who has who has been a great critic, and always an inspiration.

PublicAffairs is a publishing house founded in 1997. It is a tribute to the standards, values, and flair of three persons who have served as mentors to countless reporters, writers, editors, and book people of all kinds, including me.

I.F. STONE, proprietor of *I. F. Stone's Weekly*, combined a commitment to the First Amendment with entrepreneurial zeal and reporting skill and became one of the great independent journalists in American history. At the age of eighty, Izzy published *The Trial of Socrates*, which was a national bestseller. He wrote the book after he taught himself ancient Greek.

BENJAMIN C. BRADLEE was for nearly thirty years the charismatic editorial leader of *The Washington Post*. It was Ben who gave the *Post* the range and courage to pursue such historic issues as Watergate. He supported his reporters with a tenacity that made them fearless and it is no accident that so many became authors of influential, best-selling books.

ROBERT L. BERNSTEIN, the chief executive of Random House for more than a quarter century, guided one of the nation's premier publishing houses. Bob was personally responsible for many books of political dissent and argument that challenged tyranny around the globe. He is also the founder and longtime chair of Human Rights Watch, one of the most respected human rights organizations in the world.

For fifty years, the banner of Public Affairs Press was carried by its owner Morris B. Schnapper, who published Gandhi, Nasser, Toynbee, Truman, and about 1,500 other authors. In 1983, Schnapper was described by *The Washington Post* as "a redoubtable gadfly." His legacy will endure in the books to come.

Peter Osnos, Founder and Editor-at-Large

CPSIA information can be obtained at www.ICGtesting.com
Printed in the USA
LVOW11s1925020614

388245LV00001B/9/P

9 781586 484200